You Are Ours

Leann Lane

Leann Lane

You Are Ours

Discover other titles by Leann Lane:

Bound to Me
You Are Mine
Because I Want To

Almost Taboo

The Devil in the Black Dress

Leann Lane

<u>Disclaimer</u>

Any and all resemblances to actual people and places is unintentional. Minus the Oregon coast. That was purely intentional it's a beautiful place and everyone should go there!! But for all other things this is purely a work of fiction and should be taken as such.

Dirty fantasies that should be enjoyed alone... or with that special someone or someone's. Bondage/bdsm should not be taken lightly. Yes, it is great fun to read about and fantasies about. But, to put it to use takes great trust and communication between the sub and the Master. Remember: safe, sane, consensual. Truth and honesty. Those are the basis of ANY bdsm lifestyle and should be practiced before you move farther. Play responsibly!

Lastly, I would like to apologize for the comments made by the characters in the book towards a certain branch of our military. Jack and Jordan really need to work on their attitudes. But, you know how Dom's are. I have no such compunction towards the men and woman in the military. I hold them in high respect and regard as well as am very grateful for all they do. Please forgive my rude characters; they are such a handful.

Leann Lane

GRATITUDE

I was going to make this book dedicated to all my fans, but instead I write this as a thank you. Thank you to all who helped make this book possible and the best that it could be.

I want to say a special thanks to my wonderful sister-in-law Deanna, her mother Connie, and the rest of her family who have never stopped pushing me to finish this and the next books to come. Not to mention for being patient while I sorted it out and helping me through it not once but twice.

I would also send a shout out to the beta readers in the world without you our books would make no sense. Thanks again!

Chapter One

My heart faltered from its normal rhythm as I stared in morbid fascination at the shiny piece of metal that encircled Mia's neck. Mia had been my best friend and constant companion for over ten years now and this was the first time I'd ever seen her look this happy. She practically vibrated with joy as she gazed lovingly at her new Master as he finished hooking the chain-linked collar around her neck.

An uncomfortable spark of recognition zipped through me as I hesitantly reach up and grasp the chain-linked necklace that Master Jordan had given me, not even two hours earlier. I had thought it was just a punk-metal piece of jewelry. At first glance no one would have ever compared it to the collars that the subs around here wore. Never had I seen one that held the same two hearts and single key that mine had. However, in this moment I finally understood it signification.

"It is a collar you gave me, isn't it?" I breathlessly asked as my fingers ran over the only piece of decoration on it.

"Yes, I gave you a collar," Master Jordan confirmed. "What would make you think it was anything else? You have been in this society for three years now."

Quickly turning in disbelief to confront them making sure it was not some nasty joke or a horrifying mistake from them. The two men I was up against gave no indication that they were anything but completely serious. The outright certainty in themselves and their actions was what scared me the most.

"Why?" My voice came out as a tiny shaky squeak not even a mouse would have been able to hear.

I didn't bother repeating myself because I had no doubt whatsoever that both of these men heard what I said even over the uproar going on around us.

The club The Dungeon on a normal night was blaring. But on a night when the owner had finally collared his permanent sub, the noise levels were beyond ear-piercing. Every person was shouting and cheering, making cat calls and a few were even pounding their feet.

Unsure if they heard me, yet I wasn't worried because I knew they could read all the confusion and fear that was etched in the lines on my face.

"You are ours, Lizzie. You and I known since the first time you stumbled through that door. You are the one for us, baby girl," he said with total conviction that almost had me convinced he was right.

Panic overcame me as the world tilted on its axis for the second time tonight, honestly not sure if I had recovered from the first surprise of a second Master. It was only two hours ago that I was still kneeling in front of Jordan. Listening to his and Jacks conversation, thinking this was it he was handing me off to another Master without any warning.

Never being so grateful to anyone in my life, when Mia had pulled Jordan aside and made him see that I was completely confused about the situation. That realization spurred him and Jack to take me aside and quite clearly explain the truth of the situation.

"You are the key to our hearts, baby girl," Jordan finally finished.

The implication in his voice had me hastily retreating in an involuntary move of fear. When he reached for me I sidestepped his efforts, fearful that with his touch all thoughts would fly out of my head. His effect on my entire being is always overpowering to the point where I would end up as nothing but a puddle at his feet, awaiting to fulfill any command he would give.

I had backed up feeling as if his very essence was surrounding me and closing off every route of escape I possibly had. My body tensed ready for action as question and demands swirled around in my mind. Glancing at the exit sign not sure if I truly wanted to run away.

My back suddenly hit a wall of unforgiving flesh, I tipped my head upwards just to confirm the obvious. Jack's dark piercing eyes unnerved me as they stared down at me in an almost harsh and unforgiving way. Just as suddenly his hands captured my arms removing my only chance at escape.

The moment our skin came in contact a tingling sensation swept through me. The terrifying realization settled in me that Jordan was no longer the only man in existence that could make me crave his dominance with just a look or a touch.

My gaze traveled over his dark wavy hair down to his soul penetrating eyes that sent a delectable shudder through me before finally got caught on his lush. The vision of how they'd feel on me, set blood pounding through my already heated veins combining with the shiver of delight that raced down my back. The desire that filled me at the idea of submitting to both of them was so fierce it was like a kick in the gut.

A solid chest pressed against mine and I was surrounded by two hulking masculine bodies. It was much like being in my very own protective bubble, except I knew I was in more danger from both these men then I was if I'd just walked into a cage with a hungry tiger.

My breath caught again as Jordan leaned in close and pressed his warm lips up against my ear.

"I put our collar on you, Lizzie, because no other woman will ever wear it. Just as Reed wanted every Dom and sub alike to know Mia is not available, we want them all to know that you belong to us and only us. Apparently this is a lesson you need to learn to, sub."

Every breath and every syllable that left his mouth brushed past my ear and was ingrained on my mind and body. My heart began to pound so hard against I was sure it was about to burst out of my chest. I felt my head begin to spin and I struggled to remember how to breath, dread clutched at me as I started to recognize the signs of a panic attack.

My vision began to blur and the room spun violently as I gathered the last remaining energy and yanked free. I stumbled headlong into the crowd searching desperately for the door.

I dodged around people as best I could and somehow successfully managed to sidestep every Dom that tried to grab me. I ran, not even acknowledging the voices closing in behind me that were calling my name.

Tripping up the stairs I finally made it to the last exit door and swung it open with all my strength. The faces on the other side of the door did not resemble anything human to my blurry eyes and I stumbled away from the crowds, searching for a quiet place.

I leaned against the side of the building and bent to put my head between my legs trying desperately to draw even an ounce of air into my oxygen starved lungs.

My legs gave out as I slowly realized the only inhaler that I had brought was still downstairs. Closing my eyes and allowing myself to drop with the expectation that at any moment I'd feel the hard impact of the pavement. Instead a pair of strong arms caught me and until the tingling sensation registered I thought they were a stranger's.

When I peeked I found Jack's dark eyes swirling with concern and fear searching my face. His arms tightened around me when I opened my mouth to demand he let me go. Dismay took the last breath I had in me when I realized the only thing that was coming out was little squeaks.

"J-J-J-" was all I got out before my fight with the dark oblivion finally took its toll and I went limp.

Whispers penetrated the darkness surrounding me and slowly began to increase until I could make out bits and pieces of the conversations going on around me.

"That's ridiculous, Jordan. You can't just spring something like that on to her and just expect her to accept it. It's no wonder she panicked with your fumbling way of handling it," a voice said right next to my ear. It held a plethora of irritation that even my foggy brain could make out.

I would know that voice anywhere, Mia. She had obviously taken great exception to what Jordan and Jack had done. I knew her well enough; it didn't shock me that her mouth had overridden her brain; as it had a habit of doing on a normal basis.

It was to Mia's house that I had ran to at sixteen and had finally managed to get away from my drunken abusive father. At the time I chose Mia's house based purely on selfish reasons. I knew her parents, I knew they had money and connections and I knew they could protect me. In the end they did more than that, they took me in without hesitation and gave me a warm, loving home.

Ever since that day Mia had taken to being my champion whenever she saw the necessity of it and apparently she did for the second time tonight. I wanted to warn her that she wasn't going to get away with talking to Jordan like that again when-

"Mia!"

Jordan's voice whipped through the room with a crackle and it made me wonder if Mia would ever truly learn that she could not continue to be disrespectful to these men. It's a hard lesson for a new sub to learn, I knew from experience. The first year of my life in this whole new world was a mire of discipline and wincingly bad scenes. It wasn't until Jordan had finally taken over as my Dom about a year ago that I was able to fully submit to anyone. Jordan was a good Master, one of the best according to all the subs at The Dungeon.

He didn't have a lot of rules but was strict on the ones he did have and any breaking of them would result in immediate punishment equal to the amount of disobedience.

Early in the night Jordan had set her up on the bar, short green dress pulled up and backside out for the whole club to see and grope if they wanted to. Because not only had she not called him by his proper title of Master Jordan or Sir, she had been blatantly disrespectful during the course of the conversation. It was a wonder, with how conservative Mia is, that she would even dare that type of humiliation again.

It was that concern for Mia that finally had me struggling to pry my eyes open. I could feel the tension in the room about to break and I figured one punishment a night would do for her.

My first sight was one of Mia kneeling next to the giant leather couch I was laying on. Her face was a kaleidoscope of worried fear and I felt a sting of regret for my actions.

"Lizzie! How are you feeling?" she asked anxiously.

I took quick stock of my body just to make sure nothing was broken or bruised up too bad. I was happy that everything seemed fine, minus the pounding in my head that seemed to have absolutely no focal point.

I gave her a sardonic smile. "I'll be better once the marching band goes home."

She gave me a worried look until she realized I meant the one pacing around my head.

"Oh you're such a baby! It's just a little headache," she chided.

I had to hide a smile while pulling myself into a sitting position and leaning back against the couch. Mia should know all about headaches from passing out, it was three years ago that she had cracked her skull on the very same sidewalk. She ended up in the hospital for the night with a mild concussion. I pulled at the bottom of my skimpy nearly nothing red dress Jordan had made me wear tonight trying to make sure I was at least covered. After what had happened tonight I felt vulnerable enough I didn't need anything hanging out to make it worse.

I looked around trying to figure out what room we were in. The whole room was cloaked in dark shadows being thrown off by the fireplace making it hard to identify details, but by the large shelves that lined the wall I assumed we were in the library that Mia had told me about.

"This had better not become a habit with the subs," said a voice from the corner of the room.

I squinted through the shadows and just barely made out Reed's hulking form standing near the door way. Of course with his height I wasn't sure how anyone could miss him. However, he was wearing black like most of the Dom's around here wore so he blended in with the darkness.

I couldn't help but wonder where my own Master, or Masters, had gone to. Trying to look casually I peered around the room hoping to spot them without looking like I was trying to find them.

"Behind you," whispered Mia into my ear having not missed a thing.

Very slowly I turned half afraid of the disappointment in their eyes, or worse the anger that I would run from them when I should have stayed and talked it out.

I couldn't deny either emotion because I knew full well it was deserved. My behavior was not one befitting a sub with the experience I had, but when I felt the panic attack come on the hysteria became worse until it was like a snowball running downhill.

The panic attacks hadn't been a problem for me for a while now thanks to Mia's mother, Maggie and the therapist they had sent me to. All I could do at this point was pray that it was just a one-time thing.

My eyes finally fell on them standing near the far back of the room. Jack was right next to the window watching everything intently not missing even a single movement. His face was perfectly blank but I sensed a distinct agitation from him, however I didn't have the courage to ask him anything just yet. He turned back to the window running his hands through his hair giving it a slightly unkempt look that made me want to running to him and straighten it out again.

Just a short distance away from him, leaning against the table looking openly frustrated and annoyed was Jordan. My heart twisted painfully when I saw the disappointment that I was expecting in his eyes. I looked away hoping to hide the pain that I felt at having let them both down and twisted back around to address Mia again.

"I need to go home," I said and winced at the hiss of rejection from the two men behind me.

I glanced over my shoulder in time to see Jordan shove away from the desk and head my way. Instinctively I shrunk away from him and watched as anger and hurt filled his face. I looked away unbelievably ashamed at my behavior towards him, towards the both of them. It seemed as if I was unable to control my actions tonight and every move, sound, or step I made did nothing but harm them.

Jordan let out a frustrated growl and stalked over to the window next to Jack seemingly like he was turning his back on me. I wasn't sure if that's what he meant to do but the response I had was the same. The heartbreak got worse and tears gathered in my eyes until I was almost blinded. Fearing the dam would break and I'd end up bawling on the couch in front of everyone I looked back at Mia and pleaded with my eyes for some help to get out of here.

Mia bit her lip reaching up to grasp the collar Reed had given her and I could tell by the uncertainty in her face she wasn't sure it was the right decision for me to go home with so much left unresolved.

I wasn't sure if it was the right move or not either but the turbulent emotions rolling through me made it impossible to trust anyone or anything. Mia continued to stare at me while she was deep in thought and played with the little name plate that said "Mine" at the clasp of the chain-linked collar. I reached up in a movement that mirrored hers and grasped my own collar. Needing to feel the smooth coolness of it just to make sure it was real, but my hand touched nothing but the bare skin of my neck.

It wasn't there.

I gasped out loud and felt a new panic beginning to course through me as I immediately searched for it frantically in the couch, praying that it had just slipped between the cushions and that it hadn't fallen off in the midst of my mad dash through the crowd.

"I have it."

Chapter Two

I looked up to find Jack holding it gently, almost reverently in his hands as if it were the most precious diamond in the world.

To a sub, having your Master collar you is a big honor. It's his way of telling the D/s world that you are off-limits unless he says otherwise. To collar a sub is no little thing either, more often than not it's likened to asking someone to marry you, or move in with you. The removal or rejection of one was even more serious to both parties and not something anyone took lightly.

The shock that they had collared me was nothing to the shock that now ran through my body when I realized exactly how much I really did want them. Then again only a dead woman would be able to resist them. These men were like night and day in looks and personality, still they both were sexy as hell. Just one of them could bring a normal woman to her knees and together they would reduce her to a quivering pile.

Jordan was shorter than Jack and kept his blonde hair impossibly short but it was his eyes that got me first. One look from those steel gray eyes and a sub would drop to her knees immediately. From what I could see of Jack's eyes they were very dark almost black, and were the cause of the shivers I felt down my back at first sight. Instead of being turned off by them, I found myself intrigued.

They deserved someone better than me. It wasn't that I thought I was bad looking, it was quite the opposite, I knew I was good looking. I was constantly getting compliments on my long blonde hair, long legs, and my blue eyes. My breasts weren't big like Mia's, still they managed to get attention when I wanted them to. The only complaint I'd ever had was that I was a bit on the skinny side, although I was able to blame that on an active lifestyle and a high metabolism. On the outside I knew I was good looking. But on the inside, I still feel like that scared little girl trying to figure out why my daddy hated me and why my mommy wasn't there anymore.

The drastic crazy events of the night didn't help the insecurities that I'd try to battle for so long. This situation was so far beyond my experience and expectations it wasn't even funny.

Yet at the same time I couldn't help but wonder what it would be like to just give in to them both. Maybe I could just once, whined a little needy voice inside my head. I squelched it faster than a spider I caught racing a crossed the floor. Along with the other eerily ominous whisper that brushed through my head telling me that once would never be enough.

I tore my gaze away from the object of my longing and curled my hands into the couch to keep me on it so I wouldn't jump up and rush towards it and them.

"Please, Mia. I really just need to go home," I pleaded with her again.

She nodded finally giving in and walked over to Reed kneeling at his feet as gracefully as if she'd done it a million times with her eyes downcast in the traditional sub position.

"Is it okay if we borrow your limo to take us home, Sir?" she asked softly.

I felt a bit of jealousy run through me at the ease she'd taken to her submissive role especially when she was still in the learning stages.

The first two years for me were a mire of punishment and disappointed or outright frustration. By the time Jordan had taken over, hardly any of the other Masters would work with me. However, Jordan seemed to have a knack at knowing exactly what it took to easily bring me to my knees.

I shook my head to erase some of the memories of what had happened over the last year as some of the things we had done, now suddenly made sense. In my traitorous mind, I slowly went through them one by one and inserted Jack into those scenes. I immediately felt myself grow wet and I had to wiggle a bit to relieve some of the growing ache.

"Yes, my little sub, you may. But come straight back, tonight I am going to introduce you to a few new toys that I keep here at the club," Reed said, his voice bringing me out of my musings.

Reed had a devilish grin on his face that made Mia shiver and I saw her eyes dilate with desire.

"Yes, Master," she said softly.

Quickly she arose from the floor and up to her tippy toes to give him a gentle kiss. I watched fascinated as it only took a moment for Reed to respond, and when he did, it was with a hungry growl. Then he pinned her to his chest tightly and rapidly took over the toe-curling kiss. Suddenly I realized I was acting the voyeur on their private moment and I had to turn away. My gaze ended up being caught on the two men in the corner whose eyes were glued on me as well. My heart stopped, then sped up as I saw them blazing with identical emotions, pure unadulterated lust.

"Lizzie, come here," Jordan ordered softly, yet the tone was hard as steel.

I let my feet touch the floor and noted with a mixture of both relief and anxiety I realized I was barefoot. Probably a good thing given how weak kneed I felt, however the loss of my shoes left me feeling small and even more fragile at that moment, which was a feeling I did not need help with.

When I finally managed to step up to them, they surrounded me instantly, very effectively enclosing me between them. That didn't help the feeling of smallness one bit. All worries and fears soon flew out of my head as Jordan lifted my chin and forced me to look at him. I became ensnared in his heated eyes that were churning with desire and promise.

His gaze briefly flickered to Jack and as if it was the signal, Jack's hands came up and gripped my forearms instantly, effortlessly capturing me. I took a breath to steady myself knowing that the fear I was feeling was a normal reaction. But instead of soothing me, each breath drew more and more of their intoxicating scents until I felt branded by them.

My body tightened as a sense of awareness took over and pulsed through me as I tuned into every little movement these men made.

Jordan dropped tiny kisses on my cheeks and my tension melted slowly away until Jack shifted behind me. Stiffening, I waited for any signs of jealousy to come from Jack, but the only thing that happened was he pulled me closer.

His arousal pressed hard against my back and I couldn't believe that he was getting aroused watching Jordan kiss me, even more unbelievable was how turned on I was getting knowing that.

I watched as Jordan slowly lowered his mouth to mine, inch by sweet torturous inch and I realized he was giving me a chance to deny him. With the tight grip Jack had me in there was no way I could refuse him even if I'd wanted to. It shocked me how much I didn't want to refuse either of them. My mouth watered with anticipation for their dominance and the loss of control on my part just made it all the sweeter, heightening my arousal. I could feel myself already dripping wet and I silently cursed Jordan for a moment because he had insisted on me not wearing any underwear. Without them the dampness between my legs was twice as obvious.

When Jordan's mouth finally touched mine it was in a kiss so sweetly gentle that a small sigh escaped my lips. The feel of the kiss was so achingly familiar, along with the restrained desire that I tasted on Jordan's tongue, that it excited me and soon had me swept away.

I felt fingers brush softly across the back of my neck, sending shivers down my spine as my hair was swept aside giving Jack access to the back of my neck, which he immediately took advantage of by raining kisses from my ear down to my exposed shoulder blade. My ability to think at all quickly vanished as my body began to pulse with all-consuming desire. It took all the will power I possessed not to wriggle in Jack's strong grip just to get closer.

My knees almost gave out as my whole body became focused on the tingling sensations that were being stirred up with every touch of their lips, and when I felt a breath sweep across the back of my neck a small moan left my lips as my nipples tightened painfully hard against the constrictive material of my dress.

Instinctively, I arched my neck in a silent plea for more. Jordan chose that moment to break the kiss and a disappointed whimper popped out of my mouth. Startled, I opened my eyes and stared up at him in confusion wondering why he had stopped when it had felt so good.

Jack let go of my hands just as suddenly and gripped my shoulders and spun me around, answering my silent question immediately. I felt an almost giddy excitement as I realized it was his turn. Our eyes met long enough for me to realize that his dark eyes were actually a warm chocolate brown and they were gleaming with desire and anticipation. I couldn't help the shiver that went down my spine at the intensity that was radiating from his face. My body must have responded of its own accord because despite my reservation it didn't hesitate to lean into him.

As if it was a signal, he swooped in and kissed me hard, as if he was a drowning man and I was his last sip of water. His tongue didn't ask for permission as it plunged into my mouth and forced my tongue into a duel with his. I gladly complied with his demands because I longed to learn his taste as badly as he wanted to learn mine. The feel of his tongue rubbing against mine left me feeling hot with need, and practically begging for more. I reached up and grasped his shoulders, clinging to him.

Jordan's kiss had already started the fire that was slowly burning, Jack's kiss finished the job and stoked the burning desire to a roaring fire of lust making me so wet that even as I squeezed my legs together I knew I was going to embarrass myself.

Jack's hands reached down to cup my ass and pulled me tight against him as if he knew exactly what I wanted. My breasts felt heavy and sensitive as they smashed up against his unforgiving, hard, leather covered chest. My hard nipples getting stimulated every time they moved even slightly.

The little hairs that dotted the area not covered by his vest rubbed against my bare skin sensitizing my nerve endings and making every touch of his body more arousing. A little moan escaped from me and Jack quickly swallowed it up, his mouth devouring mine leaving no spot untouched by his exploring tongue.

I felt Jordan step up behind me and press his equally hard chest against my back, his sweet lips swiftly picked up where

Jack's had left off on my neck. Unable to contain it anymore I began to fidget causing them both to press more firmly to restrict me. I was in the middle right where they wanted me to be and I basked in the undivided attention from these two sexy men.

The hands that were cupping my ass balled into a pair of fists dragging the bottom edge of my dress up, exposing my backside.

"Spread your legs," Jordan demanded hoarsely in my ear.

I didn't hesitate, my very existence depended on the sensual delights these men were awakening in me.

I spread my legs as far as they would go and gasped into Jack's mouth when a pair of questing fingers slid between my dripping wet pussy lips. I tried to press back into the soft touch to make the fingers finally touch my pouting clit but Jack and Jordan had united. I pulled back from Jack's insistent kisses trying to catch a breath and ended up just panting soft whining breaths against his lips. Jordan kept up with his caresses until I thought I would go mad if he didn't let me come soon.

"Please, Please, Master," I begged him.

I heard a deep lust filled growl come from under my lips and my eyes snapped open clashed with Jack's. His face filled with carnal appreciation as he watched closely not missing a single twitch as Jordan brought me rapidly to a mind blowing climax.

Instead of scaring me or horrifying me, it inflamed me even more and the next pass of Jordan's fingers sent me over the edge hard and unexpectedly. My sweet climax causing streaks of tingling pleasure to radiated throughout my body starting from my core. My pussy walls squeezed together trying to milk something that wasn't there and it wept its juices down my legs when it realized it was empty, but I was too far gone to care.

Before the last of my soft keening cries spilled out of my mouth, Jack slammed his down on mine again, sucking all the noise and breath out of me. His tongue tangled with mine as if he could taste my pleasure on it and he couldn't get enough of it.

Jack finally released my mouth only to trace little nipping kisses along my jaw line to my neck once again. On the other side Jordan was doing the same and as if by some unspoken command they attacked simultaneously, biting and sucking hard marking me as effectively as if they'd left the collar on. The minute they bit me,

I cried out unable to quietly take the dual assault and my whole body went up in flames. I knew they were marking me on purpose, but instead of trying to push them away, I dug my nails into Jack's shoulders. Thinking unconsciously that if he was going to mark me, I would do the same to him. I heard a grunt and worried that I'd hurt him, but if the erection that was pressed tightly against my stomach was any indication, he was loving the feel of my nails on him.

I heard a throat being cleared off to the side causing me to jump, which unfortunately caused my shoulders to knock both of the men in the head as they hadn't released my neck just yet. I couldn't tell if the aggravated noises they made were from the hit or from the fact they had to let go of my neck.

We looked over to find Reed leaning against the doorway, Mia was nowhere in sight.

"Mia went to get the limo," Reed said as if reading my mind, his mouth lifted in a grin at one corner.

"But if you don't need it right now please let me know, I'd be happy to let you use the room in the back. Lizzie, I think you know where it is. I seem to recall finding you and Master Jordan in there about three years ago."

I jumped away from them quickly and hurriedly straightened my dress as I ducked my head as the embarrassment warmed my face. I silently cursed my skin which made the redness so obvious. You'd think after the last three years in this club I would have little left that would embarrass me. But this situation was like being caught with your pants down in the back of your father's car. At that thought my father's voice suddenly started ringing in my ears unsolicited.

"You're a slut, Elizabeth. A whore just like your mother," his voice slurred drunkenly and was angrily nasty.

If the words weren't bad enough I was suddenly overwhelmed by a strong smell of whiskey. Instantly my stomach churned and I had to slap a hand over my mouth in an effort not to be sick. I pulled even further away from the men and began taking slow, steady breath's in order to stave off the agonizing feelings as well as the panic attack I felt coming on again.

"Lizzie?" Jack inquired quietly.

I turned to him and found his perceptive gaze boring into me. I knew if I spent any amount of time with him that I may soon come to either be grateful for such insightfulness or hate it with a passion.

"Yes," I croaked, then cleared my voice knowing I wouldn't be able to fool him unless I tried harder than that.

"Yes, I'm fine I think I'm just tired, I'm still recovering from being sick. Jordan was right earlier I shouldn't have come here tonight. I just don't like the idea of other woman clinging on him like they do when I'm not around and-"

I broke off as I tried to catch my breath again from the nonsensical babble that was spewing from my mouth. I strained to concentrate on the other sounds of the room to find some way to ignore the sense of dirtiness and panic beginning to wash over me as the sound of my father's voice became more insistent in my head. No matter how many breaths I took or how much I tried to tune into the conversation that Jordan and Reed were having, it wasn't helping. My vision started to cloud once again and I felt myself slip back into the darkness.

Chapter Three

"ELIZABETH!" Jack snapped as he gripped my shoulders and shook me slightly.

My eyes flew open before I had even realized they were closed and locked with Jack's. No one had ever called me Elizabeth except my parents, which normally was a sore spot, but for some reason when he called me that it helped snap me out of the dark hole I was falling into.

"Breathe with me, honey," he whispered as he leaned his head against mine.

He breathed in through his nose and out through his mouth several times as I struggled to match his rhythm. I stared into his eyes and allowed myself to relax bit by bit, despite my head's warning that I barely knew him. My body seemed to recognize that I could trust him so I did something crazy and allowed myself to be swept away in him, quickly relaxing and breathing calmly.

"Good girl," Jack whispered.

He wrapped his arms around me and urged me to lay my head on his chest. The steady strong beats of his heart soon gave mine a rhythm to match. We stood pressed together for a moment and I felt a sense of peace come over me, as if he was the missing piece to the puzzle. That scared me more than anything in the world.

If I screwed this up by being too tired or displeasing both of them would risk losing not only one Master, but two. With so much to lose the thought of submitting to them seemed daunting.

"How long have you been having panic attacks, baby?" Jack whispered into my ear, bringing me out of my nasty thoughts.

I pulled away and shook my head unsure of what else to do since I wasn't ready to discuss my past with anyone.

I looked up at Jack with pleading eyes, silently asking him to understand why I couldn't tell him yet. I saw shadows dim his eyes, but he just shook his head and pulled completely away leaving me feeling more alone than ever. I looked to Jordan for help or understanding but instead all I got was a shake of his head.

"Go, Mia's waiting to take you home," Jordan said, disappointment evident in his eyes as well.

Pain shot into my heart at knowing I had disappointed him. I began to feel panicky again so I quickly began walking out the door.

"Lizzie," Jordan called.

I turned around to see both men staring at me, their arms crossed over their chest in exactly the same stance.

"Yes?" I said softly not sure if I wanted to hear what he was going to say.

"We will discuss the events of tonight in full detail later. This is not an escape. It is a momentary truce," Jack finished for him.

"You make it sound like a battle," I said, my throat felt so raw that it came out as barely a whisper.

Their smiles turned virile and I saw a light flash in Jack's eyes as Jordan winked at me

"Oh it is, sub, and just to let you know we have never lost a battle," Jordan said warningly.

I just looked at them while I let their words soak in. They still wanted me after everything and I had to fight the joy that began to rise in me with a large stick of reality. I couldn't think of any way for this to work.

When no answers presented themselves to me, I ran like the hounds of hell were on my heels not stopping or slowing until I all but jumped into the limo that was waiting for me. I slammed the door shut still feeling as if they were going to reach in to grab me and drag me back inside, where I would be tied up and ravished. I felt a shiver of pleasure go down my spine at that picture.

One could only hope, came a stray thought rattling around in my head. I sighed, hating the mess that my thoughts were in and stared down at my feet. A sound of distress burst from my lips as I realized I had left my shoes in the library.

"Oh, hell and those were my favorite shoes, damn it!"

I cursed and slammed my hand against the seat in agitation. There was no way I was going back in for them because I knew there was no way the men would let me leave again. Damn it, this night had not gone the way it was supposed to.

Damn it.

Leann Lane

Chapter Four

"So, are we going to talk about it or are you going to sit there and look like something the cat dragged in?" Mia asked softly.

I almost jump straight up in the air having forgotten she was there. I could hear the worry in her voice despite her angry words.

I sighed in resignation. "What do you want to talk about, Mia?"

"First I want to understand your Houdini act after Reed collared me," Mia said crossing her arms over her chest.

"It wasn't a Houdini act, I just felt closed in, overwhelmed," I said trying to find the best way to describe what had happened.

"So you what, decided to run away and knocking yourself out was a good idea?" she asked sarcastically.

"No! It wasn't like that, I didn't knock myself out, either. I-I fainted," I ended in a whisper.

The shock on Mia's face would have been hilarious if the situation had been different.

"You fainted?" she asked incredulously, her mouth still hanging open.

I sighed in frustration, not really wanting to discuss this right now. What I really wanted to do was to run away and hide from the world, at least until the echoing voice of my father was chased out of my head.

"Yes, Mia. I fainted, I had a panic attack and I fainted," I explained reluctantly.

I reached up and began playing with my hair, a nervous reaction that I hadn't done in a long time. I could see by Mia's gaze that she'd caught the action and recognized it for what it was. She didn't comment on it, which I greatly welcomed.

"Okay, so you had a panic attack. Why? Did you have a problem with the idea of a threesome?" Mia asked forwardly.

My mouth hung open with astonishment at how boldly she'd asked that. Mia had always been so conservative, the exact opposite of her parents. I couldn't count how many times we'd pick on her until she was beet red in the face and stuttering. To have her speak of something so openly and honestly was a shock to me.

"No, in general, I don't have a problem with a ménage à trois. Threesome as you put it," I explained.

"Good!" Mia said emphatically. "So what's the problem? Because, despite the punishment tonight, which I still say I didn't deserve because I was just protecting you, I still think Jordan's a great man. He has deep feelings for you and I think you should give him a chance. Jack doesn't give me that creepy, stalker vibe or the woman beater vibe. Well, not any that are out of the norm for a Master."

She ended with a wink which drew a small smile from me.

"They are both wonderful. It's just … they want to collar me, Mia. That's not a small thing and you know that, it's not just Jordan that wants to collar me it's Jack too."

"So in a ménage à trois, as you called it, is it an unusual thing for someone to be collared?" Mia asked.

I thought of all the threesomes I'd seen at the club and there were quite a few. It just wasn't a relationship I'd ever contemplated having before tonight.

"No, it's not. They were able to keep up and keep each other happy. How am I supposed to keep two men happy?" I questioned sadly and looked out the window again.

I noted we were close to my apartment and couldn't help but feel relieved knowing this nightmare was coming to an end. When Mia came and sat beside me I thought she was going to hug me, instead she pinched my arm so hard I cried out.

"Ow! Mia! What the hell was that for?" I shouted rubbing my arm.

"Lizzie! You are a wonderful, loving, smart, sexy girl. Any man, or two in this situation, would be lucky to have you. Only their opinion's matter and you know that. Jordan and Jack should get on their knees and thank their lucky stars they found a woman like you," Mia spat out fiercely.

She sounded like a momma bear protecting her cub and her gaze softened as she looked at me.

"You need to realize that you are an amazing woman and stop being so hard on yourself. I think you should give them a chance," she said softly.

She finally ended up wrapping her arms around me and hugging me then. I leaned into her allowing her calm to wash over me and was grateful to have her here right now because Mia was nothing if not a good loyal friend.

"Thanks, sweetie," I whispered into her ear before pulling away.

"I mean it, Lizzie," she insisted looking me in the eyes, making sure I understood and believed her.

"I know you do, hon. I just need to get away and have some time to think," I said.

I didn't elaborate because I knew she'd understand my meaning.

I was going to the cabin.

It was her parent's cabin yet the first time I went up there they noticed a change in me immediately. So had I, for that matter, so they'd given me a key and told me to use it whenever I needed it. I wasn't a victim; I hadn't been one in a long time. I was a survivor and I planned on staying that way, I reminded myself fiercely.

"So how long are you going to be gone?" Mia asked as she walked me up to my door.

"A week, I think," I said hesitantly.

I was looking down at my toes and cursed once again at having left my shoes back at The Dungeon.

"I see," Mia said softly. "I will let Reed know when I get back to the club."

I turned and unlocked my door, then hesitated.

"Tell Jordan and Jack I'm sorry... for everything," I said softly.

Mia stared at me for a moment longer as if she was about to say something, but in the end she just nodded and left quickly. My heart twisted since I could have sworn I'd seen tears in her eyes.

"I'll miss you," I called softly though I knew she couldn't hear me.

I walked into my apartment feeling even more depressed and alone. I began to pack enough for a few days or a week if I wanted to. Ignoring anything in my closet that even screamed sexy, I went straight for the giant winter clothes I'd bought several years ago. I didn't want a single thing that reminded me of either Jordan or Jack. Sadly, as I looked through everything that Jordan had bought or I had bought to wear for him, I'd find myself wondering what Jack would think of each one of them and wondering how he'd react if I put one on.

I viciously shoved the remainder of the clothes into the depths of the closet and grabbed a lot of warm clothes because a walk on the beach sounded just like something I needed right now. I finally finished packing and looked at the clock grimacing to see at the late hour. I still had to call Maggie and Tomas just to let them know where I was going. They were Mia's parents and my foster parents, and hopefully they'd still be up.

When I'd started in this life I'd run into a friend of Maggie's at the club and, as I had feared at the time, Maggie and Tomas had found out rather quickly what I was up to.

However, instead of being horrified Maggie was delighted. All Tomas had to say on the matter was to give threats of castration with an implement that I had no idea were still being used at the time, to any man dumb enough not to follow my hard limit list. It had been a rather horrifyingly educational conversation. Maggie, on the other hand, had been so elated that I had found my 'kink', as she called it, that we talked constantly now.

I quickly dialed Maggie's number so I could at the very least leave a message and let her know because I knew Mia would do it anyway, if she hadn't done it already.

"Of course you can use the cabin. Is everything okay?" Maggie asked.

The knowing mom tone in her voice told me she already had the answer to that question.

"No. I heard his voice again," I whispered into the phone.

She made a distress noise. "What happened?"

"Same thing as always, Maggie. He was calling me a whore and a slut-"

"You are none of those things, Lizzie Moore," Maggie interrupted. "What provoked it this time I thought you were doing better?"

"I was! Jordan-Jordan wants to collar me," I blurted out.

Maggie gasped, "That's wonderful!"

"But it's not just him, his friend Jack would be a part of it too," I said trying hard to sound scandalized.

I wasn't really sure where Maggie stood with everything having to do with BDSM. I knew she was a part of a few clubs in her area, but I didn't know if this kind of situation was still considered taboo by her.

"Really?"

I felt myself relaxing when Maggie's voice held intrigue rather than disgust.

"Yes, how on earth am I going to be able to handle two men? It's-"

I couldn't think of a word that described it beyond overwhelming, because that's how I felt. I sat down on the couch in my living room and stared over the open bar into my kitchen at the only light that was on in there and lost myself in my thoughts.

"Lizzie," Maggie's voice whispered over the phone snapping me back to the conversation.

"Not to mention the sudden reappearance of my father's voice," I finished finally, unable to hide the hopelessness in my voice.

"Lizzie," Maggie started again, "I know conventional society says poly relationships are wrong. Now I don't want one, but that doesn't mean they're wrong. I'm not gay, but that doesn't make homosexuality wrong, just different. I would prefer to see you follow your heart more than what society expects."

Maggie was a wonderful mother and I was grateful every day she was in my life. She understood what I needed to hear and I never hesitated to be honest with her.

"It also doesn't make you a whore or a slut, just different. That's a good thing Lizzie. Please, instead of listening to that bastard of a father, listen to your heart. What does it say?" Maggie urged.

As she spoke of my father I could hear the venom in her voice and it sent a fresh trail of tears running down my cheeks.

"I want to, Maggie. I just can't think clearly, I want to be with them both, but I don't know how it'll last for more than one night. Every time I try to think beyond one night or start thinking maybe I can do this... I panic and now with my father's voice... I just don't know," I whispered into the phone.

"Then let me give you some advice. Mother to daughter, sub to sub," Maggie said softly. "Tell your Masters what's going on with you. Because if you really want to make this work they need to know, so they can help you."

I hung my head and braced it against my hands knowing she was right. I knew that, yet every time I think of talking to them about it to them my fear chokes me and my chest tightens up so much I could feel another panic attack coming on.

"I know," I whispered quietly in the phone.

"So, you will talk to them?" she asked.

I blew out a breath. "I'll think about it. If there is no future for us it wouldn't be fair to them to give them hope."

"Don't you think that's their choice? How can they make a decision if they don't know your worries, your fears, and your concerns? It's a Masters job to take those into account, otherwise the things you're doing are not safe. You have to let them have this knowledge," she pointed out.

I hated when she was this rational, it made the argument boil down to the heart of it, a place I wasn't really ready to go just yet.

"What if they decided I'm not enough? What if it's too hard for them?" I whispered giving voice to my deepest fears.

"Then they are dumber than bricks and don't deserve you anyway," Maggie said fiercely.

I laughed through my tears just then because she sounded just like Mia.

"Just think on it. Use the time at the cabin to think on it and remember we love you," Maggie said.

She always reminds me of that before we hang up and it never fails to make me remember what it meant to be part of a real family.

"Love you too," I said and hung up.

I sat holding the phone for a while feeling all of my energy draining out of me like water through a sieve. I decided for my safety and the safety of other drivers that the cabin could wait until tomorrow and headed to the bedroom with every intention of going straight to bed.

On the way I walked right past my mirror and was struck by how pale I was. The two dark marks that sat on either side of my neck were visible against the stark contrast of my pale skin. I lifted a hand and touched them gently causing a bolt of desire hit me like a blow to the stomach.

I knew why they'd left the marks on me. It was their way of reminding me of whom I belonged to, even after I'd left them standing high and dry in the library. I should have been embarrassed, mortified even that they had left such an obvious sign on me. Instead I felt heat burning through me and a sense of satisfaction or even joy that they had wanted mark me so.

I laid my head on the mirror with a frustrated groan spilling from my lips. My temperature had risen as my mind played over and over again the moment when the men had surrounded me, kissed me, gave me a mind-blowing orgasm and marked me. The coolness of the mirror felt so good against my heated skin that I briefly entertained the idea of staying there resting against it longer. However, I felt the emotional roller coaster finally took its toll. I forced myself away from the mirror and went into my room where I flopped onto the bed without even bothering to undress and passed out immediately.

Standing next to my car, I took a deep long cleansing breathe basking in the early morning air that surround me in my personal fortitude. Suddenly my problems didn't seem so insurmountable and I was finally able to breathe normally.

I took in my surrounding with glee, the white foamy waves that were crashing against a bright sandy shoreline to the dark shrub filled evergreens that towered over everything and was beckoning me to explore its depths once again.

This place, this beautiful peaceful place was the epitome of nature's balance and it never failed to make me feel so small and insignificant yet mighty and powerful all at the same time.

The cabin was off to my right nestled back against the trees. There was a path that led the way off the stairs, and then split off, one side leading into the forest and the other side lead down to the beach, and I knew both paths like the back of my hand. It didn't matter that I hadn't been here in almost four years, I still knew every bump and dip in both.

The cabin itself was a natural old wood cabin that and had been built by Mia's, god only knew how many greats, grandfather. Each generation had either been replacing or upgrading pieces of it until it was the cabin it is today. The outside had been made completely out of wood even the wrap around porch and swinging bench were made of wood. The inside, on the other hand, was as modern as they came except for the wood stove, there was heating and electricity, but they were rarely used.

I rushed into the cabin and threw everything into the only bedroom and immediately headed for the beach.

The air that was rushing off the water quickly left my cheeks flushed and my lips with a salty taste on them, but I didn't mind. I felt my tilted and churning world slowly right itself as I began to delve into my whirling thoughts.

The first one that came to mind was my father's voice. It was still in the background calling me names and running me down. It was the loudest of them all and the most tiring trying to ignore.

The first time my father called me names was when I was three and I learned two lessons that day. The first, my father was a mean and cruel man to us all; the second, how to run and hide from him. A lesson I had cultivated into perfection by the time I was twelve.

I'd accidentally spilled my milk all over the table and down into his lap since he was sitting right next to me. My brother Trev was five at the time and I remember looking to him and my mother for cues as to what I was supposed to do, when I saw the unmistakable fear in their eyes I knew I was in deep trouble and began to cry.

"You stupid fucking little brat," my father slurred angrily.

36

He had been drunk at the time, not that I knew the difference. But as always when he was drunk, he got meaner. He raised his hand to slap me when my mother stepped in and took the blow herself. That only made him angrier and he proceeded to beat my mother as Trev took my hand and hid both of us in the upstairs closet. I remember burying my head in his shoulder and then he covered my ears so I wouldn't hear what was going on.

After our mother ran away when I was twelve, he started taking the abuse so my father wouldn't go looking for me. I brought him soup one night after a particularly nasty incident and he was grateful. I began cooking for him as often as I could, it was probably the only reason we didn't starve to death.

The only good thing that happened around that time was my father took his drinking to the bar every night after work, this became our favorite time of the day. That would all change once my father got home. It would become hell on earth and my brother would meet him at the front door to take the brunt of it. I loved my brother dearly, he'd become my hero and my only regret was that I had never taken the time to thank him properly for protecting me as he had.

Until the night he told me he was leaving to join the army. For months after Trev left I held nothing but animosity for him, but after a while I let it go because I couldn't blame him for finding a way out. I began counting down the days until my eighteenth birthday so I could leave as well.

Then one night everything changed.

Chapter Five

I had successfully been hiding from him for the last week. Like most nights I was sleeping in Trev's bed because, despite my anger, I missed him terribly. Also because my stupid father never thought to look for me in there, but It wasn't my father that found me; it was one of his buddies that was just as drunk as he was. I remember waking up as soon as the door opened and hid under the covers as his voice came to me from the dark.

"Hey, purdy lady. How's about you come out from under that cover and we'll talk. Yer daddy's downstairs passed out drunk and I'm getting bored," he said as he sat on the edge of the bed.

He smelled of urine, vomit and whiskey and I had to try hard not to throw up as his stench seemed to surround me. I gripped the blanket tighter and tried to sink into the bed hoping, if I didn't make any noise he might leave me alone and I'd be safe. Instead he ripped the blanket off me with a triumphant laugh.

"Oh, you are purdy. Why don't you come sit on my lap?" he sneered grabbing my arm and pulling me to him.

I struggled harshly, kicking and punching at him, but he just kept laughing until he pulled me on his lap beginning to grope savagely at my breasts and pulling at my shirt obviously hoping it would rip off. My vision turned red and the next thing I saw was my fist, balled up perfectly like Trev had taught me, going into his nose which broke with a sickening crunch. Ignoring the pain radiating up my arm as he dropped me on the floor so his hand could grab his blood spewing nose I jumped up and ran without hesitation. I raced down stairs to where my father had passed out in the chair and slapped his face to bring him out of his drunken stupor.

"What the fuck do you think you're doing, you little bitch?" he screamed at me.

High on adrenaline I found my caution was thrown to the wind.

"Your buddy just tried to rape me!" I screamed back at him.

"Bullshit! Franks a good man!" my father shouted back.

My mouth dropped in disbelief. All I could do was just stare at him trying to figure out if he was serious or if he was really just that stupid, I was pretty sure it was the latter. As my mind was still trying to figure it out, Frank stumbled down the stairs still holding his nose and groaning in pain. Pride welled in my chest at the knowledge I had indeed broken his nose, hopefully shattered it came a vindictive thought.

"Your slut of a daughter came on to me, Steve, and when I refused to screw her, she broke my fucking nose," Frank said.

His drunken slur was nasal and his hand never left his nose even while the blood trickled through his fingers.

"Don't shock me none, Frank. She's just like her mother, a little whore. Maybe I ought ta start making people pay for it," Steve said with a belly chuckle that jiggled his bulging stomach.

I grew dizzy which was always the first sign of a panic attack coming on. They had been a frequent visitor for so long now that I had gotten good at learning the symptoms.

Filled with desperation and frustrating hopelessness, I picked up the nearest lamp and chucked it at them with all my strength. The cord ripped out of the wall and barely scraped my father's face, but the lamp itself slammed right into Franks head knocking him out cold and I ran. The pounding of my feet barely drowned out the sound of my father screaming obscenities and the crash of things breaking. I didn't stop running until I passed out on the street.

When I awoke I was surrounded by the paramedics. They had bandaged up my hand and told me to come by the hospital later and get it splinted since it was broken. When they asked where home was, I gave them Mia's address in hopes they would take me there. I knew that her mother was a nurse and her father was a well-respected lawyer and if anyone could help me it was them.

I have to give Mia a great deal of credit, when she saw me pull up in the ambulance she didn't even bat an eye as she said "Yes, she lives here."

When they pulled away I began to spew out my story as fast as I could and Mia immediately went to action calling both the cops and her parents.

I can recall a brief encounter with my father a few nights later. He apparently had stumbled to their front door and was yelling at them, warning them that I was a drug addict, a whore, and would corrupt their daughter. I'd hid in Mia's bed trying to come yet another panic attack until he left.

At the custody meeting my father had a cast on and two black eyes. So I could guess from Tomas' bloody knuckles what had happened and once we left the court room I hugged Tomas as tightly as I could.

Ever since that day I had done my best to make the Johnson's proud of me and to put that bastard out of my mind as well as my life.

"SO LEAVE ME ALONE, YOU FUCKING DRUNK ASS PIECE OF SHIT!" I screamed to the sky.

As soon as the words were out of my mouth my memories came to a halt and I felt like a million tons of weight lifted off my shoulders leaving me able to breathe once again.

It was getting dark by the time I made it back to the cabin and I quickly went in and built up a fire. I got caught up in the colors of the flames as they danced through the darkened house. I decided to sit in front of it leaving the lights off. I laid down on the couch, staring at it for a while not really thinking about anything, just letting my tired mind relax. Of course being the traitor that it is, it brought up Jordan and Jack making my heart ache and wondering what they were doing and if they missed me too.

I sighed in frustration calling myself a million kinds of idiot for missing them both as well and threw my arm over my eyes trying hard to block out the images of their faces. My mind didn't stop there, it brought up the memory of the first night I'd ever seen Jordan.

I couldn't believe this was happening, I hadn't meant for this to happen. It was her birthday and I'd wanted her to wear this sexy little corset I'd never been able to fill out properly and this cute little mini that showed off her assets to the max. The end all had been a set of stilettos that had been held together with a few dinky straps. I should have known better than to make her wear them, Mia had never been coordinated or graceful and I'd made her wear the worst possible shoes.

I was in a panic as Reed, the owner of the club, came out and carried her gently through the club into a room in the back. They sent me into a kitchen through the back so I wouldn't stay out in the club with everyone else because you weren't allowed in until you signed the confidentiality agreement. I didn't care, I was glad that I wasn't out there with all those people. I wanted to drown in my own self-pity.

I sat at the small table, my head lying on my arms and trying hard to stem the tears rolling out of my eyes. I hated to cry, I had been taught young that crying would never get me anything. Anxiety of not knowing how Mia was and the frustration of my own guilt had the tears rolling at a steady pace.

I felt a hand on my shoulder and I spun around quickly thinking it was the owner with news about Mia. The owner of the hand jumped out of the way just in time as my elbow passed within an inch of his stomach.

"Holy shit!" he shouted.

"Oh my God!" I cried as I stood up. "I'm so sorry, I'm just really jumpy tonight."

He wasn't nearly as tall as the owner was, yet he still had a few inches on me, even while I was wearing my heels. His hair closely shaved to his head, however I could still tell it was a blonde. His eyes were an interesting gray color that I could get lost in. I was enthralled immediately, unable to keep my eyes off his very muscular physique. He had to have been a full six foot of solid muscles. He was wearing a white T-shirt that stuck to every imaginable surface on his chest. I was certainly imagining it, but it was his biceps that were almost my undoing and sent delicious shivers down my spine. The salacious image of him picking me up and putting me on the counter floated through without much work.

My eyes continued downward taking in every titillating sight like the sweet little eye candy that the man was. Most of the men that I saw here were wearing a pair of skin tight leather pants. Not this man, this man wore faded jeans with holes in them making him look as if he'd just come from a construction site, which for all I knew he could have. I noticed he was barefoot, odd for a man, yet it gave him a more heathenish appearance.

"Are you okay?" he asked, breaking me out of my admiration of him.

My mind was already foggy due to all the alcohol I had shoved into it tonight and I didn't need a hot, sexy man clouding my judgment. I shook my head in an effort to try and remember why I was here.

"Yes, I'm so sorry. I'm just really anxious to know how my friend is doing," I said with a nervous shake to my tone.

I grabbed a napkin off the table and wiped my face with it praying my makeup wasn't too beyond repair. I felt an immense need for this man to find me beautiful even as I chided myself for thinking such a thing.

"She'll be fine, I'm sure. Master Reed is going to check on her and the ambulance is on the way as we speak," he said trying to reassure me.

"Ambulance!" I squeaked, my hand flying to my mouth. "Oh no! What have I done? I just wanted to show her how cute she could look and now she's going to the hospital and -"

"Stop," he said firmly.

My mouth snapped closed so fast I almost bit my tongue off.

"The ambulance is strictly precaution. She did hit her head when she fell and Master Reed would feel a lot better if she was checked out. As for you, yes, it was a dumb thing to make your friend wear shoes she couldn't walk in. But you didn't push her down or trip her, it was an accident and I'm sure everything will be fine, so calm down."

I nodded miserably feeling only slightly better. I sat back down and pulled my cup of coffee closer. They wouldn't give me anything stronger, believe me I asked.

"What's your name?" he asked sitting down across from me.

"Lizzie," I said staring into my cup of coffee miserably.

"What's that short for?"

"It's short for Elizabeth. Elizabeth Moore, and you are?" I replied irritably.

I tried really hard not to glare at him since I hated my full name and never used it if I could help it.

"You can call me Master Jordan or Sir. Whichever you prefer," he said with a shrug.

I raised my eyebrow. "Master Jordan? Now we aren't full of ourselves are we?"

His eyes darkened to a steel gray as he straightened in his chair and stared at me. As for me, I squirmed in my own, hearing warning bells going off in my head and feeling distinctly uncomfortable. I lowered my gaze to my coffee cup and refusing to look at him, caving under the harsh glare of his gaze. Suddenly he threw his head back and laughed making me jump straight up in the air.

"Yes, I am full of myself and I have every right to be. You can ask any sub here; they'll tell you I am one of the best. Do you know what that means?" he asked leaning in closer.

There was a whole table between us and I still felt as if he was crowding me. I leaned back and folded my arms then watched as his eyes followed the movement appreciatively. The shifting had caused my breasts to swell up and almost over the top of my corset, inadvertently I had given him an unhindered view of my cleavage. I dropped my arms down quickly and felt a flush of heat as he smiled at me with a distinctively predatory grin.

"No, I'm sorry, I don't," I lied.

I was desperately trying to distract him from whatever thoughts were running through his head and hoping he would drop the subject.

"Have you ever heard of BDSM?" he asked with a knowing grin.

That bastard was on to me, I realized with dire certainty. If I were honest with myself, his attention was arousing. Still, I couldn't help hear 'he's way out of your league' run through my mind. I shook my head, as much to answer his question as to knock the warning out of it.

"It's a form of erotic play," he explained as if that told me everything.

"Erotic play? What do you mean like... spankings and ropes? Because let me tell you, I know all about those and it's not all it's cracked up to be," I spouted out haughtily.

He smiled and shook his head. "Baby girl, this goes way beyond some little light rope play, so far beyond, that you may get scared."

The fire in his eyes made me catch my breath as my blood began to heat up. He grasped my hand and began rubbing his thumb gently across my knuckles each pass sending another spike of fiery lust through me.

"But feeling fear is normal. In fact, some subs say it heightens their arousal."

My mouth went dry as he gazed across at me from under his lashes, his gray eyes sparkling with mischief. Annoyed, I realized he knew exactly what he was doing to me and he was doing it on purpose, the freaking jerk. I snatched my hand back and had to curl it into a ball to keep from slapping him.

"I don't enjoy being played for starters. I can tell you right now, you son of a bitch, yes, I know what a sub is and there's no way in hell I'm ever going to submit to you," I growled at him.

I saw several emotions cross his face anger, disbelief, and another one that made me quake. His eyes became hard as rock and his mouth clenched in determination and I felt myself stiffen.

"Oh, really?" he said softly.

Yeah, I'm in deep shit. I thought to myself.

Leann Lane

Chapter Six

I pinched the bridge of my nose trying to figure a way out of this so I could find out how Mia was doing and get the hell outta this place.

"Look, I really appreciate your-" I waved my hands at his body, "manliness."

Even in the white T-shirt and faded torn jeans his manliness was very evident and I felt another shiver try to crawl its way down my back. He raised an eyebrow at me and ignoring him and the shiver, I continued.

"I really was not coming here to submit to a man. I was actually coming here to ah-" I broke off realizing I had nothing else coming to me.

I bit my lip trying hard to come up with a believable reason to be in this exclusive club that apparently was all about bondage. I'd tried bondage once and it had turned out terrible, giving a man two black eyes was not exactly my idea of a good time. I winced inwardly at that thought and what completely unexpected turn of events this was. I was going to have a long chat with Bethany when I saw her, the tricky wench. She had probably thought that this whole situation would be so funny when she had sent me here.

"A friend of mine said that this was the best place to find a man who could-"

I scrambled for a good explanation because saying 'who could get your panties soaked' to this man suddenly seemed like a

47

terrible idea. I stuttered and stumbled over my words for a bit longer as his eyes bore into me.

"A man that could make a girl melt," I ended lamely hopelessly embarrassed.

The laughter started from Jordan's eyes, the hard gray went to soft twinkling silver and his mouth which had been set in a harsh line softened to turn upward. The rumbling in his chest broke into a flood of full out belly laughter.

If looks could kill, I'd be giddily watching him wriggling around on the floor in pain. I'd probably be dancing around his decaying body right now.

"I don't see what's so funny, asshole," I snapped at him.

Just like that, the laughter died and once again I felt my stomach tighten in impending doom.

"No person, sub or otherwise has ever given me as much disrespect as you have and gotten away with it. I have half a mind to put you over my knee right here and now," he stated leaning back in his chair, a deadly calm shrouding him.

My temper now had me in its destructive grasp, and despite knowing I was in deep trouble as it was, it's clutches tightened and I found myself leaning towards him to glare daggers at his chest.

"Better men than you have tried," I said softly.

I knew it was a dare and maybe I had meant it to happen and looking back now I could see the self-destructive spiral I was spinning into. Maybe I had needed what would happen next, God knows I'd wanted it.

Jordan stood up and walked around the table until he towered over me. My heart sped up, even as I struggled to keep a calm facade in place so as not to let him know I was being affected by him. Unfortunately, he leaned in so close that his breath bathed my ear causing little goose bumps to break out across my shoulders as my breathing to become ragged in a way that I could not hide. I could feel his smile radiate through every part of me and just like, that my anger vanished and was replaced by something more destructive, desire.

"Baby girl, there is no man better than me and I think you know that," he whispered.

With each of his words, his mouth brushed around the shell of my ear sending tiny shivers down my back. I turned my head

48

slowly with the only thought being to get his mouth, and its tormenting effect on my already aroused body, away. Our eyes clashed and I knew that had been small compared to the response that was stirring deep within me now. The image of some of the things I wanted him to do with this particular body part came to mind and I stilled as an alarming realization hit me. I wanted him, I wanted him as much as I wanted my next breath.

"Is that so?" I whispered sealing the challenge.

He stared at me and I could feel the electricity zapping around us as if it was its own separate entity. In a snap he grabbed me out of my chair and spun me around, my arm pinned to my back. I reached around with the other one to free myself, but he snagged that also. A few clicks, a cold hard metal pressed against my wrist and I knew he had cuffed me. I began to struggle earnestly still cussing at him when he slid in front of me and grabbed my hair holding it tightly in a closed fist.

"Stop! You're doing nothing but hurting yourself and I won't allow it, Lizzie," he said harshly.

He pulled me tight to his body and held me so hard it was difficult to breath, but I couldn't tell if it was excitement, fear or how tight he held me that was causing it.

"Then, let me go," I whispered desperately.

A part of me was cheering at this masculine show of strength and another part of me started shivering in fear, at least I think it was fear. His eyes were showing signs of distress as if he was waging some inner battle against himself.

"I can't," he whispered back.

His mouth swooped down and captured mine in a harsh punishing kiss. I was stunned for a moment because this reaction was not exactly what I was expecting. Anger, annoyance, maybe even frustration, not this all consuming passion. My startled body was being tossed between fear and desire, a startling combination that had it throbbing in awareness of each twitch and tightening of his powerful body against mine. The only thing that rivaled the feel of his body against mine was his lips, they were devouring mine in a rampant fashion. I melted against him unable to fight the rising passion within me and the unyielding cuffs that bound me. I felt his hard erection pressing against my stomach and feminine joy washed through me knowing he was affected as well.

His mouth parted and gripped my bottom lip between his teeth, nibbling on it gently. It grew swollen and raw, but he soothed that feeling away with a swipe of his tongue. I opened my mouth and practically begged him to take advantage of the opportunity. He was a smart man, I could tell, because he did so without hesitation. His tongue swooped in almost as aggressively as the rest of him had. Rubbing and dueling with my tongue making my already hyper aware body restless and needy. My nipples hardened into peaks and I knew if my hands were free I would tear off the constricting corset, mainly so I can beg his hands or his mouth to touch them. I felt my self-control slipping as I was being swept away by the desire he was stirring up in me. As if sensing my imminent surrender, he pulled away slowly.

"You are submissive, baby girl. You just need to find the right Master to top you," he said with an odd look.

You would have thought he would have looked more victorious, however instead he just looked disturbed. On the other hand, I became pissed that he had the audacity to prove me wrong. I fiercely shoved my passion down and let my anger consume me until I was almost seeing red.

"I am not submissive and I would rather cut out my tongue then try that again especially with you," I said harshly. "Now, release me from these damn handcuffs."

Jordan growled and grabbed my arm again yanking me towards him and I knew he had something less pleasant in mind this time. A voice came from the doorway just in the nick of time to save me from whatever terrible punishment Jordan was about to inflict on me.

"Jordan, when I asked you to keep her out of trouble I didn't realize you'd become the trouble."

Jordan's eyes never left my face as he spoke, "I'm sorry, Reed, but this woman was a little too mouthy. I had to shut her up somehow."

My face flushed in anger and embarrassment as I yanked my arm out of his grip and turned my back to him indicating the cuffs as best I could. Luckily he gave in this time and undid them, I promptly crossed the room to be as far away from him as I could.

"Maybe I wouldn't have been so mouthy if you hadn't been such an arrogant asshole," I snapped back glaring daggers at him.

I didn't know what it was about this man, but he was getting on my last nerve. I heard a sharp intake of breath from Reed, but I ignored both of them and folded my arms across my chest.

"You're right, Jordan. I do believe this little one needs a lesson almost as much as her little friend does," Reed said, though his voice held more amusement than anger.

"How's Mia?" I asked changing the subject before I had any more 'lessons' from either one.

"She's fine, the paramedics are checking her out right now and you can go join her in a second," Reed said.

"Thank you so much for all your help Mr.-?" I said.

I stopped trying to remember if I'd heard his last name. Come to think of it I didn't know either of their last names and that was more than a little disconcerting, leaving me a little ashamed of my behavior. I couldn't remember the last time I'd jumped a man without knowing his full name and address.

"You may call me, Sir or Master Reed if you feel that necessary," Reed said with a knowing look in his eyes.

"Great another one," I murmured disgustedly then turned to leave.

One arrogant, know-it-all, stubborn male a night filled my quota nicely; deal with two went above and beyond the call of duty.

"We are not through yet, Lizzie," Jordan warned.

I looked over my shoulder at him. "I think we are, Jordan."

I saw him stiffen and my heart began to race thinking I'd finally hit rock bottom with that last comment. Then a smile crossed his lips and I realized he was laughing at me instead. I let out a growling noise which only served to make the men laugh harder. Throwing my hands in the air in frustration, I stormed off cursing all male species especially the handsome dominating kind.

Leann Lane

Chapter Seven

Two months after that, I went back to Reed and asked him if he wouldn't mind letting me try the club out for a while. When he asked me why I opted to be completely honest with him. I told him that I liked submitting, just not to Jordan. Despite the disbelieving look he gave me, he didn't say anything as he pulled out the paperwork I needed to fill out. Reed explained a few rules about the place, like the dress code for example Masters could wear what they wanted, but subs must wear fetish wear and/or whatever their Masters require of them. Or the fact that I was to do anything that I was asked to by any Dom or Domme as long as it was something I had previously agreed to or it was not pushing my hard limits. As always it stated the club safe word, which was "Red" then asked me to pick out a safe word. I declined that on the basis that I was not going to play outside the club anyway, Reed gave me a disapproving look; yet didn't say anything at all thus allowing it.

I shook myself out of my memories and realized how late it was. I dragged myself off the couch and into the bedroom. My phone still sat on the bed where I had tossed it earlier in my dire need to get away from it all. I spied the flashing red light and let out a moan of irritation. I didn't have to open my phone to know who had been messaging or calling me. Mia was probably blowing up my phone because she was pissed I forgot to call her. I set my phone aside and flopped on to the bed. The moment my head hit the pillow I was out, but once again the memories betrayed me and I was back to the night Jordan finally became my Master.

This time I had truly thought it would be different. I had picked a Master who had sparked my interest to play with and I had picked the St. Andrew's cross because I had always liked the idea of being tied to the big giant x shaped thing. Now, however I just really wanted to kick it.

No matter what he had done or used, he hadn't gotten anywhere. In the end he just untied me and left with a frustrated growl. I couldn't blame him though. Instead of feeling a sense of surrender, I had felt very disconnected as if I was sitting back watching the whole thing on a T.V. show. Sadly, it was the same feeling I'd gotten with everyone the last two years.

Movement in the door way caught my eye and I turned to find Jordan leaning up against the door jamb of the private scening room I was in. Barely even half dressed, I pressed my clothes tight against my chest insanely aware of his eyes on me.

Honestly I couldn't count the amount of times I'd been naked at the club, but with Jordan's eyes on me, I felt more exposed than ever.

He wasn't in his customary attire of jeans and a t-shirt and instead was wearing a pair of slacks and a button up shirt that hung loose. It looked as if he'd just come from the office which considering he was Reeds right had man in most everything, including this club, he very well might have. Either outfit was a stark contrast to the leather and chains that most of the other Doms or Dommes wore around here. He cleared his throat loudly, making me jump and snap myself out of my thoughts. Immediately I straightened my back and gave him a cool look.

He had a smirk on his face though, one that I wanted to reach out and slap off him. Somehow I managed to contain myself which was a feat I thought I should be proud of.

"What do you want?" I said snidely tightening the hold I had on my clothes.

"I want to know if you are done screwing around with all these pansy little men?" he asked so directly that it shocked me and I was unable to think much less speak for a moment.

"What are you talking about? I haven't been 'screwing around'. Each one of those men are Masters with a ton of practice," I threw back at him astonished at his attitude.

"They each have some practice, but they are nowhere near what you need, Lizzie," he said softly walking up to me.

"What do you know about what I need?" I said trying hard not to sound as breathless as I felt.

Jordan just smiled smugly before suddenly ripping my protective covering away from me so fast all I could do was gasp. My hands instinctively flew up to cover my breasts but with look from him I was dropping them again. My nipples tightened into hard points and I couldn't be sure if it was the air or his heated gaze. I had to ball my hands into a fist to keep from cupping them trying to find a way to easy the ache in them.

"You won't be needing those," he said with his eyes never leaving my exposed breasts.

My body cried out for him as it had been doing secretly for the last two years. In all that time I had been avoiding him like the plague. Right now, however, I had a feeling that was no longer going to be possible.

"I really don't think this is a good idea, Jordan," I whispered.

I was purposely using his name knowing it was one of the things that would annoy him. I was hoping that if I pissed him off enough my own anger would rise up in defense and override the arousal that was slowly burning its way through me.

"Master Jordan, or rather call me Master, since that's what I'm going to be from now on," he corrected patiently.

My eyes widened in surprise at his tone. It was like he'd suddenly found a hidden reserve of patience. He began to slowly walk around me, his steady, calm, movements making me nervous since I couldn't read his intent.

"You see, I'm on to you, Lizzie. I slowly began to realize that you were pushing me away. Sorry I'm so thick headed, but it happens in Masters sometime. Reed let it slip the other night that you asked for a different Master. 'Anyone, but Jordan' I believe is what you said. That's when I realized that you were scared of me. Why? I asked myself." he whispered the last part in my ear making me jump.

A strangled noise broke from my chest as I slowly began to understand that he was right, he was indeed on to my game. A little chuckle brushed over my sensitive earlobe as he walked back in front of me.

"I began to look back over the last few Masters you've had and it hit me, you played the other Doms like a fiddle and they didn't even realize it. But, you knew I wouldn't let you get away with it."

He turned and aimed an arrogant, self-satisfied smile at me.

"You have never truly submitted, Lizzie. That's why you feel unsatisfied, but that's all about to change, Lizzie."

Fear was threatening to choke me, fear at having been found out by the one man I wanted with every breath. Jordan did indeed scare the hell out of me, he was the one person in the world that wouldn't let me get away with anything.

"Do I have any say in this, at all?" I asked quietly even though I already knew the answer.

"Of course you do. You have the option to leave."

"I really don't think this is a good idea, Master Jordan," I said feeling suddenly apprehensive now that the reality of what was happening started to sink in.

"Lizzie, it's not about what you think is a good or bad idea. I'm not asking you to give up control to me because I want you to. I'm demanding it because it's what you need and a good Master knows the difference," Jordan said.

My mind began screaming obscenities at him and telling me to just hit the road. It was quickly out voted by my body as it politely reminded my logical part that if we really wanted to submit, this man could make us do it. With the weight of defeat pinning my shoulders down, I sighed and nodded.

"That's not going to work. If you want me to be your Master after what you have said about me, you'll have to ask me very nicely," Jordan warned.

Damn it, he was asking me basically to beg him to top me. I swallowed a growl that arose at that thought and gathered up my courage.

56

"Please, Sir. I want you to be my Master," I said softly.

"Tell me you need me," he whispered stepping closer until his mouth was just a breath away.

"I-I- need you, Sir," I whispered back.

A satisfied grin broke across his firm lips before pressing a gentle kiss to mine. I realized that this had just been a test, he was establishing his dominance first off and putting me in my place. Instead of being pissed it gave me hope that I could in fact submit to a man. He stepped back and was transformed right before my eyes to the quintessential Master.

"Good, baby girl. Stand next to the bed and take off your underwear. Only your underwear, I like that little skirt on you."

I had decided to go with the classic naughty school girl outfit tonight, seeing as the vacated Master had a soft spot for that look. I had found it so cliché it was embarrassing, but knowing Jordan liked suddenly had me excited and pleased.

I watched as he walked over to the only table in the room and put a black leather bag on the table before he turned back to me and lifted an eyebrow when he saw I hadn't moved. Despite the fact that I had agree, begged him, worry still had me in its grasp and I hesitated.

He began to walk towards me slowly with the rope in his hand. With each slow, purposeful step he unraveled the rope bit by bit and I felt myself getting wound up tighter bit by bit.

"I know your list of hard limit's by heart. You are going to have to trust me to not push you too hard too fast." Jordan explained stopping in front of me and forcing my eyes to his. "What's your safe word, Lizzie?"

"Red, Sir," I said dutifully half considering using it right now.

"Very good. If you're in too much pain or if it's something we cannot work through use it. Otherwise, if it's something we need to discuss or adjust use the word yellow. If I ask and you're good to go, use green. Understand?" he asked.

I took a deep breath and nodded.

"Good, now do as I've said and don't make me ask you again," he said pushing me gently towards the bed.

I did as he asked, as he put it, and took off my underwear. The air rushing in immediately and I realized my backside was completely bared to him.

"Now that has to be the sweetest sight I have ever seen," he commented.

I looked over my shoulder at him not having to guess where his eyes were. I decided to do a little shimmy to get them all the way down and was rewarded with a sharp intake of breath from him. Pleased with myself, I stood up quickly and adopted the traditional sub pose of legs spread shoulder width apart, arms crossed behind the back and eyes on the ground near my Masters feet.

"Nice pose, but eyes on me unless I state otherwise. I want to know where your mind is," he said walking toward me slowly.

I peered up at him and allowed myself to study him in a way that I had never had the courage to do before. He was quite a handsome man, he still kept his hair short though it was a bit longer now. There was a hard edge to him that only came from a man that had seen some terrible things in life. I'm not sure if it was the few stress lines on his face or bump on his nose that indicated it had been broken a time or two, but I fully believed the military rumor. Despite all this harshness, as he looked at me and I could see a soft calm come over him as if he was looking at something precious and it made the anger and resentment I'd felt for him over the last few years melt away.

"I'm very proud of you for taking this step, Lizzie. However, I do believe we have unfinished business, so as much as I hate to start off with a punishment we must," he said as he reached up and began removing his shirt.

My eyes widened and my jaw dropped.

"What? Why?" I cried softly.

Jordan shook his head as he hung his shirt up on a hook beside the door.

"You have a selective memory, baby girl. Every time I have talked to you in the last two years you have been completely disrespectful to your Master."

"You weren't my Master then, Sir. I think it's you that has the selective memory," I shot back defensively.

"I was, Lizzie, and I think we both knew it. You were just the one avoiding it," Jordan said.

I said nothing in response to his words, there was no way I was going to agree with him out loud.

"Now, for your punishment. Since you've decided to show me a vast amount of disrespect. I have decided you will show me just how respectful you can be," he circled around behind me.

I had clasped my elbows behind my back and knew he had decided to use that to his advantage when I felt a light scraping of the rope. He wrapped it around my forearms quickly and precisely as if he'd done it a hundred times over. I felt him run his hands over the rope that bound me and, though I had no doubt he'd done it right the first time, it made me feel protected that he wanted to double-check.

"You do that very well," I said then winced when it came out sounding more sarcastic than I had intended.

"Yes, I have had much practice in rope bondage. It's one of my favorites," he said as he finished checking the wrappings.

"I'll just bet it is."

I couldn't hide the sarcasm that time and in response he grasped my arms and jerked me back against him, his lips pressed up against the shell of my ear.

"I have to say, though, there has never been anyone I wanted to tie up more than you. Since the first time I saw you all I could think about was how gorgeous you'd look bound up in my ropes," he whispered.

His breath caressed my ear sending tingles running down my neck into my shoulders and ending in my arms. His words, however, sent the tingles straight down to my toes making them curl and making me wet.

He walked around me slowly taking the time to admire his handiwork. His sharp gaze took in appreciatively how my breasts thrust forward now that my arms were behind my back. I wiggled for a moment feeling myself grow restless and achy under his silent appraisal. I had never understood the joy of just standing there as your Master inspected you. I'd always felt like a piece of meat. Now, in front of Jordan I felt like an unfinished work of art impatiently waiting for the last finishing touches.

Everywhere his eyes touched seemed to immediately jump to awareness. My breasts tightened while my nipples hardened to tight aching peaks that begged for his attention. He stopped in front of me and his hands reached up to simultaneously stroke the sides of my breasts. His thumbs barely touching the nipples, yet it was enough to make my breath catch in my throat with anticipation. I closed my eyes to better concentrate on the feel of his hands and the pleasure it sparked in me.

"Look at me, Lizzie," Master Jordan ordered gently.

My eyes felt heavy as I opened them slowly. On the surface he appeared to be controlled, but you could see the desire etched into his features.

"Good, baby girl. I need to know you are enjoying my touch and when you look away from me I can't tell if you're just humoring me or if you're honestly enjoying it," Master Jordan explained as if this was all new to me and I couldn't help feeling as it was.

I had heard Jordan was one of the best Masters at the club and so far I had to agree, never had any of them taken the time to go through this much explanation with me.

The subs had helped as much as they could and as long as their Masters agreed to it. Still never had I felt so cared for or able to understand exactly why I was being asked to do something. I thawed even more towards him and felt his command of me go deeper.

"Those nipples are just begging for me aren't they, baby girl?" he said licking his lips as if he could taste them already.

I bit my lip hard because the words 'do it now' which were poised on the end of my tongue. I nodded eagerly hoping he'd put action to his words at my agreement. His thumb left its continued torment of my breasts and reached up grabbing my chin and gently pulling down until my teeth let loose. He rubbed a finger over my lip soothing the ache from my bite. I opened my mouth slightly and I sucked his thumb in, tasting its saltiness and feeling the roughness of his fingertip over my tongue. His eyes dilated slightly as he watched me sucking on his thumb, a bit of a nibble and a swipe of my tongue caused his throat to produce a deep growl of appreciation.

"Enough," he said hoarsely as he pulled his thumb back which I released with a quiet pop.

He turned away from me for a moment to grab a few pillows and put them on the floor next to the bed.

"I am putting pillows on the floor so you will be comfortable when you're on your knees. It's time for your punishment," he explained as he looked down to make sure everything was set according to his silent expectation.

I stiffened at the mention of this punishment he was going to give me, but I kept quiet knowing better than to argue. Not to mention when he stood beside me and began to pull his jeans off in such a sensual fashion I lost the ability to speak. Watching him undress was like watch your own private strip tease and I loved every minute of it.

My mouth went dry and my eyes widened as I saw his erection for the first time. It was thick and hard and reached to the top of his belly button. He sat down in front of me slowly allowing me a good long look at him which I had to say I didn't mind at all. Then he beckoned me over with the crook of his finger.

It wasn't hard for me to understand what he wanted and the idea was scary, yet thrilling at the same time. He helped me kneel down in front of him and I was grateful because the thought of falling on my face was not one I wanted to entertain here.

Once I was in position my eyes were glued hungrily to the delicious erect length of flesh sitting in front of me pulsating and waiting for me to devour.

"Now suck it, sub," he demanded.

His words instantly made my pussy contract and immediately I leaned towards him. My tongue slowly reached out to swipe at the swollen tip and I watched intently to his reaction. His eyes closed as his hand reached up to grasp my hair tightly so he could direct my movements. I allowed my tongue to flicker around the head, as much to tease him as to taste him. His hand tightened in my hair fractionally and satisfaction coursed through me. I gently took the head into my mouth nipping at it, repeating the movements I had used on his finger seeing as it had pleased him. A harsh groan broke from deep inside his chest, which heightened my excitement. I sucked gently and a little drop came out of the tip which was quickly gathered with my tongue greedily because I was desperate to taste the essence of him.

"Yes, that's it baby," he whispered.

I gradually began sucking harder and deeper until he almost hit the back of my throat causing me to gag and instinctively pull back. The hold he had on my hair did not allow me to go to away before he was pulling me back again.

"Breathe, Lizzie," Jordan encouraged breathlessly.

It took a moment for me to figure out what he meant. Not understanding how I could breathe when his huge cock shoved deep down my throat.

It soon became clear when my nose took over that he meant to remind me I could still breathe. I took him deeper earning myself a rather crude word that forced its way out of Jordan's lips. His breathing had become ragged and his body was moving with me trying it's hardest to be thrust deeper into my mouth. I did it again and again, each time remembering to breathe through my nose; each time taking more and more of him in until he did actually hit the back of my throat again and I prepared myself to start gagging once more.

"Swallow, honey," he groaned out.

His other hand reached up and grabbed the back of my head and I felt him swell in my mouth. His movement became more erratic underneath me and knowing he was coming to the explosive end; I began to pull away. However, his hands held fast not allowing me much farther away than the very tip. I looked up with shock in my face, but his gaze held on to mine letting me know that in this moment, this was my true punishment. He had made me start it and he wasn't going to let go until it was completely done, my anxiety began to rise.

"Breathe, baby girl. I know it's hard, but you can do this," Jordan said sensing my problem.

His voice held such a belief in me that I was able to draw strength from it. I was going to do this; I wasn't going to let him down. I turned back to the task at and sucked him hard, fast and deep.

A heart beat later he stiffened suddenly and with a hoarse shout as I felt his hot saltiness hit the back of my throat. I continued sucking through every last thrust and every little noise he was making as he found his release. My own sex was pulsing with desire as if I was on the verge of joining him.

Leann Lane

Chapter Eight

"Stop!" he gasped finally.

He pulled my hair hard forcing my head up to look at him. With a lustful growl he swooped down and captured my mouth like a soldier capturing a war criminal that he had been searching for.

"God, I can taste myself on your lips," he whispered, his breath ragged.

My pussy clenched again at his words as they fanned the flames burning inside me. He picked me up effortlessly and straddling him I pressed my body tightly against his, more to enjoy the hardness of his solid frame than from fear I'd fall since I knew he'd never let that happen. His mouth captured mine once more and his tongue invaded my mouth instantly as if he couldn't get enough. I let out a gentle moan as our tongues sparred and danced together. Finally, he captured it and forced it into submission then, seemingly pleased with himself, he pulled away.

"That was amazing, sweetheart," he whispered leaning his head on mine. "You made up for your insubordination very well."

I smiled happily, feeling the immense joy of a sub that has pleased her Master.

"Sweet little sub, you're soaking wet," he whispered as he spread small kisses over my face. "I think someone liked their punishment, despite her reservations. Are you about to come?"

I moaned my answer as he grasped my hips and thrust his still hard cock against my throbbing clit. I threw my head back, the pleasure unbelievable, mind blowing, and still it was not enough.

"Please! Oh god, Sir, please," I began to beg when it wasn't working.

"Yeah baby, get it. I want to feel your hot come on me," he growled into my ear then bit it hard.

My back arched again as my movements became erratic and hurried trying hard to do as he wished, but I just couldn't get close enough. I needed more I just couldn't figure out what it was I wanted more of.

"More! Please, Master," I pleaded with him.

"I know, baby," he whispered, "I know what you need."

He began kissing my neck with such exuberance that if I hadn't been so aroused I would have easily noted the excitement in his voice and might have been worried.

He lifted me up until he could reach my dripping pussy between my legs. He rubbed it gently spreading my juices all over until my back hole was soaked as well, then he slowly pressed a finger in without warning.

I squealed and jerked away almost falling off his lap. His free arm tightened around me trapping me on his lap so I couldn't even wiggle.

"Whoa, baby. Don't worry I know you're going to like it, just relax," he said with a wicked grin on his face.

I looked away, feeling ashamed suddenly. "I've never liked it before."

"It has never been done right then that's all, Lizzie. Trust me, I've had a great deal of practice and one day I'm going to bury myself deep in your tight ass," his eyes gleamed with a promise of more to come.

I swallowed my mouth suddenly dry at the image he had invoked. This sort of thing had been a hard limit for me from the start, but apparently, Jordan hadn't read that portion of my contract.

"I'm not sure, Master," I whispered shameful of my hesitation.

"What is your safe word, Lizzie?" he asked once again as a reminder.

"Red, Master," I dutifully replied.

"Relax and let me help you. I promise you'll love it," Jordan promised.

I had a safe word, I reminded myself with a deep breath to build up my courage. I nodded and allowed my body to relax into his as he had requested.

With a gentle kiss, he picked me up and laid me face first onto the bed, my backside tilted up in the air and quickly grasped a wedge from under the bed and shoved it beneath my hips making sure I was comfortable before he moved away.

I turned my head so I could watch his movements as he wandered around deliciously naked. His ass was a perfect shape for a man nice and round, nevertheless you could see the muscles in it flex as he walked, I found myself wanting to reach out and bite it.

I giggled softly causing him to turn back to me. My breath caught as I got my first full on look at him, he truly was an excellent specimen. Strong and muscular, not an ounce of fat on him, his six pack beckoning me to touch them or lick them. He had two scars on his chest one high up by his shoulder and the other one was a thin slash from the top of his left pectoral muscle down almost to the top of his stomach. I felt a chill go down my spine thinking of ways he could have gotten those scars, I almost asked him about it when he turned around and the beauty of his back took my breath away.

Every muscle was spelled out in perfect detail and I could hardly wait until he allowed me put my hands on him. I had never been that attracted to a man's back before, now seeing Jordan's, I knew it would live forever in my fantasies.

"Enjoying the show?" Jordan asked, a smirk turning up the corner of his lips.

"Yes," I answered truthfully. "You are the most beautiful man, I'd ever seen."

I was quite amused to see a blush creep into his cheeks.

"Thank you, baby girl. You happen to be the most beautiful woman I have ever seen, so I guess we're even," he said as he picked up a tube from the table.

He walked over and knelt behind me where I couldn't see him anymore, his hand pressed firmly against the lower portion of my back. I felt a glob of cold gel hit my puckered entrance and gasped, if his hand hadn't been holding me down I would have jumped up and off the bed.

"Easy, baby," he said softly.

His fingers began to rub the slowly warming gel in between my upturned cheeks and I began to relax. I had just started to enjoy the touch when his finger began to slowly press against my hole, I instinctively tightened against the invasion waiting for the pain. His other hand reached under and began thumbing my clit quickly, I cried out and arched back against his finger pressing it further into my backside. I gasped, feeling a pleasure and pressure combination that I'd never felt before. I wanted to hate it, but I couldn't. Not when it was quickly ushering me to a peak that I had never known existed.

I began to moan and accept his touch even pressing back to get more of it, an action that caused him to groan.

"God, baby I wish you could see how sweet this looks my finger sliding into your hot, tight, ass," he groaned out.

I moved against his fingers, my arousal at a fever pitch again as he quickly brought me closer to the edge once more, a thing I wouldn't have thought possible with what he was doing. I was on the verge of coming when he stopped suddenly and withdrew. I let out a protesting whine when he pulled his fingers back.

"I have to be inside you this first time, baby. I want to feel you when you come," he said his voice husky with desire.

I wholeheartedly agreed with him and sat quietly wanting for him. I heard the quick rip of foil and then he slammed inside me along with the finger plunging back into my ass. Both of my holes were sensitive and the hasty invasion drew a harsh scream from me.

His thrusts were quick and hurried as if he couldn't wait for my release either, my moaning and cries became incoherent as his other hand reached around and began flicking my throbbing clit. I let out another scream and came harder than I have ever before in my life. Each movement of both his hard cock and his penetrating finger caused more ripples to radiate inside me and from what seemed like a million miles away I heard my name being ripped from between his teeth and with hoarse shout as he came once again.

When I finally returned to my body the only sound in the room was rasping of our breaths and after what seemed like forever he slowly pulled out causing little spasms of sensation to run through me as he slid past the super sensitive tissues from both ends.

He quickly untied my hands and began rubbing my wrists and hands then let them drop as he covered me with a blanket and held me close.

I awoke at that moment back in the cabin, alone. My pussy was throbbing and backside was puckered as if ready to be penetrated. That night seemed such a long time ago yet from the emotions rolling through my taunt body, it might as well have been yesterday. I groaned when I saw that it was still dark outside and threw a pillow back over my head.

I entertained the thought of taking care of myself for a moment, but Jordan's voice reverberated in my head and effectively crushed that idea.

"You do not touch yourself unless I'm present. I don't dominate over the phone, or over the internet like some Masters are willing to do. If I'm not right there watching every movement, it doesn't happen. Do you understand me, sub?" his warning resounded in my mind.

"Yes, Master. Damn it," I shouted out loud and listened to the sound echo back to me off the bare wall.

The sky was barely pink when I finally gave up on sleeping any longer and got out of bed. After having an extra strong cup of coffee, I braced myself and checked my messages on my phone. Four calls from Mia, she was in an uproar as I had expected because I haven't checked in with her. Five from Jordan, I deleted those instantly, there was no way I was ready to talk to either him or Jack yet. The last one was from Maggie, she just wanted to let me know that the kitchen was pretty understocked and if I needed anything to let her know.

I left my phone on the bedside table after shooting a quick text to Maggie and Mia, letting them know I was fine and I'd call them tomorrow. Scrounged up some breakfast and I decided to head to the store about thirty minutes away and do some binge grocery shopping, maybe a little sightseeing as well.

The best find in the sleepy old town was a bookstore, delight warmed my heart and by the time I left there I had so many books that it took two bags to carry them, and the thought of trying to lug them around town was not one I wanted to contemplate.

I went back to my car and decided it was home time, there was a trail that led to the forest that was calling my name.

After putting the groceries away in what must have made a speed record. I grabbed the first book off the top of the bag and set off on the path that led to the forest. It twisted and wound its way throughout the dense pine tree filled woods that was so dense with foliage that at times it resembled a jungle.

At one point a fallen tree seemed to be trying to block my path as if telling me not to go that way, but I just glared at it as I stepped over it. There was no way I was going to let some big burly tree tell me how to spend my day, this day was just for relaxing, and by god that was what I was going to do.

Not too far away there was another fallen tree, however this one looked as if it was going to be the perfect spot to sit and read. I noticed once I sat that, there was a little gap in the trees giving me a perfect view of the ocean and the beach. I saw several couples strolling hand and hand, a few kids playing with their pets chasing the waves back and forth, and occasionally the lone person staring out at the waves.

I wished at that moment that time would stop for a while. I wanted nothing more than that moment keeping me in it forever; No more worrying about my past, no more stress about my future just the peace I'd found in the waves as they rhythmically rolled in and out.

I shook my head at my foolishness, there was no way I could stay here forever unless I wanted to sign myself off as a recluse. I opened my book and I decided that if I couldn't lose myself in the woods of the real world, maybe I could lose myself on a pirate ship in the mid-1600s where a captain of the British Royal Navy and the dashingly handsome scoundrel of a pirate fought for the heart of a sweet innocent young girl.

Hours later I finally gave up on the book after realizing there was no way I could choose between the two strong virile men in the story, who were currently engaged in an avid sword fight in a vain attempt to win the heart of the girl.

I kind of wished this was one of those alternative stories Mia had told me about. That way once I got to the end I would happily find the girl had picked both of them. That thought had me a little disturbed seeing has I'd ran from both of my men. Maybe you should call them, said a tiny voice in the back of my head. And tell them what, I answered back, that I haven't decided anything expect I'm scared shitless.

I got up and dusted myself off feeling distinctly more depressed as I started back down the path.

Out of the corner of my eye I caught a view of the beach once again and noticed there was a single lone man walking on it. I stopped to watch him as a sense of recognition came over me, the broad shoulders, the short crew cut hair, and the tight T-shirt with the jean pants that if he turned around would probably have holes in the knees.

"Oh, shit," I whispered.

Jordan was here.

Leann Lane

Chapter Nine

My heart started pounding and I was frozen mid-step watching as he gazed out at the ocean. From this distance I couldn't tell what the expression on his face was, but somehow I knew he was worried, probably frustrated as well. I wondered if I could sneak over to my car and get out of here before he could catch me.

I knew the instant that thought crossed my mind it was a pipe dream because I had a feeling that if Jordan was here, then so was Jack. And if Jack wasn't on the beach as well, he was probably still at the cabin. I grasped the book tightly to my chest and began heading back along the path chewing on my lower lip in trepidation.

I hit the end of the trail before I had finished my inner pep-talk and was stopped in my tracks by the sight of Jack leaning against the post at the top of the stairs. He was wearing a pair of jeans as well, but he had just a pullover shirt on, the black colors on him gave him a dangerous and foreboding look that sent shivers down my spine.

His dark eyes pinning me to the spot like a deer in a passing cars headlight. I paused not knowing if I should run to him or back into the forest that I just came out of. Maybe that wasn't too bad of an idea, after all I knew every trail from here to the road and every place to hide in between. I was pretty sure I could disappear in less than a second and they'd never find me. Even as my memory began to shuffle through the best bushes and trees to hide in, I decided against it. In my heart I knew that this was fates way of telling me it was time to face my fears.

Forcing my knocking knees to move, I shuffled closer watching closely for some indication of his thoughts. His eyes traveled down the length of my body taking in my baggy jeans and the sweater that hung down almost hitting the top of my thighs. I suddenly felt shy, my hold on the book tightening and my eyes dropping to the spot where the grass met the sand. I jumped a little when Jack let out two short whistles and I wondered silently what the purpose of this move was; if he was whistling at Jordan there was no way he'd be able to hear him over the ocean waves.

"Hello, Lizzie," Jack said stiffly as if he didn't know what to say any more than I did.

"Hi," I said softly looking up at him slightly.

There was an uncomfortable pause and I shifted restlessly under his penetrating stare as if he could read my thoughts.

"What are you doing here?" I asked redundantly mainly to break the tension.

He raised one eyebrow, understanding as I did that the question was completely unnecessary.

"We came here to find out why our sub ran away from us instead of coming to us with any of her problems. Do you have any insight to share?" Jack asked pushing away from the pole.

Footsteps interrupted us before I could answer, much to my relief. Jordan came strolling up the path, his gray eyes filled with the powerful turbulence of a gathering hurricane. Pain squeezed my heart then released it but left a dull ache in its path. His face showed his uncertainty and I hated myself for causing them so much grief. When his eyes rested on me, I could see relief touch his features before they turned into a stone mask and I was unable to read anymore from him.

"Lizzie, you want to tell me why you felt the need to hide all the way out here?" Jordan asked stopping mere inches from me.

"How did you guys find me?" I threw back at him.

"We told you, you can't run from us," Jordan said by way of explanation.

"Mia," Jack clarified.

74

"Is she okay?" I asked, worried about the punishment she would receive for keeping something like this from them.

"The last we saw of her on our way out of the club, she was cussing up a storm at Reed," Jordan said with a chuckle. "Should have seen Jack's face, his mouth 'bout hit the floor when she called Reed a son of a bitch."

I shook my head and smiled. "That sounds like Mia."

Jordan nodded solemnly. "Yeah, I hear that by the end of the night she didn't have much to say at all. Apparently Reed gagged her and tied her to the Saint Andrew Cross, do you remember that one?"

My body clenched at the reminder of the dream I'd had just last night. It had taken most of the day for my body to stop throbbing and at Jordan's words I felt it starting to heat up again.

"If you recall correctly we've never actually used it, Sir," I whispered to him breathlessly.

"We will have to remedy that in the near future," he said gruffly. "Besides, Jack's better at the cross than I am. I'd hate to spoil his fun."

I looked up at Jack and was caught up in the intense craving I saw in his gaze as if he could see me on it already. Licking my suddenly dry lips, I cleared my throat trying to think of something to say that would sidetrack these two men and my own naughty thoughts.

"I don't believe we've had a proper greeting," Jordan said. "Do you, Jack?"

Jack just shook his head and hung back watching the scene play out between Jordan and I.

I made a noise in the back of my throat. This is definitely not what I meant when I said I needed a distraction. I cried out at them silently.

Instead of the passionate feverish kisses I was expecting for him, he grabbed me up holding me tightly and laying a gentle kiss on the top of my head. After a long confusing moment of wondering why he hadn't done more I gave up and snuggled up to him laying my head in the crook of his neck and just enjoying being held by him again. He smelled like the ocean, sand, and a purely masculine scent that was uniquely Jordan.

He let go of me slowly then gazed into my eyes for a moment before he turning and walking to the Jeep that was sitting behind my car. From what I could tell by what Jordan was grabbing out they had apparently made arrangements to stay with me for the rest of the time I was here or maybe longer. I tried be angry or upset, but I couldn't be. I was surprise that what I felt was suspiciously close to excitement.

"Would you allow me to hug you as well?" Jack asked softly.

He stepped around in front of me with his arms crossed over his chest. It melted my heart to see a bit of hesitation in his eyes.

"I'd like that, Sir," I said with a small smile.

I saw his face brighten like a child's that had been given a piece of candy, it was so sweet that I almost giggled as he opened his arms to me.

I stepped forward eagerly wrapping my arms around his trim waist and laid my head on his chest. I could hear the beat of his heart skip the moment I pressed my body against his, but otherwise it was a strong soothing sound that helped curb my turbulent emotions.

Jack was quite tall; I could barely have reached the top of his chest. Somehow it was comfortable, it was like his body was made to accommodate mine and I smiled at the foolish thought. Jack kissed the top of my head as well before pulling away, though he left his arm slung over my shoulder as if he was afraid I was going to run away again.

"Hey, lazy ass. Get over here and help me," Jordan called as he walked by us.

Jack smiled at him then looked back at me. "Nah, I think I'll have our girl here give me a tour of the place."

I watched Jordan pause while he was unloading and flip Jack the finger. He just chuckled and started pulling me towards the house, but I shrugged his arm off and step back a little upset that he had felt the need to volunteer me for such a task.

"I will leave you both to have fun with that, I've got to go get things ready for dinner anyway and find out where you too are going to sleep," I said turning to walk up the steps.

Jack and Jordan both refused almost as soon as the words were out of my mouth.

"Don't worry about dinner, Lizzie. I've got it covered," Jack said grabbing a box from the back of the jeep.

"As to our sleeping arrangements, we are sleeping with you," Jordan declared.

"No, you are not," I said turning on them, "for one thing the bed is not big enough and for another thing I need my space, hence me coming out to the middle of nowhere."

The men apparently hadn't expected me to protest because they gave me blank stares. That and my aptly put statement had me feeling rather victorious and, with my head held high, I strutted into the cabin leaving them to handle the rest of whatever else they'd decided to bring along. Although as a gesture of generosity I decided to put together a mass of blankets and pillows and other things they would need in order to sleep out in the living room.

A part of me felt terrible as I looked around and it became obvious one of them was going to have to sleep on the floor. But another part of me felt suitably justified and smug about the whole thing as if saying silently serves you right for crashing in on my quiet time. On the other hand, said a little horny voice in my head, it would be a great opening for me if one of the men complained, I could offer a back rub to help them ease that.

Leann Lane

Chapter Ten

After what seemed like hours of avoiding them, because some naughty little voice kept whispering about all the ways I could enthusiastically help them with their aches and pains; the sound of the shower brought me out under the pretenses I'd be safe to roam without prying eyes. It was the sounds coming from the bathroom that had me walking towards it cautiously, becoming the prying eyes.

Deep guttural moans of pleasure came from inside and I knew instantly that it wasn't Jordan, so that only left Jack to make such animalistic sound of passion. Its tone reverberated throughout my body hitting me in the gut leaving me breathless causing me to begin panting as if I'd run a marathon. The blood coursing through my veins surged as I snuck closer and closer praying he was so caught up in what he was doing that the creak of the floor boards would not be heard.

The door had been left part way open and I stopped just short of it wondering if I really should look in. I bit my lip until the point of it almost bleeding unable to come to a decision as to whether to run back to my room or to step an inch to closer and sneak a peek.

A hard groan followed my murmuring words raised my curiosity until I couldn't ignore it anymore and I stepped up to the crack. The water from the shower was pounding down on Jack's head that he had bowed behind the curtain with one hand braced against the wall. His other one was down pumping himself with long sure strokes and each time it got to the head it circled slightly making his hips jerk.

"Fuck," he cursed softly.

I gasped as his hand started to speed up. There was no way he could possibly hear me, but when his head jerked up I knew I had underestimated him. I stepped into the shadows hoping he hadn't seen me and slapped a hand over my mouth to steam the threat of noise.

"Lizzie, get in here now," he growled.

I groaned inwardly in absolute embarrassment and slapped the same hand over my eyes as I stepped in.

"I'm sorry... I was... trying to find... my...ah-"

"Look at me, girl," he snapped the growl in his voice never dropping.

I stood stock-still for a heartbeat wondering if it was too late to turn and run, then slowly lowered my hand my need to comply overwhelming. Trying hard not to look anywhere lower than his head but I couldn't help but notice when he faced me that his stiff cock was being squeezed hard by his hand the tip of it bulging. I licked my suddenly dry lips unable to look away from the sight.

"Did you enjoy the show?" he asked.

I balked at answering him, unsure if I would be saving or condemning myself at this point.

"Answer me, girl. Did you enjoy the show?" he asked again more sternly this time.

I nodded my head, unable to vocalize the words I wanted to say.

"Did the sight of me fucking my hand get you wet?" he asked as he stroked his hand up and down once more.

Once again I hesitated to answer.

"You will answer me or I will come out there and find out for myself then punish you for disobeying. I will ask you again are you wet?"

My eyes widened in fear at his threat and quickly nodded. Even through the shower curtain I could tell the smile that crossed

80

his face was nothing short of feral as he looked down at my pants and back up.

"Show me," he demanded.

I felt a flush spread across my cheeks and slid a trembling hand down my stomach then under my pants. I bit my lip to contain the gasp that wanted to burst out as soon as one small finger brushed against the tingling button between my legs. He made a noise of longing as if he could see through my pants and knew exactly what had happened.

I knew I should have ranted at his directions but my body had a mind of its own right now and it was overriding the logical one.

I slid the hand back out of my pants, fingers glistening with my own juices and held it out for him to see. He made an appreciative sound and then braced his legs to lean back against the shower wall. I wanted to tear the shower curtain off its rings just so his body would be completely visible to me; with it in the way all I couldn't see any sensational details.

"Good girl. Now since you have not yet allowed us to be your Dom's I will not touch you," he said with a tinge of sadness in his voice.

That sorrow resonated through me until I opened my mouth to beg him to touch me, take me, make me submit, anything and everything.

"So you are going to have to touch yourself."

My already open mouth dropped down. "What?"

"Touch yourself. I want to you to drop your pants in front of me and use those fingers on that wet little pussy you have," he growled.

Carnal desire slammed into me with each word and I noticed his hand had begun to move faster as if his words were arousing himself as much as they were me.

My hands moved the waistband and slowly pushed the pants down my legs until I could step out of them. I kicked them off to the side but couldn't help cupping my hands in front of my sex as if I was ashamed of it.

He let out a harsh chuckle and shook his head. "Shy now, girl? Get to it, I wanna hear your pretty moans as you play. After all it's only fair since you were spying on me."

Another flush crept up my cheeks at the mention of that little blunder. I wanted to run and hide, but I also wanted to please him. It was as if the sub in me already recognized him as my master; a fact that I was going to have to examine a little more closely when I could think clearer. Instead of giving into the fear I spread my legs as far as they could go while I stood upright against the wall and drew my courage up to obey him.

I slid a hand up my legs until it reached the juncture between my thighs. My mouth parted on a sigh as I caressed the lips of my weeping slit before slowly slipping my fingers inside and promptly finding my nub that was begging to be touched. My hips twitched forward at the first tentative touch and a gentle moan burst forth.

"Yeah baby," Jack groaned with me.

I opened my eyes so I could watch him as he continued to pump himself, his hips jerking forward every other stroke.

I moaned at the erotic sight in front of me and realized this was something we all had in common. We loved to watch as our partners engaged in self-pleasure, that sort of thing was a huge turn on for us.

I slid a finger deep inside and began to thrust it in and out quickly in time with the rhythm he was setting for me. I slide my other hand down and began strumming my clit letting the sweet pleasure wash through me as I watched him.

When his hand sped up so did mine own wanting to keep up with him. I sagged against the wall grateful it could hold me up so I could lift a leg onto the sink and spread myself open even further as our mutual self-pleasuring became more intense. My breath came out in short heated pants and my movements accelerated as my inner walls began to clamp down on the penetrating finger seeking a release. Each pass with my finger over my swollen clit drew a harsh cry from me which harmonized with each groan of ecstasy from Jack.

I could feel the crest nearing as my hands became more frantic and it was almost the undoing of me when I saw Jack's hand going just as quickly as mine.

I tipped my head back unable to keep my eyes opened as I felt the climax come to a head.

"Yes, baby. Come now," Jack commanded in a gravelly tone.

Always the good sub, I did as I was told. With one final swipe of my fingers, a loud cry burst from my lips and I shattered hard; harder than I had ever thought possible from only my touch. My hips bucked slamming into the thrusting fingers again and again until the last twitch had gone. I opened my eyes just in time to see Jack rinsing himself off and concluded, with disappointment that I had missed watching him come.

The pleased smile on his face warmed my heart and I was glad to have been able to witness it.

"That was very beautiful, sweetheart. We still have a little while longer before Jordan gets back, did you wanna join me in the shower?" he asked pointing to the stall next to him.

At the mention of Jordan's name, I stiffened. What the hell are you doing, Lizzie? I thought to myself. You were supposed to figure all this out before you submitted to them, remember? You're not ready for two Dom's yet.

I backed away slowly, shaking my head then I quickly gathered up my pants before racing back to my room. I slammed the door shut with a resounding thud and leaned against it as if Jack was going to come bursting in after me demanding my submission right then and there. When no sound came but the sound of the shower I began to relax once again and reaffirmed my choice to hold up in the bedroom at least for tonight.

Leann Lane

Chapter Eleven

I heard rustling in the kitchen and curiosity got the best of me. On my tippy toes, almost like a teenager trying to sneak out of the house, I walked quickly and quietly into the room to find Jack padding around barefooted and deliciously shirtless still. Speechless, I allowed my hungry eyes to devour his chest and back now that I finally had the chance to see it in more detail.

His hair was still damp from the shower and it hung in a dark curly halo, I wondered if he ever managed to tame it or if it was always a wild mess that begged a woman to run her hands through it. Every muscle on his body was well defined; evidence of a man who knew how to work hard and, from what I've heard, play harder. His waist cut in and then gave way to a nicely rounded ass that made me think of digging my heels into it as he was pounding into me.

In my pursuit of this decadent piece of eye candy, my attention became snagged on a small tattoo situated right between his shoulder blades.

"It's a dream catcher," he said suddenly not even turning around.

I jumped then flushed at being caught lurking in the doorway once again.

"I'm sorry to keep ah... bothering you," I stuttered out trying not to say anything about before.

"You don't. Sit down," he said clip as he gestured to the kitchen table but otherwise barely paused in his task.

"Dream catcher? Isn't that unusual for a man to have?" I asked snagging up a very innocuous topic.

I sat down as he had indicated and watched as he brought me a cup of coffee with the cream and sugar just the way I liked it. It made me wonder exactly what he and Jordan had discussed when they'd talked about me and when exactly had my coffee preference come into play. Before I could question him about that he went back to the cutting board and began to chop up some vegetables.

In the silence I ran my eyes over his lean, sinewy chest gobbling it up like I had his back, and finding not a single thing wanting on either side. His skin was lightly tanned and smooth with only a small dash of hair on it, but it was his nipple rings that made my mouth go dry as I imagined how the cold hard metal would feel against my tongue or even running my fingers over it.

I took a quick sip of coffee to put moisture back into my dry mouth, desperate for some sort of relief from the burning desire that was trying to boil in my stomach at the tempting sight in front of me. Unfortunately, instead of feeling relief, the burning went into my mouth after having forgotten that the coffee was scorching hot. I began to choke and spit the coffee out over the table. Jack rushed over and began to harshly pat my back until I stopped choking and handed me a glass of cold water. Gratefully I drank trying to cool the heat in my mouth as I watched him clean all the liquid off the table.

"Thank you," I rasped out my throat feeling raw.

"You have to be more careful," he chastised me with a disapproving look.

I nodded in agreement deciding that if I'm going to have hot coffee, or anything hot for that matter, I needed to keep my eyes to myself for safety reasons.

"My grandfather told me it'd help with the nightmares. He's full-blooded, Navajo, I went to see him after we got out of the Marines," he said.

I looked at him confused until I realized he was talking about the tattoo. My chest tightened with sorrow for him and before I knew it, I was up wrapping my arms around his waist. I laid my head on his back willing the pain to go away inside him, wishing I had a magic eraser to erase the horror he'd seen. He stiffened for a moment then relaxed into the hug. He turned in my arms and held me tight, almost squishing me into him and I reciprocated the strength of the hold hoping that it was enough to heal him even a little.

He pulled away and looked down at me, I thought I saw a little tear in his eyes, yet he blinked and it was gone leaving me thinking I'd imagined it.

"Thank you, sweetheart. I needed that," he said softly.

He tilted my chin up and gave me a gentle kiss which sent my heart racing. Wanting more I stood on my tiptoes hoping he'd get the hint and take it one step further. All I got for the effort was a small kiss on my nose, leaving me frustrated.

"Go sit down and carefully, enjoy your coffee. Why don't you tell me about yourself?" he said with a pat on my bottom.

There was a delicious smell in the air that radiated from the stove and I began to watch his movements avidly trying to figure out what he was cooking. He started grilling the vegetables on the stove top and slid a baking pan in the oven, he turned back to me as he shut the oven door and stared at me with a raised eyebrow at me before I realized I hadn't answered him.

"What do you want to know?" I said reluctantly.

"Where are you from?" Jack asked starting out easy.

"Same place as Mia. Washington, you?" I asked.

"Arizona. Any siblings?"

"One brother, older. You?" I answered, countering as fast as he could with his clipped answers.

"None. Where's your brother?" He asked turning to look at me.

"I have no idea, he left to join the Army at 18 and I haven't heard from him since," I answered shrugging it off.

He paused and just stared at me for a moment. I could almost see the gears turning in his head, fearful of what question his would ask next I decided to derail his line of questioning.

"Why'd you join the Marines? Is that where you met Jordan?" I asked.

"I met Jordan when we were kids and his family kind of adopted me. We joined the Marines because we thought it would be a great adventure and to get out of the small town we lived in."

I nodded my head in understanding since that was the reason Mia and I had gone to college in Oregon.

"Where were your parents?" I asked not waiting for his next question.

There was a pregnant pause as he started grabbing the plates out and putting them around the table. I got up to help but sat back down when he gave me a pointed look.

"My parents died when I was three, a car accident. I moved in with my grandfather."

There was a look in his eyes that spoke of a deep soul biting sadness and loss.

"When did he pass?" I asked compassionately.

"Last year."

I put my hand on his arm as he placed a plate in front of me.

"I'm so sorry, Jack."

His breath came out in a hiss as if someone had just punched him in the gut and when his eyes came back to me they were flashing with a strange emotion. I felt myself wither slightly under his gaze realizing I'd called him Jack not Sir, or Master as I was supposed to.

"I'm sorry, Sir," I corrected quickly.

It took a moment but a sweet smile relieved the stern edges on his face and he reached out slowly and caressed mine.

"It's alright, Jordan told me that when you are not playing, he allows you to use his name. I was just letting it sink in, I usually am very strict about protocol. I was just shocked at how much I loved the sound of my name from your lips."

His finger ran across my mouth before laying another gentle kiss on it so full of promise that it sent my blood pounding again. As quick as the kiss was, he left me even quicker to finish what my nose was telling me would be a delicious dinner.

"Where are your parents?" he asked.

I got distracted by whatever he was pulling out of the oven; it smelled like heaven and calories needing to be burned all in one.

I sniffed at the air feeling my stomach grumble as if I hadn't eaten anything all day.

"Mmmm, that smells so good. I'm starving," I said eagerly.

"I was the cook on duty while we were on a mission I learned to cook on basically anything from a roaring fire to barely a candle."

The smile on his face was nothing short of pure pride and I smiled sweetly back at him.

"If it had been left to anyone of our other men we would have starved or died from food poisoning. Do not ever ask Jordan to make more than a cup of coffee, you'll find yourself in deep trouble," he warned on a laugh.

I laughed. "I kind of figured that out on my own. It's a good thing he has Mrs. Lichten, even if she does refuse to let even me anywhere near the kitchen. I think there were a few times when she even waved a knife at me, though that may be foreplay in her world."

Jack started laughing with a full on belly roar, it was a deep husky sound a little on the scratchy side. It was such a wonderful carefree sound that I promised myself that I'd try to make him laugh more often.

"Yes, she does tend to have that type of personality. She must love you, she's only mean to those she loves," Jack agreed as he set the food on the table.

Meatloaf and grilled vegetables and I knew I had died and gone to heaven. Suddenly he let out two sharp whistles I recognized from earlier; he was calling Jordan.

"Where is he?" I asked.

I hadn't seen hide nor hair of Jordan since I had run away and hid in the bedroom earlier.

"He went to scout out the area. He really didn't like the idea of you being up in BFE, as he called it, alone. He barely slept last night and I could hear him pace the living room for hours," he said.

He threw an accusing look my way that also let me know he hadn't approved of my little disappearing act either. I could feel my face flush with embarrassment. If he continued to look at me like that I would find myself kneeling on the floor next to him and begging for forgiveness. That would have been the right thing for their sub to do, but instead I quickly changed the subject.

"How do you know he can hear you?" I asked.

"We both have always had amazing hearing. It was a signal we came up with when we were kids and it served us well in the Marines. Jordan is actually right out on the porch. I heard him walk up while we were talking," Jack answered with a slight grin.

I shook my head at him and at the nosy man that walked through the kitchen door at that moment. Jordan stopped and sniffed the air for second before letting out a loud appreciative breath.

"Damn, man, you have the touch when it comes to food," he exclaimed appreciatively.

Jack accepted the compliment with a nod of his head as he began to put food on my plate, however I quickly stopped him.

"I can handle that, Jack. I'm not helpless," I said reaching out for the spoon.

He pulled it out of my reach. "I will do this, Lizzie. It's my duty to take care of you and I do my duty well."

I turned to Jordan for help, he just sat back holding his hands up in the air and shaking his head. The bastard was biting his cheek to keep from laughing though, I could tell by the gleam in his eyes. I took a deep breath to control my temper and turned back to Jack determined to win this battle. I decided the best course of action to win a battle with a Master was to become the sub.

"Sir, I know you wish to take care of me. But I really do wish to do it myself, seeing as I am perfectly capable of handling a little bitty spoon," I said.

I made a split second decision not to end my statement with a bat of my eyes figuring that would be over kill, especially when I heard Jordan desperately trying to cover the snort that was currently choking him. Jack, on the other hand, stared at me with a mixture of confusion and disbelief before turning to Jordan and jerking his head at me as if asking Jordan's opinion on the matter. I was offended by the doubt that I saw on his face and bit the inside of my cheek hard in an effort to stay quiet and wait for them to work it out.

Jordan nodded and cleared his throat a couple of times before he could speak.

"Yes, Jack. I knew you'd find out eventually that our little sub is very self-sufficient, it took me threatening to tie her to the bed the other day before she agreed to stay home when she was sick," Jordan said still chuckling over that fight.

Jack was silent for a while as he took in Jordan's words. They must have done their mind meld thing again because Jordan's eyes suddenly narrowed at him.

"She's nothing like Molly, Jackson," Jordan said firmly.

Jack stared at him a moment longer and I could see the struggle on his face as if he was having hard time believing Jordan's declaration; finally, he nodded and handed the spoon to me. I wanted to ask who Molly was since it was the second time I'd heard a reference to her and I wanted to know exactly what she had done to my men and where she was so I could kick her ass for causing the pain I'd seen in Jack's eyes at the mention of her name.

My men, that stunning thought came out of nowhere, but for the first time it seemed like a solid idea that had some merit and an attainable goal. Joy and hope welled up inside me and I smiled a sweet victorious grin at Jordan and Jack, thought I wasn't sure if the victory was for the spoon or the hope I was suddenly feeling.

"Thank you, Sirs." I said happily.

Hopping out of my chair as fast as I could, I rushed around the table serving the men before sitting down and serving myself. Feeling very satisfied as they stared at me with identical astonished looks. I have to say, it was the most enjoyable dinner I'd ever had and the food was delicious as well.

Leann Lane

Chapter Twelve

After dinner was over Jordan volunteered to clean the dishes and instead of arguing with him I took my coffee and went and sat on the porch swing. I curled my feet underneath me and just listened to the sounds of the ocean as it blended into the noise from the forest to create the most beautiful music I'd ever heard.

"You know you never answered my question."

I screeched and almost fell off the swing, cursing as I righted myself and looked over my shoulder to find Jack a foot away from me with his hand outstretch like he was going to catch me if I fell.

"Damn it, Lizzie, you need to be more careful!" he growled at me with a glare.

I flushed in embarrassment and glared back at him with as much heat as I could muster, trying to pretend he couldn't see how red I was turning.

"How long have you been there?" I asked accusingly.

He shrugged then walked over to the railing and leaned his back against it, folding his arms over his chest. He just stared at me with an expectant look on his face, just waiting. When it became obvious he wasn't going to answer my question, I gave up with a sigh of frustration.

"What was it you wanted me to answer?" I asked.

"Where are your parents?" Jack repeated.

I felt like a deer in the headlights again or even worse a fly on the wall that someone was trying to swat. I wasn't sure if I was ready to answer all his questions about my past just yet and this was quickly going to a part of my past that I certainly wasn't ready to talk about just yet. But, if I deflected him I had a feeling he was going to go all pit bull on me and not let it go. As if every thought that I was having showed on my face Jack straightened as his piercing eyes took it all in.

"I really don't want to talk about this right now, Jack," I said, going with honesty.

"I can see that this is hard for you, Lizzie, but I really think we need to. I have this feeling that, whatever it is, it's something Jordan and I should know," Jack explained to me.

I really hated how rational he sounded right now, it made me want to throw my coffee in his face. Instead I put the cup on the railing and wrapped my arms around my knees to brace myself for the argument that was coming. Jack took the opportunity to sit on the bench as well filling up the space with his body, leaving almost no room for me to spread out again and not touch him. He grasped my feet to pull them onto his lap and start rubbing them. Inch by minuet inch, I began to relax and leaned back against the armrest again.

"There's nothing you can't talk to us about, sweetheart. We are your Masters. Granted we don't know everything, but we want to help you if we can," he coaxed.

I wanted to hate Jack for being right, but the delicious feel of his hands on my feet quickly stole the thunder of my proud anger.

"My father is dead. He died a while ago and my mother... my mother ran off when I was 12," I explained finally.

"See... was that so hard?" Jack said smiling encouragingly. "What did your father die of?"

"He died five years ago of liver failure," I said on a sigh.

Jack was quiet, just pushing the swing back and forth. I closed my eyes and just listened to the sound all around me, loving the feel of his hands on me and just the fact he was next to me.

"Was he an alcoholic, Lizzie?" Jack asked quietly.

"Yes," I answered on a sigh as his fingers found a very sore spot on my feet and soothed.

"Did he hurt you?"

"Yes," I whispered almost falling asleep.

A loud curse and the sound of a fist connecting with wood snapped me out of my reverie. My eyes flew open and connected with his as they flashed with anger and determination. What the hell had I said? I thought and replayed the conversation in my head. When I heard myself answer his question, anger rose up and took control.

"See?!" I cried jumping off the bench and pacing away from him.

He stood up as well, coming close enough to crowd me, causing me to become even more irate as I was overwhelmed by a feeling of being trapped.

"You can't just leave well enough alone!" I shouted shoving at him.

To his credit he didn't stop me from venting. He just stood there like a stoic solider, keeping an eye on me as I continued to rant at him slowly getting closer to me.

"You're just like Jordan, you have to dig and dig and... Maybe I don't want you to dig?! Maybe I'd rather you left well enough the hell alone?!" I continued shouting.

I was too busy shouting at him that I didn't notice someone coming up behind me until I went to shove Jack again, trying desperately to get him to move back and give me some space. A set of strong hands gripped my wrists in an unyielding hold and gently yet firmly twisted them around behind my back. The hold did hurt, but only because I was fighting against it as the rage filled me past the point of reason. I looked back to see who held me and realized my shouting had brought Jordan out of the house. My breathing was ragged and broken, but I couldn't tell if it was from fear, or anger, or my futile struggles against Jordan's unrelenting grasp.

"Elizabeth!" Jack snapped.

I ignored him until he gripped my chin hard and forced me to meet his gaze. His dark eyes blazed with fear, worry, and anger but he finally had my attention.

"Shh," Jordan whispered in my ear. "No one's going to hurt you."

There was a pause as Jordan's words sunk into my screaming brain and I stopped struggling in his grip.

"Good, baby girl. Now listen to Jackson," Jordan urged.

"Breathe, Lizzie. Remember the other night at the club?" Jack whispered.

He leaned his head down to mine and pressed his chest against me so I could feel both of their chest rising and falling in sync, a perfect rhythm. I let my eyes fall closed so I could concentrate on them. Quicker than I thought it would happen, my breathing calmed along with the frenzy of emotions that had been drowning me.

"Good girl," Jordan whispered into my ear.

"Thank you, Sir," I whispered feeling more submissive now than I ever had before.

Jack backed away slowly, looking more and more frustrated until he finally exploded and his fist slammed into the wall on the side of the house. I jumped and unconsciously pressed closer to Jordan, he wrapped his arms around me and held me tight.

"Jackson!" Jordan barked.

I looked up at Jordan in time to see him give Jack a pointed look in my direction.

"How are we supposed to do this, Jordan? We can't even get to the bottom of her fears without her having a panic attack," he asked, his voice sounding hopeless.

My shame began to swallow me up and I laid my head on Jordan's chest trying to hold back the tears.

"Lizzie's a tough girl, Jack, she can handle it. We just gotta help her past her fears," Jordan said calmly.

"I cannot stand the thought of hurting her," Jack said leaning against the railing refusing to look at either of us.

"I know," Jordan whispered against the top of my head. "I can't stand the idea of hurting her either."

He reached down and lifted my chin up to meet his eyes so I could see how sincere he was.

"Now, do you want to tell us what happened to cause this and perhaps the other panic attack?" Jordan asked letting my arms fall from his.

Both Jack and I stiffened instantly again. Jordan caught sight of our agitation and pulled away a bit, I could see the wheels in his head turning and I braced myself for the question I knew was coming.

"Who was it?"

His tone was so cold and dangerous that it sent shivers down my back just hearing it, I'd hate to be on the receiving end of his anger. I waited to hear if Jack would answer for me and when he didn't I realized he was giving me a chance to do it myself. I wasn't sure if I was grateful for this chance, however I knew that this was an opportunity for me and I had to snag it even if I didn't want it. I walked over to the swing again this time to look beyond it out to the ocean where the moonlight was playing among the waves and drew strength from the current.

"My father," I conceded finally, "It was my father, he was a drunk, abusive, son of a bitch."

The silence behind me was tangible and as deadly as the eye of a hurricane until it finally exploded.

"That fucking bastard. I'd kill him if he was still alive now," Jordan growled out.

His dark tone had me turning around to make sure Jordan was still there and hadn't been replaced by a demon. Over the last year I would have sworn he was an extremely calm and collected man, despite the times before that where I kept pushing his buttons. Even then I had never seen him this angry at anyone and it throw me for a loop.

"What happened?" was all Jack said, his tone was deceptively quiet again.

I looked over to find Jack's hands squeezing the rail tightly as if he was already ringing someone's neck.

"No, that's enough for tonight," I said.

I was beginning to worry about how much bigger the rising storm in their eyes could get. I wondered briefly if they were phasing into werewolves since they both looked about ready to howl at the moon and tear someone apart.

"Now, Lizzie!" Jordan snapped at me.

"What do you want to hear, Jordan? You want to know how my drunken father abused me? He'd beat me if he could find me, reason or not. Do you honestly want to hear all the names he used to call me? Do you wanna hear about how I was nothing but a 'fucking whore' to him and how he threatened to sell me because, 'I was already whoring it out, might as well make some money at it'? That was the night his buddy tried to rape me," My voice grew louder with each sin of my father's that I cast at them until I was almost screaming it to the sky.

"What was his name?" Jordan said calmly the smoothness of his voice, a deceptiveness I immediately saw through.

He had begun pacing the porch after my screamed confession and seemed to be almost stalking back and forth like a caged tiger about to pounce.

"Who's?" I asked, my hands on my hips.

"The man who tried to rape you," Jack asked through gritted teeth.

I was pretty sure by now his white-knuckled grip had probably squeezed a really good notch into the rail.

"I-I don't remember," I lied.

"Bullshit," Jordan spat out making me jump.

He stalked up to me holding one finger up in the air, "that's one, Lizzie. You remember how I punish you for lying."

I nodded and swallowed past the lump that had suddenly built up in my throat. The last time I lied to him it had been about something so small that I couldn't even remember now what it was about, still he had made me wear a gag ball around the club for most of the evening until I learned that my mouth was only used for pleasure and honesty. I also remember how many times I had bitten that very same gag ball trying to hold back the screams as he'd brought me to the edge over and over again without letting me fall. I could tell by the dilation of his eyes that he was remembering that night as well.

"Yes, I remember. I just don't want you guys to get in trouble for something that happened in the past. He tried to rape me but he didn't succeed. In fact, he got a broken nose and a concussion from his attempt. From a girl who was 16 and tiny, I think he's suffered enough," I said letting the pride show in my voice.

They both turned and stared at me, their mouths dropped open with astonishment leaving me feeling even more proud. Little ol' me had shocked two big tough Dom's like them.

98

Like rolling thunder, the laughter started quietly, just a few chuckles here and there that I managed to stem with a well-placed glare but soon, as rolling thunder will do, it burst and was echoing throughout the porch. I crossed my arms over my chest and waited until their laughter stopped before I said anything.

"I'm glad you had a great laugh at me but I assure you it's all true," I said snottily.

Jordan was the first one to recover as he straightened and wiped his tears from his eyes.

"Oh, baby girl, we believe you," he said still chuckling.

"Bullshit," I repeated Jordan's term as I continued to glare at them.

"No, honest we do. We're not laughing at you; we're laughing at him. Good for you, baby," Jordan said as he rushed over and swooped me into his arms to twirl me around.

"Let me down, idiot," I cried laughing.

Jordan put me down right next to Jack who promptly threw his arm over my shoulders. Jordan looked at me in disapproval and I wondered if Jack was keeping me close so I couldn't run away. I shouldn't have called him an idiot and I knew that, I haven't actually meant to it just kind of slipped out.

"Did you hear that? She called her Master an idiot," Jordan said with false astonishment.

"I did," Jack agreed immediately then made a tsking sound with him tongue. "We are going to have to teach her some respect."

I shied into Jack's side with a little epping sound of panic. Jordan laughed out loud again and I felt Jack's side tremble with poorly contained amusement.

"I'm sorry, Master," I said quickly.

Jack's hand slide down and grasped my elbow effectively pinning me against his side. I wanted to pull away but I knew it would be a bad idea, given the fact that Jordan had some sort of punishment in mind. He reached out slowly and I stiffened with unease until he suddenly tweaked my nose.

I jumped and squeaked which caused both men to break down laughing again. My temper hit the melting point, I let out an ear piercing shriek and stomped my foot; the temper tantrum I threw would have made a two-year-old proud. Storming off, I pushed passed them and left the pair to laugh themselves silly. In fact, I hoped they fall off the porch in their hysteria and roll into the freezing ocean only to be swept away where the sharks would eat them one little piece at the time, preferably starting with their hard heads.

I slammed and locked my bedroom door with a resounding, satisfying, click before I flopped angrily on the bed and punched the innocent pillow into a shape that met my approval.

"Jackasses." I swore at them, quietly of course, but only because I didn't feel like yelling.

Chapter Thirteen

I awoke to the sounds of birds chirping outside my window. It was a pleasant peaceful sound that drug me outside with a cup of coffee in hand. Of course I had to sneak past the two loudly snoring men in the living room. I tried hard not to look, really I did, but the men obviously had no idea what pajamas were.

The half-naked view was so sweet and sexy that I found myself stopping just to get a glimpse of everything. Jordan was on the floor sprawled out, his awe-inspiring back bared for my hungry eyes. Jack had engulfed the tiny couch, his normal hard face relaxed giving him a slight fallen angel look. At some point in the night he'd thrown the covers off and all he had on was a pair of boxers that really should have been silk, if only so they'd cling to him better. Still, his morning erection was outlined quite nicely.

I sighed as I looked at his chest again and wanted desperately to go over there and finally satisfy my curiosity about those damn nipple rings that I was slowly becoming obsessed with, or maybe even run my fingers through the small patch of hair to see if it was as soft as it looked.

Realizing how close I was coming to waking them up, I forced myself to move. Sneaking past a couple of guys that were known for their keen hearing was hard, but it was well worth it as I drew a deep breath of the fresh morning air. I sipped my coffee and watched as the birds dove and tumbled playfully in the tides, enjoying their early morning jubilee.

That was until I saw three birds sitting on a tree right next to the house. Two giant crows were picking on a little swallow that was precariously close to the edge of the branch. The similarity to my situation was vastly unsettling for me and it hit so close to home I found myself growing angry on the poor little bird's behalf.

"Hey! Leave that little one alone you bastards!" I yelled at them.

Unfortunately, all the good that did was scare off all the birds in the area.

"Don't you think that was a little harsh?" came an amused voice from behind me.

I spun around to find Jordan lounging up against the door jamb looking far too sexy for his own good. My pulse began to race the moment my body realized he was nearby.

"What were you doing, Lizzie?" Jordan asked breaking into my train of thought.

"I was protecting that little bird from the two crows?" I said softly, slightly embarrassed he'd seen my rant.

"Why did you feel that was necessary?" he asked.

He stepped closer to me and grabbed my coffee cup out of my hands so he could take a sip out of it. He turned the cup in his hands so he could drink out of the same side I had been as if he could taste me on the rim. I licked my suddenly dry lips and tried to remember what we were talking about. When it came back to me I shook my head and felt slightly defensive.

"The little bird was scared, overwhelmed and they weren't giving her the space she needed," I said folding my arms over my chest.

"Is that how you feel?" Jordan asked handing me back my coffee cup.

"Yes," I murmured looking down at the coffee left in my cup.

"Why?"

I sighed and leaned against the railing resigning myself to the fact that this conversation was going to happen whether I wanted it to not.

"How on earth do I keep up with two men? You both are strong healthy men and I'm just one woman. What happens when I get tired? Or sore? What then?" I said sadly.

102

"Then you tell us," Jack said from behind Jordan.

I wondered how long had he been there especially since apparently he was very good at sneaking around without a sound.

"I just don't want to disappoint you guys," I practically whispered.

My voice grew higher desperate for them to understand. "What happens if one night I'm just with Jordan? Or just with you Jack? What happens then do I owe you one? Do I have to start keeping track?"

Jordan leapt at me and wrapped me in his arms before I could even get the last words out of my mouth.

"Baby girl, no. No one is keeping score if we were you'd owe Jack a lot right now, but he doesn't care. All that matters right now is that you are with him. If you get too tired or sore one night, you need to let us know. We are your Masters not your slave drivers. If for some reason it ends up with just Jack one night but the next night you are too tired, I'm not going to be offended at all, I'd be more than happy to just hold you."

It couldn't be that easy, I thought to myself. No man I'd ever been with had just been content to just hold me without demanding something in return. What these men, these two men were offering was too good to be true. There had to be a catch somewhere and I was scared as to what that was.

"I'm sorry, Sirs," I whispered to both of them.

My eyes dropped to the ground as I struggled to contain the tears that were welling up as my jumbled emotions once more threatened to overwhelm me.

Jack tipped my head up and forced me to look at him. "What's wrong, Lizzie?"

I shook my head not sure how to begin to explain my thoughts without hurting any of us.

"Does the idea of being with two men disgust you?" he asked hesitantly.

"No!" I said horrified, jerking my gaze back to him.

"Alright. Then what?" Jack asked.

"There is no way men as..." I waived my hands at them struggling to find the right word again, "manly as you both are would ever just be content to hold a woman. It's just impossible, don't you see?"

Jack's jaw dropped and Jordan snorted out a bark of laughter. I glared at Jordan and watched as he raised an eyebrow at my attitude. I immediately glance away I knew well the meaning behind that look and had only tested it once.

"Oh, good. I thought it was something terrible," Jack said softly.

I lifted my gaze to his and saw his eyes crackle with amusement.

"So you like the idea of submitting to both of us?" Jordan asked again and I turned towards him and nodded.

"Good!" Jordan almost shouted. "That's what we want, what we were hoping for. So what's the problem?"

"You want me to submit to Jack as well?" I said making sure he understood that I was specifying him in particular.

"Yes, baby. I know it sounds crazy and it's not normal, but for us it is," Jordan explained.

He laid his hands gently on my shoulders as if he was waiting for me to break down. I let his words roll around in my brain, I wasn't repulsed, just the opposite in fact. I was interested, excited and very much turned on by the idea. I just couldn't wrap my head around the fact that these two, huge, passionate men wanted me. I was still uncertain about keeping them both satisfied, yet I knew I wanted nothing more in this world than to try.

"I'm sorry, Lizzie," Jack said his voice tearing at my stomach with the sounds of desolation.

He turned away from me, shoulders sagging. He looked so defeated that I felt my heart die for him. I looked over at Jordan to see the mirror image emotion blooming on his face.

"What the hell for?" I said harshly.

"That we are different, I wish we weren't. But we are. This is something we have fought and have tried hard to change. We even separated a while after we got out of the military but it didn't do any good neither of us were happy. I'm so sorry that we can't be normal for you, truly I am," Jack said sadly.

As he began to turn and go into the house as Jordan started shaking his head in disbelief and followed him. My mouth dropped open as I watched them go into the house. My shock was so all consuming that I just stared at the empty space that had been occupied by my Masters.

Yes, my Masters. I told myself firmly. I was not shying away from this anymore and I was not going to allow my fears to run my life. It was time to stop being a wussy and suck it up, especially if these men were the ones I wanted to be with.

I heard noises coming from inside and I realized they were getting ready to leave. I ran into the house and slid to a stop in the living room when I saw the two men were in the process of getting dressed. Neither looked up as I entered, they just continued getting dressed and then proceeded to start folding up the blankets.

"Stop!" I shouted loud enough to stop a herd of charging elephants, yet I was still surprised when they looked up at me and actually stopped, giving me a confused look.

"Drop that stuff, you are not going anywhere," I stated in a firm tone.

Leann Lane

Chapter Fourteen

They raised eyebrows at me in an identical questioning action as if they were wondering whether or not I should be talking to them the way I was. Despite all that, I had their attention and I wasn't about to waste it.

"Excuse me?" Jordan asked quietly.

He crossing his arms over his chest and adopting his normal Dom stance. Jack just stared at me, his dark eyes a churning mixture of hope, fear and confusion.

"I said you two are not going anywhere. Jack, you can't just assume you know what I'm thinking and Jordan, you should be ashamed of yourself. After all this time together, how can you believe I would think so harshly of you. Let me be as clear as I can be," I walked closer as well until I stood directly in front of them. I crossed my arms trying hard to imitate Jordan's stance, "I do not think you guys are perverted, I think you guys are amazing and sexy as hell. Every time you guys look at me I want to melt and submit to both of you. So if you guys are perverted I think that makes me a nympho."

As I spoke, the tension in their bodies began to melt away proving that I was doing the right thing. I knew there was only one course of action left to show them how serious I was. Keeping eye contact, I slowly knelt at their feet and bowing my head, showing them the only way I knew how that I was agreeing to be their sub.

My long blonde hair pitched forward covering my face completely hiding them from my view. Right now with the raw emotions that were crossing it I was happy to be hidden until I could get under control.

I heard shuffling then I felt a hand on my shoulder, I lifted my head to see the men kneeling in front of me as well.

"Are you sure about this, Lizzie? Because once we get started, Jack and I are not letting you go because you get scared. This is your last chance to change your mind," Jordan warned, his gray eyes serious as they drilled into mine seeking out any hesitancy that might belay the truth in my words.

"Yes, Master. Please, this is what I want. I am terrified, but I can't stand the idea of not having either one of you in my life. When I first started being a sub, I was scared I'd never be able to submit to anyone and that was all I ever wanted. It wasn't until I met you, Master Jordan, that it finally became a reality."

My voice grew stronger and the words began to flow from me like a river breaking through a damn, "Then when you brought me Master Jack and I got scared because I didn't know how I was going to keep up with you both. Now, you both are giving me a chance to live a fantasy I was too frightened to acknowledge. But I want to take that chance."

Tears began rolling from my eyes unabashedly and Jordan reached over to wipe them away almost as fast as they were falling. I closed my eyes and laid my cheek against Jordan's hand feeling soothed by the warmth of him touching me.

"May I put this back on you?" Jack asked softly.

I looked to see Jack holding up the collar they had put on me the other night. My breath caught as the sunlight hit the two hearts and making them shine brightly beckoning me. The hearts on it held even more meaning today than they had ever before. I nodded, not trusting my voice to work while it was so choked up with tears. The men stood up and then had me stand so Jack could walk slowly around behind me.

Jordan eyes were shining with something I had never seen before and it took my breath away. I drew a deep, painful breath as Jack move my hair out of the way and slipped the collar around my neck. I felt his fingers trembling against my skin and it made me relax a little knowing that he was just as scared, excited, apprehensive, and joyful as I was. Jordan grasped my chin gently and gave me a sweet little kiss of abject gratitude.

"Thank you, baby girl. I promise you won't be sorry you put your faith in us, you will never go unsatisfied," Jordan whispered his thumb rubbing against my lips as he seemed to have a habit of doing.

"Silly man, it's not me I worry about going unsatisfied it's you two," I whispered back giving his thumb a gentle kiss.

Jordan chuckled and bent down pressing another kiss on my lips. It started out as gentle, teasing, but it quickly became deeper. His tongue reached in and began a foray with mine bringing me to a fever pitch as I felt another kiss being planted on the back of my neck above where the chain for the collar lay. Goose bumps spread rapidly down my entire body with every gentle kiss and nip on my neck. It quickly became impossible for me to do much else besides make continuous pinning noises as Jordan's tongue playing its usual game with me and Jack's mouth seeking out the most sensitive spots on my neck.

I waited for Jordan to get mad that I wasn't kissing him back yet all that happened was him stepping back and watching with his blazing eyes as Jack continued to rain burning hot kisses down my neck. My head tilted back of its own accord to give him better access to every sensitive spot on my throat. My eyelids closed half way and Jordan's lust-filled gaze was the only thing in my line of sight. I searched his eyes for some sort of anger, his gaze only held passion as he continued his voyeurism. I was astonished that the feel of Jordan's gaze just heightened every sensation that Jack's lips evoked.

The thin t-shirt I was wearing was no barrier at all from Jordan's heated gaze. His eyes moved down my body and took in the straining of my breasts and the nipples as they stiffened into a hard nub that begged for some sort of attention.

Jordan glanced up at Jack and did their mind meld, I quickly found myself spun around with my back press hard against Jordan's chest. Jordan ran his hands down my arms to grasp my wrists pulling them up and around his neck. The move made my breasts press forward even more and treated Jack to the same view as Jordan had just enjoyed.

"That's a beautiful sight. Isn't it, Jack?" Jordan asked his voice growing deeper in my ear.

He pressed his body completely against my back letting me feel his hard erection nudge itself between the cheeks of my ass. I tried to slowly rub against it, but he pulled away slightly making me whimper in frustration.

"Ah, ah, ah, baby girl. This is just about you right now, you've denied Jackson here the joy of your submission and I know he's been wanting it for a long time. You may have just met him, but I have been telling him all about it since we first talked and now it's your turn to show him what an amazing little sub you are," Jordan said.

Chills ran down my spine from his hot breath caressing my ear and from the implication of him words. For the first time since I'd met Jackson the hesitancy and the uncertainty were gone; all I saw was the ridge control that every true Master had. My stomach clenched and my body began to burn, I bowed my head submitting to his control.

"Yes, Master," I said softly lower my eyes to the ground.

"Eyes on me, Elizabeth," Jack said softly almost echoing Jordan's exactly words the first time we were together.

The name Elizabeth brought everything to a halt inside me. I could feel my body stiffen and my blood freeze as it ran through my veins. I hated that name, it represented everything I had ran away from and everything I never wanted to be.

"Please, Sir, do not call me that," I asked in a strangled voice.

I was trying hard not to let the anger and fear show itself on my face. They noticed it anyway and I could tell by the narrowing of Jack's gaze and the flickering glance towards Jordan which meant that they were silently communicating together.

"My father called me that and it reminds me of him," I explained hoping that they would understand.

"So this name bothers you to the point that it's almost a hard limit for you," Jack asked to clarify.

I nodded emphatically, I had never thought to make it a hard limit but if that's what it took, I was going to.

"I would like to work on that with you, Lizzie. If you would allow me, too?" Jack asked.

110

I bit my lip in hesitation.

"I love your name, it was my mothers and she was a strong, beautiful woman just like you. I want you to wear that name proudly and it kills me that you hate it so much," Jack explained raising his hand to my cheek trying to brush the worry away.

My breath caught in my throat at his words. He thought I was strong and beautiful even when most of the time I'd acted the opposite. This really meant a lot to him, I could tell by the look in his eyes as he spoke to me about it. I wanted to let out a sigh yet I held it in, if he'd made it an order I probably would have said no. Instead I nodded my head wishing nothing more than to please him.

"Good, baby girl," Jordan whispered into my ear. The pride in his voice was giving me strength and warming my insides.

"Thank you, sweetheart. It means the world to me that you're willing to try," Jack said.

He stepped up to me and kissed me gently on my swollen lips. My eyes dropped closed and I kissed him back thinking it was ending there but as ever my Masters surprised me, Jordan's hands ran slowly down the sides of my arms, tickling and sending chills everywhere, making me feel like laughing and moaning at the same time; a strange combination that had me titillated and confused.

"I think she likes that, Jor. Do it again," Jack said as he pulled away and laid his mouth against my ear.

Jordan did it again and this time I did moan louder laying my head back on Jordan's shoulder. Jack rained kisses down over my neck again until he reached the neckline of my shirt, that's where he flipped sides and began kissing back up until he reached my lips that were parted on a gasp. He took that as an invitation and kissed me deeply stealing away what little breath I had from Jordan's soft caresses.

I was intrigued by the difference in each man, Jordan's kisses were sweet, playfully, sensual, combination that always had me thinking of a spontaneous in- the- middle-of-the-day-can't-stop-touching-you encounter. It was an addictive and something that I had found myself longing for as time went on with him as my Master. Jack's taste was darker, more sensual, it had me begging for red satin sheets and candlelight. Both had their merits and I was elated that I was enjoying both of them right now.

Jordan's hands made one last trip down my arms and Jack's tongue gave one last thrust into my mouth before they both finally pulled away. Jack stepped aside to make room for Jordan as he moved in front of me.

"Please Masters," I begged reaching for them again.

"No, Lizzie. You see, we have waited a few days for you to finally decide to submit to us. More often than not in the same position you are currently in now. I think it's your turn to wait for us," Jordan said staring at me.

Eager to please I folded my hands in front of me awaiting impatiently for whatever command were going to come from them, my body cheering at the attention it was getting from these two powerful Masters.

"Good, now that we have all that squared away. I think it's time for breakfast." Jordan said nodding in satisfaction.

Jack nodded back at him as my mouth flopped open over and over again. Little noises of protest were all that came out even as I tried to stop it so I wouldn't get into any more trouble.

"What's wrong, Lizzie? Aren't you hungry?" Jordan asked innocently.

I could tell by the amusement on his face that he knew exactly what the seemingly innocent question really meant. I wished fiercely that I could tell him exactly where to shove his question, however I knew all the good that would do me is to get punished by two Dom's.

"Yes, Sir. I'm starving." Was all I said trying really hard not to hang my head.

They lead the way into the kitchen giving me a wonderful view of their backsides which my hands had to curl into a ball to keep from touching.

"Just not for food." I whined softly.

I followed the objects of my arousal and frustration into the kitchen before I gave up being a good girl and seeing where the bad girl could take me.

Chapter Fifteen

Just like last night Jack cooked a delicious breakfast that had me moaning in rapture with every bite. After the third sensual sigh Jack paused in the middle of getting a fresh cup of coffee and leaned down behind me to bite my neck which elicited another moan for an entirely different reason.

"Next time it won't be my food that causes you to make that sound," Jack whispered into my ear.

I looked up at him and opened my eyes wide, hoping he'd see the pleading in them for him to make me moan again. He just chuckled and sat down again with his coffee cup full, happy that his threat was issued to his satisfaction and my further frustration.

The men struck up a conversation about some of their old military buddies, however I couldn't figure out who they were talking about because they used nicknames like Spider, Animal, and Sparky. Their voices became a very pleasant background noise as I quickly finished up the dishes. I looked around wiping my hands on the dish towel trying to find something else to do since I still felt restless and aroused as hell.

I went into the bedroom and changed my clothes then put my long hair up in a single ponytail. I noticed my phone on the bedside table was blinking indicating I'd missed a phone call or maybe more than one if Mia was really worried.

As soon as my feet hit the sand, I called Mia anxious to hear the sound of her voice.

"Lizzie! I am so sorry! I tried, but Reed... he... well... he got it out of me and then I tried to warn you but you didn't answer!" Mia spouted the instant she picked up.

"Don't worry, Mia. It's alright and for the record don't bother trying to hide anything from them or lie to them because it doesn't really work. Been there, done that," I said letting out a little laugh.

"Are you okay?" Mia asked.

A twinge of guilt ran through me at the sound of concern in her voice. I really should have called her the other day and let her know that I was alright at the very least.

"Yes, for the most part I'm fine. I just need to adjust to all of this, Jordan can be overwhelming by himself and then to throw someone like Jack into the mix just adds a hundred times more to that."

I shook my head despite the fact I knew she couldn't see me and stopped in my walk to gaze out over the rolling waves.

"Lizzie, you have always been the extreme kind. Extreme anger, extreme excitement, extreme happiness. I don't know what makes you think you'll be happy with anything less than extreme love," she said bemused.

"Is that really how you see me?" I asked surprised.

I'd never in a million years look at myself that way.

"Yes, you have lived through a horrible abusive situation and came out on the other end even stronger than before. I think instead of asking yourself if you should do this you should ask yourself why you're hesitating, and why you're scared," Mia said adamantly.

I couldn't help but chuckle, "Do you know how much you sound like your mother?"

"Lizzie, you maybe an hour away but I'll still come down there and kick your butt if you don't watch it," she growled menacingly into the phone.

I laughed out loud the sound startling the birds drawing my attention their way. My heart began to race as I looked over to see Jack and Jordan with a heated look on their faces that, from the stance of their bodies, I knew had nothing to do with passion.

"Mia, I gotta go," I said and hung up quickly before she even could say goodbye.

I walked slowly up to them, my heart still pounding as if I had just gotten done running a marathon, although I wasn't entirely sure that it would slow down anytime soon. Their eyes were flashing at me warning lights telling me that if I hadn't run yet I probably should, run far away from my two angry Dom's.

"Lizzie, you are a very bad girl," Jordan said softly, the anger behind his words were as pronounced as if he had been yelling at me.

My voice shook as I spoke, "what did I do wrong, Master?"

"Did you ask our permission to leave?" Jack spoke this time, however his voice was as soft and deceptive as Jordan's.

I shook my head and stared at their toes almost amused to find they had no shoes on.

"You are going to be punished for this, little sub. I'm sorry, but we have been over this already and you know how much I hate repeating myself," Jordan said sadly.

I lifted my head in a flash. "But, Sir-"

He lifted his hand and cut me off before I could say anything else.

"No, Lizzie. There is a reason behind my asking to know where you are and you should have already known this. When I became your full time Dom, I told you that I wanted you to be available at anytime and you agreed. That meant you should be informing me when you leave and get home. When you get up and go to bed. Now I have never been that extreme with it. But I do require knowing when you're going for a walk, especially when I'm sitting in the kitchen. Obviously you don't see how nice I have been, so I guess I'll have to remind you," Jordan said harshly, growing angrier and angrier as he spoke.

I looked to Jack for help but saw rather quickly I wouldn't be getting any. His dark eyes had gone all the way to black which I was rapidly realizing meant he was not to be toyed with.

"I'm sorry, Masters. I really am, I wasn't doing it to be disobedient," I said pleadingly.

I could see Jordan's anger visibly melt and be replaced by sorrow.

"I know, baby. But what kind of Masters would we be if we allowed you to be disobedient at all?" Jordan said putting his hands on my shoulders.

I thought for a second trying hard to come up with a response.

"The best kind?"

The men stared at me for a moment in disbelief before Jordan's lips began to twitch and Jack lifted a hand up to cover a smile. I just gave them my most innocent of looks and even threw a few eye bats in for good measure.

"I only hope you are just as sweet and wonderful after we are done," Jordan said shaking his head but still smiling.

"I should have known that wasn't going to work," I grumbled silently as I allowed the men to pull me back to the house.

Chapter Sixteen

As we stepped through the front-door my phone rang again and I saw it was Maggie. I showed them the phone and asked if I could answer it, not wanting her to worry anymore.

"Of course, it's your mother," Jack said as he pulled Jordan into the kitchen to give me privacy.

I sent a grateful smile towards their retreating backs and answered it quickly.

"Lizzie, Mia just texted me and told me your Dom's are up there with you right now. Are you alright?" Maggie asked anxiously.

"Yes I'm fine. I told Mia I was fine she didn't have to sick you on me," I said exasperated.

"She didn't. I just had to hear it for myself, call it mothers reassurance."

I smiled into the phone, "I know, Maggie, but honestly I'm fine. Jack and Jordan being here is honestly for the best. I have finally agreed to let them be my Masters and I think that's called progress."

"It is, Lizzie. Have you talked to them about your concerns yet?"

"Yes. More like I yelled at them," I said giggling.

"Yes, well, as much as we sub's try not to, sometimes we do lose our tempers," Maggie commented laughing herself as well.

The wisdom in her voice made me wonder how often poor Tomas was at the brute end of Maggie temper; she was a red head like her daughter after all.

"How are things this morning?" Maggie asked.

"Good," I chewed on my bottom lip. "Sorta."

"Uh-oh. What happened?"

"I left to go on a walk... without asking," I said whispering the last part almost ashamed of my actions.

"Oh no," she said my mistake evident to her.

"Yeah... I know," I said dejectedly.

"Lizzie, honey, hang on Tomas wants to say something," Maggie said, so abruptly that I felt my head spin a little.

Tomas got on and almost immediately requested to talk to one of the men. I walked into the kitchen and held the phone out to the first man in front of me. The lucky winner happened to be Jordan. He must have known what was in store for him because he stared at the phone for a moment before reaching for it. Jack raised his eyebrow at me in question and I just shrugged.

"Yes, sir?" Jordan said.

My mouth dropped at his respectful tone as if he was a sub and the man on the other line was his Dom. I slapped my hand over my mouth to hold back the giggle I felt mounting in my chest. It still threatened to burst as I watched a pained expression begin to appear on his face. He shoved the phone at Jack like it was an adult version of hot potato and Jack held the phone up to his ear looking twice as bad as Jordan.

"Yes, sir. No, sir. Absolutely not, sir. Yes, sir I believe you. Like a princess," Jack continued.

The panic in his face doubled and he began pulling at his shirt as if it was suddenly extremely uncomfortable. Then he started running his hand through his hair making the loose curls almost frizz out. I lost the fight right then and ran outside, collapsing on the swing laughing until I could barely breathe.

"That is cruel and unusual punishment, Lizzie," Jordan accused me as he stepped out on the porch his arms crossed over his chest and a look of hostility on his face.

"I'm so sorry, Jordan. I had no warning, suddenly Tomas was there and he demanded to talk to you both and I- I-" I stuttered to a stop.

I tried to sound as sorry and empathetic as I could, however I just couldn't stop giggling. He shook his head as a smile slowly broke out over his face and then came over to pull me close.

"You did the right thing and so did he. When I have a girl I'll do the same thing to her boyfriends."

I giggled imaging these two men standing guard at the front door with duel shot guns in their hands waiting for a little blonde haired girls date.

"I'd be sitting in the kitchen doing her hair and trying hard not to laugh. I'd tell her the same thing Maggie told Mia when she complained about Tomas' protectiveness," I said still giggling.

"What's that?" Jordan said pulling away to look down into my eyes.

"It's the only thing your father's are really able to do so let them have it," I said laughing harder.

Jordan laughed as well and he hugged me again. "That's beautiful, Lizzie."

"That was beautiful," said Jack as he stepped out.

"I'm so sorry, Jack," I apologized to him as I went to hug him as well.

"It's okay, sweetheart. Like Jor said it's what we expect a real father to do. The most beautiful part was listening to you two talk about us having a daughter one day, I like that idea."

His voice held hope and fear but his eyes looked at me with something that was completely impossible for him to feel so fast. However, I completely understood how he felt. When I looked back to at Jordan and saw the same look in his eyes, I knew it was too late. I couldn't help it, my heart was theirs and suddenly I realized I never wanted it back. I knew I should listen to the warning bells in my head telling me once again that I was in way to deep but I buried the fear and pain that came with it.

"I like the idea too," I said quietly afraid that if the words were too loud it'd spoil the mood.

Jack and Jordan's face's brightened with unabashed joy and I noticed a little tear gather in Jack's eyes before he quickly looked away.

Jordan's gentle side sat right on top and he was the first to crack a joke and make everyone around him feel comfortable. It was something I noticed he used quite often with the new subs at the club. He always made the nervous ones feel welcome, and the scared ones feel safe. On the other hand, though, I knew from personal experience that Jordan's temper was not something to rile up, he was not one to take disrespect or put up with lying, cheating, or stealing.

Jack, he had an aura of a ticking time bomb, one he liked to throw around quite regularly I noticed especially when he felt something was getting to close. Over the past few days, I'd seen a softer side to him that intrigued me, it was as if he was a teddy bear wearing a big giant steel coat. I wanted to hug that teddy bear forever and a day.

With a sweet contented smile on my face, I lead the way back into the house and I could hear the mummer of quiet conversation from behind me.

"Oh, really?" Jordan commented, suddenly speaking loud enough I could finally make out the words.

"Yes, he said it has never been used so if we'd like to take a crack at it he was just fine with that. However, there are no toys down there so we may have to become inventive," Jack said with a laugh.

The word toys had me turning around immediately, stopping the men in their tracks. Jack and Jordan each had a look of unadulterated delight on their faces mixed with a wicked mischievousness that had me backing into the counter half afraid they were about to gobble me up.

"What's going on?" I said breathlessly.

"Apparently, not too long ago, Tomas had the cellar revamped in this place. Do you remember where the cellar is?" Jordan asked.

I nodded and pointed to the hallway. There had always been a lock on the door since and Tomas would tell us it was because the cellar was unsafe and we were to stay out of it. Since my priority had been exploring and Mia's had been tanning, we never really cared that it was off limits.

Jordan walked down the hallway and looked at the door for a moment before reached above the ledge to find a hidden key. He held it up with a wide victorious smile. The only way he could act happier about finding it was if he had kissed it before he putting it in the lock, which opened with a chinking sound. My heart started racing as possibilities ran through my head as to what was down there that would produce such a reaction from the men.

Jordan slowly walked down the stairs and was only gone for a moment before he came back up to wave us down. I stepped back hesitating, but Jack came up to me and grasped my arm gently steering me towards the doorway. Even still I dragged my feet, apprehensive to see what had excited the men so.

Through the doorway, the stairs curved back under the house, making it hard to see beyond them. We slowly descended the stairs, the light that Jordan had obviously found and turned on was gradually growing brighter and brighter until we hit the bottom of the stairs.

Once we stepped into the room my jaw hit the floor. I had thought they were leaving any renovations to Mia when she inherited it but apparently they had changed their minds.

They had renovated the cellar into a playroom.

Leann Lane

Chapter Seventeen

The playroom had a saw horse, a swing, a chair that had restraints along the arms and the legs designed to restrain a person at different points or possibly all at once. It had a chain running along the length of the ceiling that dropped down in the middle. I knew this one well, it was a hoist, and it was meant for you to hold your arms over your head and generally went with a spreader bar at the bottom, to keep your legs spread about shoulder width apart. It was one of Jordan's favorite techniques, he'd keep me on the edge for what seemed like hours before he'd lay me down on whatever surface he could find and take me from behind. A shiver went through me and I had to bite my cheek to keep from begging him to do that again.

My eyes looked from station to station growing bigger with each and every piece of equipment that I recognized. I looked over to find Jordan and Jack engrossed in a conversation about the carpentry on several of the items. The innovation and imagination that went into every piece seemed to impress them greatly. I looked at the piece in front of it and recognized it as a kneeling chair. It was designed for the sub to kneel and bend over the flat surface on top, presenting her backside at the perfect position for a spanking or other various torturing ideas.

"That's a beautiful piece of work," Jordan said coming up behind me.

I looked over my shoulder at him and watched as he gazed at this chair in appreciation. Jack walked over and stood next to it looking it over from top to bottom.

"Hey, Jordan, look at this," he said excitedly then messed with something on the back.

The platform at the top immediately folded down making it into an odd looking kneeling saw horse, an ingenious move on the builder's part allowing the piece of equipment multiple uses. Jordan walked over to the kneeling bench and started looking underneath it and must have found a lever under there because, the kneeling board immediately parted. In awe, I stared at it imagining the reasoning behind splitting the bench like that.

Jack let out a whistle. "Nice."

"I wonder who made these for them. We are going to have to let Reed know about them and see if we can't get some for The Dungeon," Jordan said.

He stepped away from the newly modified chair and walked over to a gigantic bed that covered one side of the wall. It had four posts that held a railing along the top. Each corner of the railing held what looked like spokes, since they came together around a circle that sat dead middle of the bed. Behind the bed, was a set of curtains that were meant to be drawn around it for privacy.

Jordan looked over at me with a smile on his face that was pure mischievousness and he wiggled his eyebrows at me.

"Shall we try it out?" he asked Jack.

I felt a rush of desire run through me at the mention of using any piece of equipment in the room.

"Hell yeah," Jack agreed immediately.

He anxiously stared at the kneeling chair as if he was already picturing exactly how he wanted to use it.

"Where?" he asked.

"In the back of the Jeep," Jordan answered immediately.

I watch confused as Jack jogged up the stairs and disappeared from sight.

"What's he doing?" I asked.

"He's going to grab my big black bag of fun," Jordan said with a playful smile and a wink.

A shiver ran up my back as I remembered every little thing that was in that black bag, which was probably every toy that had ever been made and a few bundles of ropes as well. Excitement began to buzz through me knowing that he had his black bag with him. The playful look in his eyes rapidly turned to heat as they leisurely studied the clothes I had on as if he could see through them.

"While we wait for Jack to bring it down here, take off your clothes," he commanded, obviously unhappy with having to use his imagination.

I grasped the bottom of my shirt and slowly, teasingly, pulled it up. I locked my eyes on him enjoying his rampant attention as the material revealed inch by slow inch of my bare skin. I was lifting it over my head when hands on my arms stopped me, effectively trapping me and leaving me unable to see anything.

"Don't move," Jordan said harshly.

His fingers slid down to my rib cage causing my stomach to tighten as his rough hands gently scraped down my sides. They slowly slid around to my back until they quickly and efficiently unclasped my bra then glided around front to cup my breasts. My nipples hardened instantly against the heat of his hands as he slowly began to fondle the rounded globes causing the normally inert flesh to become more sensitive with each little squeeze. When his fingers found my tingling nipples, I tipped my head back letting out a small moan of pleasure and arching my back pressing my breasts more firmly into his hands begging for more.

I heard quiet footsteps come up behind me and the close proximity of both my Masters sent my nerve ends tingling. I felt my bra slowly being pulled upwards to connect with my shirt that was still caught on my arms and both of them were lazily hauled up until my top half was bared to their hot devouring gazes which fanned the already burning fire inside me.

My eyes took a moment to adjust to the suddenly low lighting in the room, Jack must have found a way to dim it when he had come back. Right now it was just a muted glow that reminded me of candle light. The gentle lighting contrasted with the harsh features on Jordan, softening them and causing my heart to skip a beat just looking at him. The desire and determination gleaming in his eyes gave me joy that his feeling had not changed in the last year especially since mine hadn't either, if anything they had deepened until I was borderline obsessive.

Jack pulled me back flush against his hard chest and the warmth of his bare skin against my back let me know that he had taken his shirt off. I felt only slightly more comfortable knowing we were all topless. Jordan chose that moment to tweak my nipples hard and I let out a soft cry tipping my head back to rest against Jack's. A deep rumbling growl came up from the middle of his chest and my eyes flew open. I lifted my chin up to meet his dark gaze which was churning with the same desire I felt pulsing through me.

"See how much she likes that?" Jordan asked his eyes never leaving my nipples as he continued to play with them.

"Yes I do. You never mentioned how responsive she was," Jack murmured slightly accusingly.

His eyes stayed locked on my aching nipples as Jordan continued playing with them and they became ten times more sensitive knowing he was watching.

Jordan just looked up and grinned, "I wanted you to have a pleasant surprise."

Jack nodded as if he understood or maybe he agreed it was a pleasant surprise. I wanted to ask but I knew we were in the middle of the scene and one of Jordan's rules was unless it was an emergency or I didn't understand something I was not to speak without permission. Jack circled my waist with one of his arms aligning our bodies and I felt his erection rub against me. Helplessly, I pressed back against him wishing adamantly there were no clothes between us, so I could see or touch that wonderful protuberance desperately trying to press its way between my ass cheeks.

"You like that don't you?" Jack whispered into my hair.

His hot breath tickled my ear sending goose bumps down my chest and making my already tortured nipples harden even more. I whimpered as the next pluck of Jordan's fingers was even more breathtaking than the first hard twist.

"Lizzie, I do believe your Master asked you a question?" Jordan warned.

"Yes, Master Jordan, Master Jack." I whimpered.

Jack chuckled softly, "I think we need to do something here, Jor. I have a feeling as we get farther along she's going to find it hard to keep saying Master Jordan and Master Jack."

"I think you're right. Lizzie, you are to address me as Sir from now on and address Jack as simply Master. Do you understand?" Jordan asked.

"Yes, Sir," I answered immediately back.

I didn't care what I called them, I just didn't want them to stop. As soon as the thought crossed my mind Jordan stepped back and Jack dropped my arms. I almost whined at the loss of contact from the both of them and I had to curl my fingers into tight balls to keep them from grabbing out.

Jordan began to walk around me in an act that was reminiscent of his usual pace when he was inspecting me. As automatic as breathing, I linked my hands behind my head, thrusting my breasts fully for their view. I spread my legs until they were about shoulder width apart whimpering softly as the air caressed the heated area between my thighs. Jack came around in front of me and smiled his pleasure as he took in the sight I was presenting him.

"That's very pretty, sweetheart. I see Jordan did train you well," Jack said warmly.

His praise made my heart swell with pride and I gave him a smile in return. Jordan slid behind me pressing his smooth chest against my back much as Jack had done. The contrast between the both of their chests was both shocking and fascinating. It was more than just the fact that Jack had his nipples pierced and Jordan didn't. It was deeper than that, it was in every line, crevice and, every curve. I wanted to beg them to stand side by side so I could explore in more depth the difference between the two men, with my eyes, my hands, and especially, my tongue. Before Jordan I didn't think there was this level of all complete consuming desire and now I've found another man that I could have such an obsession with. I was distracted when Jack moved off and picked up the infamous black bag from where he had obviously dropped it when he had come in.

"Alright, baby girl, I think it's time to show Jack that sweetly, tasty little pussy I've been telling him about," Jordan said right next to my ear almost startling me.

"Yes, Sir," I breathed out.

I grasped the button on my jeans and slowly began undoing them. I knew Jordan loved it when I went really slowly and if the flash of enjoyment in his eyes was any indication, Jack was loving it too.

I pushed my pants down my legs keeping them as straight as I could. The position allowed me to press my bottom against the stiff erection that was straining against the material of Jordan's pants. I heard him make a noise in the back of his throat before he pressed himself harder against me.

"Watch yourself, baby, or I'll shove something deep in there before we even start to play. After all, I know how much you love it when you come with me buried deep in your tight little ass," he growled.

Looking back, I gave him an inviting smile and continued to pull my pants off until I was able to kick them free. I quickly grasped the top of my panties silently wishing I had decided on a sexier pair, then deciding it didn't matter since they weren't going to be on for long anyway. As it was the sturdy cotton did nothing to hide the wet spot that sat in the middle of it, proof positive that these men were driving me crazy. Now completely naked, I stood up once again and turned to face Jordan anxiously awaiting his next order.

"Take the position again, only this time over by the bed," Jordan said stepping to the side.

I almost whined at him but I did as he asked because I knew he wanted another "inspection". This was an anticipation technique that most Dom's used to take a moment and plan out what was going to happen next. I was surprised, however, when Jack came over and was the one to walk around me.

His dark eyes ran down my body as he walked around me slowly taking in my body from every angle that he could. He stepped behind me once more and proceeded to palm my ass cheeks, squeezing them tightly then caressing them gently. The contrast between his touches had me biting my lip at how wonderful it felt and I wished I could beg him for more as he released them.

"You're right, Jor. She does have a fabulous ass, it really does make a man want to bite it," Jack commented.

His words made me almost flush and I wasn't sure if it was from joy or embarrassment. They also sent a wave of heat through me at the image he built in my head. Suddenly he grasped my hips tightly and his mouth laid a gentle kiss on one cheek drawing a quiet moan from me before the sharp cry his hard nip caused.

"Oh, do that again, Jack, our little sub liked it," Jordan said with a wicked smile on his face.

He moved to the other cheek and repeated the ritual which had me almost dropping my hands to try and grab onto something.

"Ah, ah, ah," Jordan admonished. "Don't break your stance, baby girl. You don't want Jack to have to punish you even more do you?"

Leann Lane

Chapter Eighteen

"Punish? Why?" I cried in surprise.

Jordan shook his head. "Oh how quickly you forgot. You left the house without permission and did not tell either one of us where you were going,"

I closed my eyes at the reminder of what had occurred before this little trip down stairs. I guess it was too much to hope that they had forgotten it as well, obviously my luck was not that good today.

"What is my punishment, Sir?" I asked sadly.

Jordan's smile went from wicked to downright evil causing a shaft of fear to bloom inside me. I felt Jack stand up behind me and he leaned in really close.

"You are going to walk around naked for the rest of the day. No matter where you go or what you do, you will be undressed."

My mouth hit the ground and I immediately started to try to stutter out a protest. We were relatively secluded out here, but it wasn't like no one ever went by the house on the beach side. A single look from Jordan warned me if I didn't shut up I was going to lose more than just my clothes. I just silently prayed if someone did show up out here they would call first so that I might have some chance to beg for my clothes back.

I sighed and gave up. "Yes, Master."

"Nicely done, sweetheart," Jack said as he came around.

His hands immediately came forward to cup my breasts as if he couldn't wait one more moment to touch them. He gently squeezed them and rubbed his rough palms across my nipples drawing a whimper from me. I watched as a sweet smile crossed his face while enjoying my reaction to his caresses, yet his gentle touches were not enough. I arched my back deeper into his palms hoping he'd take the hint, but like every other Master he took his own sweet time doing as he pleased.

"Please, Master," I finally begged daring to break my silence.

"What do you need?" Jack said never taking his gaze off my breasts.

"I want your mouth on me. Please, Master."

Jack finally met my gaze with a smoldering one of his own.

"Not yet, little sub, although I love your enthusiasm."

A whine finally popped out of my mouth which only served to bring a chuckle from both of them as Jack continued his slowly burning torture of my body. His hands left my breasts and followed my soft stomach down as he knelt in front of me making his face level with my throbbing pussy. My body stilled as his hands slid even farther down until his thumbs were just brushing the trembling lips of it and softly began stroking them. I sucked in a breath trying hard to remember how which wasn't easy with his feather light caresses combining with his heated gaze making me feel as if I was burning from the inside out.

He slowly leaned forward as if wanting a better look and I watched intently waiting impatiently for him to make his next move. Finally, his fingers gently parted the folds to find the engorged clit in between then paused leaving it exposed to the air in the room. I let out a frustrated sound and had to reminded myself not to stomp my feet like the bratty sub I wanted to be. Jack's gaze flew to mine and I saw a crinkle appear next to his eyes along with a barely noticeable smirk around the lips that I so desperately wanted on me.

"What's wrong, Elizabeth?" he said his voice way too innocently for my pleasure.

"Master, you're killing me," I whined not even caring that he had used my full name.

"Jordan has never been very good at holding out, but you will find that I am not quite so impatient with my sub's pleasure. I will give it to you when I'm ready not the other way around," Jack explained.

Unfortunately for my sanity, every word and every breath blew across my exposed clit making it tighten even more and I felt myself grow even wetter.

"I am quite enjoying the show, sweetheart. You are wonderfully wet down here and you smell so delicious that it's making my mouth water just being this close," Jack complimented me.

His blunt words sent more bolts of lust coursing through my body and I let out a little moan at how erotic they were. I felt Jordan come up behind me once again and he gripped my forearms indicating I was to lower them. He pulled them behind my back and I felt the rough scrapping of a rope as he began to wrap it around my forearms, not tight enough to cut off circulation, yet secure enough that I knew I wouldn't be able to slip out of it. Jordan was really good at making sure that my bonds were perfect. I knew from previous experience that if I winced once he would undo them immediately and either redo the binding or find a different rope. As soon as I felt him tighten the knot I tested them and as usual I wouldn't easily slip from them. I took a moment and allowed the feeling of submission to run through me.

First was fear because I was at the mercy of these two Masters. Then came excitement at no longer have to make any decisions and of course desire heightened the combination of the two. Jack suddenly brushed a gentle finger over my clit making me cry out and sent my thoughts scattering until I could barely remember my own name. My hips must have had a mind of their own because they began thrusting forwards trying to encourage him to move his teasing along and I felt my inner muscles clench, just begging for something to fill the emptiness.

"Hey, Jordan, as soon as you began tying that rope she became drenched, isn't that just sweet?" Jack said his voice displaying his awe as he continued to lightly stroke my clit.

With a chuckle Jack stood up and abandoned his tormenting all together. Shocking me, they both pulled me across to the bench and helped me onto the kneeling board on the front before pushing me down so my breasts were squished to the flat surface on top. Then they put a soft strap across my back and my knees to keep me safe for whatever they had in mind for me.

Jordan came around front and I realized he had finally taken off his pants so his wonderful cock was exposed for my own perusal. I licked my lips as I remembered the last time I'd had it in my mouth. It wasn't so long ago now that I thought about it, but it felt like forever and I found I didn't want to wait anymore.

"Please, Sir, may I suck your cock?" I asked knowing he liked it when I was blunt about what I wanted.

"In a moment, impatient sub. First I think Jack has a much better idea in mind," Jordan said with a chuckle.

His face clearly showed the strain it was costing him putting of both my pleasure and his own. I decided to make it even harder hoping he'd be able to rush things along. I stared at his swollen cock and continued to lick my lips making it obvious that I could already feel his velvety steel rod across my tongue. I heard him groan as he gripped the base of it hard and I knew it was a desperate attempt to keep himself in check. Pleased I was getting to him I continued my own form of torment until suddenly there was a sharp smack across my bottom making me squeal and thrash against my bindings. I looked back at Jack standing behind me with an admonishing look on his face.

"You will stop teasing Jordan, girl. He will not give you what you want, I promise you that and if you don't knock it off I will make sure that you not only stay naked all day, but considerably frustrated as well," Jack warned.

I looked back down, but this time it was to hide the tears in my eyes at his punishment. I never liked a lot of pain and that spanking hurt like hell leaving my bottom still stinging from it. Jack came around in front of me and squatted down so I couldn't hide the tears that were being to run down my cheeks.

"Jordan told me that you weren't really into pain and I'm sorry for having to cause you any. However, that being said, you should know better than to try and rush this along when we've already told you no, girl."

I groaned and closed my eyes unable to look at his face which was filled with much compassion as determination. I hated that he was right, I really did know better. My body was throbbing with need and I didn't know how much more I could take without going crazy or maybe I already had to disregard such an important rule.

"Yes, Master, I'm sorry," I finally whispered.

I felt a gentle touch on my tear stained cheek and opened my eyes in surprise to find Jack was still in front of me. He reached up gently and brushed the back of his fingers across my face clearing of the remaining wetness. His eyes had softened in forgiveness and I was relieved that I was in no further trouble. I felt the last of my anger diminish and I gave him a small smile letting him know that I had also forgiven him, mostly anyway. He returned my smile with one of relief before giving me a gentle kiss and stepped back to finally give me full view of the strong, chiseled body that was now revealed and not blurry from a shower curtain. His legs were not as thick as Jordan's yet each muscle was still clearly defined and well formed. My mouth began to water as I lifted my gaze to where his legs met unable to wait one more second to see the part of his body I'd only pictured in my imagination.

His erection was long and hard as a rock, jutting upright and laying flush against his stomach like a flesh colored flagpole. I had known from the few times I'd felt against me that it had to be impressive but when it suddenly bounced against his stomach a few times as if waving hello to me, I was thoroughly impressed.

"That's quite a trick, Master," I said on a giggle.

"What do you mean, little sub? He's just happy to see you," he said winking at me.

I giggled again, loving the fact that he could play even in the midst of the scene like this, it was a pleasant surprise from someone as serious as Jack was. Jordan stepped up beside him and was shaking his head even though his lips were curved up into a smile.

"You can't help but show off can you?" Jordan admonished him.

Jack just gave a shrug and an arrogant smile as he moved back to his original position behind me. Jordan took up the spot in front of me and I made another lazy perusal of his hot as hell body despite the fact that I knew it almost by heart now.

"How are you doing, baby girl?" Jordan asked.

"I'm fine, Sir, thank you. I'm sorry for trying to rush you," I said looking up at him repentantly.

"You are forgiven, baby, just don't do it again," he said giving me smile of approval.

"Yes, Sir," I quickly agreed.

"Good, now that that's outta the way, let's get on with the fun," Jack said from behind me.

I tried to turn my head around to see what he was doing only to feel a hand grip my hair, forcing me to face forward again.

"Eyes on me, Lizzie," Jordan demanded.

"Yes, Sir."

There was a slight scraping from behind me making me wish I could disobey my Master and look back to see what Jack was doing, but I knew better. With my luck being what it was I may very well get another spanking from Jack and there's no way in hell I wanted that.

I kept my eyes on Jordan as he'd told me to and was treated with a sensually arousing show from him. He wrapped one big muscular hand around his hard cock and began slowly stroking it as I looked on. I narrowed my eyes at his blatant teasing and opened my mouth to speak when I felt Jack's fingers ran the length of my sensitive pussy lips with a caress that could barely be considered touching. My breath caught and the muscles inside clenched hard with each pass.

I closed my eyes to concentrate on the caresses only to feel a light tap on my cheek causing them to pop open again. Jordan's swollen cock was a breath away from my face, close enough that I could see each and every straining vein as he ran his hand up and down it. Still it was far enough away that even if I stuck my tongue out I couldn't touch it. He stroked it and I saw a pearly white drop pop out of the tip before he quickly swiped it away leaving me with a sense of loss.

I was lost in the sight in front of me when two fingers spread me wide and there was a gentle buzzing a moment before a hard object was pressed lightly against my engorged clit. A sharp cry burst from my lips at the vibrations that were riding through my already sensitive clit to drive deeper inside my drenched channel.

"Do you like that, Lizzie?" Jordan asked with a knowing grin on his face.

"Yes, Sir," I gasped out.

Jack used the little vibrator to continue with the gentle stroking trip his fingers had taken and every time he came to my hole he'd press it in. When I clamped down on it trying to suck it deeper inside me, he'd pull it out and run it slowly down to my pebbled clit again where he'd let it sit for a moment. I tried to press back against the tormenting piece of equipment, yet the straps they had over me were keeping me still, making it so I was unable to do anything but take whatever my Masters wanted me too.

"Please, Master," I began begging once more.

"What do you need, Elizabeth?" Jack asked not stopping his play.

"I want more, Master, please I can't take it," I whimpered as I felt him choose that moment to push the little toy slightly inside once again.

"Oh, you can, little one. I know you can and you will. Do you know why?" Jack replied evilly.

I nodded unable to speak since he was once again working it over and around my throbbing clit.

"Why is that?" he prompted.

"Because you want me too, Master," I said almost morosely.

Jordan and I have had this conversation a million times over and each time I'd thought Jordan's tormenting had been inhumane. Now I realized they hadn't even brushed the surface of inhumane. I moaned in passion filled agony which once again only served to make the men chuckle and continue on.

After what seemed like an eternity, Jordan finally stepped within reach and I lifted my eyes to his face anxiously awaiting the command I knew was coming.

"Yes, my love, it's time for you to suck," Jordan said.

Leann Lane

Chapter Nineteen

The look on his face was pure anticipation as he stared at my lips which I'm sure was swollen considering how many times I'd bitten them to keep from screaming, crying, and begging.

However, this time it wasn't Jack's administrations or Jordan's tempting erection that had me caught off guard, it was his casual usage of an endearment. I didn't know if he realized he'd called me his love or if he'd truly meant it. All I knew was that he'd never called me that before and somehow this seemed a lot more meaningful. I stared up at his face trying to find the answer buried deep in his eyes, but no matter how hard I stared I couldn't see anything passed the desire.

"Open wide," Jordan demanded snapping me out of my musings.

This wasn't the first time I would deep throat him and it certainly wouldn't be the last. The whole experience was a turn on for me; from the feel of his velvety hard cock rubbing across my tongue, to each ragged breath that he took in whenever I'd play with the fleshy ridge that circled the top, to each moan that burst from his chest whenever he'd get closer and closer to coming.

As Jordan slowly feed me his ridge cock, Jack gently pressed two fingers into me as far as they would go causing me to cry out. It wasn't exactly what I'd wanted and yet I knew Jack was enjoying watching as his fingers slowly disappeared deep inside me. The dual assault sent me reeling and I almost forgot to breathe as Jordan's rod hit the back of my throat. It only took a moment for Jack and Jordan to begin a rhythm that was pushing me towards the edge. My mouth and my aching pussy were being filled at the same time, but it wasn't enough, I wanted, needed more.

As soon as Jordan speed up his thrusting I knew he was getting close and I clenched my mouth around him as my tongue rubbed along the ridge of his cock. Behind me I felt Jack move just slightly and the next thing I knew there was a warm wetness that began to flicker against my clit. My mouth immediately unclenched and I cried out around Jordan who took advantage of that moment to pull away from me.

"God, baby, you know just how to suck my cock," he said as he turned away to catch his breath.

I wasn't listening anymore because Jack had removed his fingers and was using his tongue to explore every inch of my pussy making me whimper for an entirely different reason. His tongue alternated little flicks on my clit with wide strokes that started from the top and went to the bottom.

"Oh, Master!" I cried.

Jordan turned around immediately to watch and he gripped the base of his erection as if trying to stave off his own orgasm. His eyes took on an appreciative look as he watched Jack's movements as he brought me higher and higher.

"She loves that, Jack. Doesn't she have the sweetest tasting pussy in the world? Just wait until you get inside, it just clamps down on you and wrings you dry," Jordan said hoarsely.

His words must have been as much of a turn on to him as they were to me because he closed his eyes and tossed his head back as he started stroking himself harder. I watch awe struck as the head turn purple and I knew he was about to come.

"Sir, please," I begged and when he looked at me I opened my mouth.

"Oh, no little sub. I'm not going to come yet," he said even as he gritted his teeth and squeezed his cock harder.

Chastised, I looked down at the floor and went back to concentrate on what Jack was doing with his wonderful tongue. It circled my ultra-sensitive nub a few more times before running upwards once again sending bolts of pleasure through me continuously. Suddenly he withdrew his fingers and tongue leaving me feeling confused and frustrated, I turned my head to look back and I saw a mischievous smile cross his face before he opened my labia wide and promptly shoved his tongue deep in me as far as it would go.

I threw my head back and cried out as he started to thrust into me with his tongue. I began panting with the need to strain back against him hoping for more, my clit was buzzing as if it still had the toy on it and I wanted him to play with it more.

"Mm, Jordan, you were right. She does taste wonderful," Jack commented his breath washing over me.

I moaned as the erotic words hit me making my tight channel clench around his tongue and for the first time I heard him groan.

"Make her come, Jack, and you'll be in for a real treat," Jordan said around his gritted teeth.

"I can't wait. Have her suck on you again, she got soaked last time she did that," Jack said on a chuckle.

I immediately opened my mouth and I felt Jack slide first two and then three fingers into me causing me to spout a muffled cry as Jordan rapidly slammed his cock deep in my mouth. My mouth and my pussy began to milk the two invading objects as they both set up a harshly paced thrusting rhythm designed specifically to get me off. I felt myself wind tighter and tighter and I couldn't help the incoherent moans that were making it almost impossible to keep sucking on Jordan.

Jack's mouth immediately went to my clit sucked on it as his tongue began once again hitting it with quick light strokes. The edge I felt myself teetering on became sharper and sharper. I heard myself begging them both around the thrusting cock in my mouth and with a few more strokes I was holding my breath, my whole body became focused on that one area that was being worked by Jack's tongue as fast as it could go.

Like a wave breaking against rocks my release hit, consuming me and pulling me under with a high pitched scream and wave after wave of pleasure soared through me. Jack pulled his fingers out only to quickly replace it with his tongue once again. My hard climax had me spouting moans and high whining noise that sent vibration down Jordan's shaft. In turn he was making harsh growling noises deep in his throat as his thrusts became hard and less coordinated. Suddenly he slammed deep in my mouth and stiffen before hot burst of come began sliding down the back of my throat. I hastily swallowed to avoid choking and sucked harder hoping to milk him dry.

He pulled away all too soon and I could see a sheen of sweat covering his face as he sat back just to watch while he caught his breath. I closed my eyes and laid my head on the table underneath me surrendering to the pleasure Jack was still evoking in me. The sweet torment on my sensitive pussy had me twitching and keening softly. Just when I thought I had finally lost touch with my sanity he pulled away before gentle hands began undoing the straps that held me down.

Drowsily I opened my eyes only to find that Jordan was no longer in front of me, gazing around I spotted him digging into his bag again. Almost triumphantly he held up a little tube and came hurrying back with his treasure. My eyes slipped down his body only to notice he was still stiff as a rock and I smiled inwardly knowing that he could almost keep up with me.

"Stand up, sweetheart," Jack ordered.

I did so on incredibly shaky legs and had to grip the bench so I wouldn't immediately fall to the ground, thankfully Jordan stood close by so when he saw how unsteady I was he grasped my shoulders to help keep me upright. I let go of the bench and gave him a grateful smile before he dipped his head and granted me a deep toe curling kiss. The minute his tongue plunged into my mouth a rumbling groan burst forth from deep inside his chest and he pulled me tight against his chest and the kiss turned harder and more passionate. My knees dropped out from under me and I was forced to cling to him, helpless against the onslaught. I was amazed that I could even be aroused again after the mind blowing orgasm I had just had.

"I think Jack has more in mind, baby girl, don't you?" Jordan asked huskily when he finally pulled away.

"Yes, Sir," I breathed out.

The excitement was obvious in my voice as I turned back to Jack. He smiled tenderly at me before stepping up slowly and leaning in to give me a gentle kiss of his own. I melted into his chest and was surprised that I found the taste of myself on his lips a highly erotic mixture that left me begging for more. More than willing to oblige, He answered my plea by thrusting his tongue deep into my mouth and holding my head still so he could take control of the kiss.

Our tongues met and began an intimate dance that once again sparked the passion that was roiling around in the lower part of my stomach. Almost impossibly, I felt myself grow even wetter. I lifted my arms up and wrapped them around his neck so I could press my body against him, feeling every inch of skin rub together. The sprinkling of hair on his chest teased my nipples mercilessly and his erection nestled sweetly against my belly as I rubbed up against it.

He broke the kiss to lift me up and walk backwards towards the bed and he let us tumble on it. Then lifted me up and situated me on top of him before he pulled my mouth down again and continued with his heart pounding kiss like nothing had ever happened.

It was my turn to break the kiss to gasp as I felt a set of fingers slide between my ass cheeks and found the swollen opening that was nestled between my legs begging to be filled again. Jack pulled back slightly to watch my face as Jordan slowly slid his fingers in and out. I leaned forwards bracing myself on my arms and my knees to give Jordan more access as I began to thrust back against his penetrating fingers.

"You like the feel of his fingers in that pussy don't ya, sub?" Jack suddenly growled.

I whimpered at his words nodding, my breath coming in harsh gasps making actual speech almost impossible.

"I'll bet it's just so sensitive that you are almost ready to come on his fingers aren't you?" Jack asked again.

I started to nodded again but Jack reach up and tweaked one hard sensitive nipple rough enough to catch my attention.

"Yes, Master," I gasped out.

Despite the slightly painful tug of my nipple I shoved my breast into his hand silently begging him to continue playing with it.

"Tell me what you want, girl," Jack said harshly.

"Please, Master, suck on my nipples. They are aching," I whined out.

Jack's smile was nothing short of triumphant before he lifted his head and began leisurely sucking on them. His tongue swept around the aureole before flicking across the nipples with the same precision it had when he had flicked it across my clit.

A deep powerful tug on my breast caused me to arch my chest into his mouth. My movements caused Jordan's fingers to slip out of me and earned me a growl from him. I jumped when a small smack landed on a sensitive spot between my thigh and ass. A curse flew from my lips when my actions caused my Jack's mouth to pop off my nipple and earned me an evil growl from him as well.

"Don't move, sub," Jordan ordered harshly from behind me.

"I'm sorry, Sir," I whimpered.

Jack wrapped his arms around me and lifted his head again to suck my nipple deep in his mouth while his tongue continued its quick stroking. I gripped his shoulders hard, digging my nails in deep, so I wouldn't disobey him and arch even farther into his sweet mouth. A whimper broke from my mouth when he let my nipple slide out with a pop, although the protest broke into a moan when he immediately attached to the second nipple with the same hungry determination as he had the first.

A cold drop of gel slid down between my ass cheeks and I squeaked but somehow managed not to jump as a finger ran over it spreading it all around before pressing forward. I gasped at the pleasure that spiked through me as he began the act of stretching the back hole. Just when I thought I couldn't take any more he pulled out seeming satisfied that he could use it for his purpose. It must have been a silent signal to Jack because he let go of my second nipple laid back. The lust blazing in his eyes and I looked down noticing his erection was jutting up harder than a rock. The swollen head was purple with the strength he was using to hold back.

"I need to be inside you," Jack grunted through gritted teeth.

He grasped the base and held it upright so I could lower onto him slowly, relishing in the feel of him as he slid into me. I moaned at the intense feeling of fullness that came over me once he was fully seated. I wanted to move but Jack had grasped my hips forcing me to stay still.

Jordan moved in behind me and pressed me forward until I was draped across Jack's chest. I held my breath knowing that this was what I had been waiting for ever since the first time I saw them together. My heart began to pound as a moment of apprehension came over me.

"It's okay baby, I know this will be difficult at first but you are honestly going to love it," Jordan whispered into my ear.

I took a deep breath and nodded knowing he was right since this was not the first time I'd had dual penetration. Looking back now it was blatantly obvious that he had been preparing me for this all along, I'd always just thought he had a fascination with anal.

Fascinated with Jacks reaction, I concentrated on his face and the whirlwind of emotions cross it. There was an intense pleasure on it almost to the point of pain and his mouth was set in a harsh line as he struggled to hold onto his control.

"God, Lizzie. You're so fucking tight already," Jack breathed out through his gritted teeth.

Jordan wrapped his arms around me and began playing with my sensitive nipples that were already hard little points from Jack toying with them.

"I know she is, isn't she?" Jordan said obviously amused by the hard time Jack was having. "Now imagine how much tighter she's going to be once I'm deep inside her tight ass."

"Quit fucking talking about it and get in," Jack growled back.

I looked back over my shoulder and watched as he smoothed more lube on the condom he had put on before touching the tip of his erection against my back hole.

"Ready, my love?" Jordan asked before pushing in.

I nodded and took a deep breath hiding my face in the crook of Jack's shoulder. I gritted my teeth as he began to slowly push inside, Jordan was not a small man anywhere and here was no exception. On a normal day I would feel the pressure/pain until it was slightly overwhelming, however, right now with Jack's large cock deep inside me I wasn't sure if I could hold them both.

I heard Jordan take a shuddering breath as he continued to press in and out slowly stretching the tight channel over and over again until he finally pushed past the ring with almost an audible pop. Although I was pretty sure it was a moan from both men and he was finally seated at least partially inside. Jack pushed me up until I was leaning braced on my hands, this position made his pelvis press hard against my already throbbing clit.

As the sensation of being overly full ran through the bottom part of my body and seemed to steal what little breath I had in me. Swallowing several times, I tried hard to adjust to the feelings coursing through me and was extremely grateful to the two wonderful Dom's that surrounded me, sitting perfectly still allowing me time to make the adjustments.

My body melted into them the moment the sensations turned from unwanted invasion to unimaginable pleasure. I nodded to the men to let them know they could finally start moving. Jack was the first one, he slowly pulled out to give room for Jordan to press in finally completely filling my back hole. The rhythm they started was slow, each taking their own sweet time to press in and out of me, I wasn't sure if they were just out of practice or if they were honestly both trying to drive me out of my mind but if they didn't hurry I was going to die, I just knew it.

I closed my eyes and gritted my teeth to keep the screams inside even as they built more and more. Suddenly fingers gripped my nipples and twisted barely to the point of pain making me finally let go of the screams I was holding in. I threw my head back and began pushing against the hard cocks that were thrusting inside me as I felt my body tighten in an impending explosion.

"Fuck," Jordan swore in my ear. "I have no idea what you did but do it again she squeezed me hard man,"

"I know, she almost strangled me down there," Jack agreed.

He pinched my nipples again and began rolling them roughly between his fingers as I jerked on them trying to get them to move faster.

"Please, Masters, Please!" I screamed at them when my movements didn't rush them.

"You know what I want to hear, baby girl. Say it," Jordan commanded me.

Not hesitating since I did indeed know what he wanted to hear me say, Jordan loved it when he made me talk dirty. It was the way he knew he'd finally made me submit and it just so happened I never felt wilder and out of control in my life.

146

"Please, Masters, fuck me hard I wanna come," I cried.

If there had been a loud snap of a rubber band, it would have been nothing compared to the moment I realize Jack had finally lost control. A deep growl burst from his lips and his hand let go of my nipples and immediately gripped my hips in an almost punishing grip holding me still as he began to slam inside me. Jordan began to copy his frantic movements as he moved in and out of my ass until they both became synchronized once again.

I began to hurtle towards my climax faster than I ever have before, tightening and tightening. My cries became louder and louder as I grabbed the closest thing to my fingers and dug my nails in holding on for dear life. With an inarticulate scream I reached the pinnacle and flew over with a burst of blinding pleasure that was a breath away from making me pass out.

I heard two deep shouts and felt the men stiffen one by one and finally finding their release shoving hard and deep inside me. I collapsed on top of Jack, who immediately wrapped his arms around me, and laid my head on his chest listening to the rapid heartbeat that seemed to beat at the same pace as mine.

Jordan groan softly as he pulled himself out and laid down beside us both. I lifted my nearest hand and rested it on his sweat covered chest needing to feel close to him after the events of the day.

My eyes caught sight of five half-moon shape marks on Jack's shoulders some of them had a little bit of blood bubbling to the surface, horrified I quickly looked to where my other hand lay and saw identical marks in his flesh.

"Oh my god, Master, I'm so sorry," I cried.

Mortified at my uninhibited behavior I was unable to take my eyes off the wounds that were still spilling small amounts of blood.

Jack glanced down and I watched as his face went from curiously confused, to morbidly fascinated, to sexually aroused. In an instance his erection that was still buried deep inside me, went from mostly flaccid to hard as a rock and he flipped me over on my back so he could tower above me.

I looked over at Jordan for help not sure if I could come again yet the only help I got was him coming around to the top of the bed and pinning my arms above my head. I opened and shut my mouth a few times trying to say something but I wasn't sure if the words 'no wait' were going to come out or if it was going to be 'yes please'.

Jack grasped my legs until they were open as far as they could go spreading me wide. His eyes were glued to where he was inside me then started a harsh almost punishing rhythm, slamming deep inside me again and again causing my already sensitive channel to clamp down on him.

My head fell back as I was immediately swept away again. My body felt as if it had never completely come down from the most recent amazing climax before Jack hurled me into another one unexpectedly. A scream echoed in the room and I came hard drenching Jack's cock as he slammed into me one last time. My eyes drifted closed and I wasn't sure if I passed out or just drifted to sleep, not that I cared either way.

Chapter Twenty

I awoke slowly wrapped tightly in a familiar set of arms and legs, I snuggled deeper not really wanting to be awake yet. A few urgent needs that required addressing pressed in on me, the top of which was the fact I was sweating fiercely. I wondered how I could be so blasted hot when it was just Jordan in bed with me. Until I realized I was missing one of my Masters and I peeked an eye open to see where he had gone to. I saw him standing in the far corner of the room talking softly on his cellphone. He had put is pants back on but not his shirt and I took a moment to ogle him as he stood with his back to me.

"Alright we'll see you then. No, I promise I'll have her back in just a few days, we just need more time with her, apparently we went about this all ass backwards," Jack said so softly I barely heard him.

A soft snore in my ear drew my attention away and I looked back at Jordan lying next to me sleeping away. I smiled softly loving how relaxed he looked, he was barely over thirty but the lines on his face said that he was years older. Not wanting to disturb his rest, I slowly slid out of the bed trying hard to be quiet and gentle. His snore broke off midway as his eyes flew open glazed, not focusing as a snarl crossed his lips.

For a moment I found myself truly afraid of my Master, his face had a murderous tint to it and I shrunk back with a quiet whimper. The fearful sound somehow managed to jolt him out of whatever land he was in and also caught Jack's attention. Without even saying goodbye he snapped his phone closed and came rushing over to me.

"Lizzie?" Jordan said softly, blinking a couple of times before his eyes focused on me.

"Y-Yes," I stuttered out.

Jordan looked around the room for a moment as if trying to remember where he was before his eyes finally landed on Jack. Jack's eyes held concern and a tinge of fear as they assessed Jordan from head to toe making sure he was alright.

"You good?" asked Jack softly.

Jordan set his feet on the floor and braced his elbow on his knees, then ran his hands over the top of his spiky head before nodding. Jack didn't make any comment just watch him cautiously for a moment before turning to me and lifting an eyebrow as if asking the same question of me.

Jordan let out a frustrating noise before bounding out of bed and grabbing his pants to race upstairs. Confused and hurt at his sudden exit I couldn't move or think as I listened to the sounds of his stomping feet cross the living room and then the slamming of the front door.

Jack let out a breath before turning back to me with a sad look on his face.

"Are you sure you're alright, sweetheart?" he asked looking me up and down much as he had Jordan.

"Yes," I insisted. "What the hell was that about?"

Jack just shook his head and held out a hand to pull me out of the low bed. I grasped it gratefully not sure if I could have sat up otherwise with how sore I was.

"Let's go get a cup of coffee and wait for him on the porch."

I sighed and like a good sub didn't argue with my Master as I allowed him to guide me upstairs. I went to the bathroom so that I could cleaned up before I joined him outside.

I stepped outside a short while later to find that we had slept the day away and the moonlight was shining down on the waves as they crashed into shore. I looked around and spotted Jack, who had taken over my favorite spot on the swing. The moment he saw me, he moved his legs and indicated I was to sit down.

I sat down right next to Jack and snuggled up to his side, he gave me a pleased look that made me feel warm and melty inside. He kissed my forehead before sending the bench swinging again.

"Why are you dressed?" he asked almost casually.

I bit my lip and let out a breathless curse, I hadn't really expected him to remember since I myself had forgotten as well.

"Well, you said for the rest of the day and as you see, it's night."

I patted myself on the back for the quick thinking in coming up with that response. Also crossing my fingers hoping and praying that I wouldn't get into any more trouble for my sass. I watched him closely for any sign of retribution while he mulled over my words.

"I see," he started slowly, "that from now on I'm going to have to be a little more specific when we discuss your punishments."

All the breath rushed out of my body as I relaxed once again into his arms knowing full well I had dodged a bullet on that one.

Silence ensued for a while as we both sat listening to the world outside and letting the contentment of being with each other settle in.

"Jordan was right," he said suddenly.

I looked up at him trying to read his expression, but it was blank almost devoid of emotion. Terror built up inside me and I thought about how to pose my question before I said it. Although I worried for half a minute it would be too quiet for him to hear.

"About what?"

"You are the most wonderful sub we have ever had. I could see myself doing this with you thirty years from now."

His words sent a burst of joy through me landing deep inside my heart that was already lost to both of these wonderful men. I smiled up at him and the love I felt for him to shine brightly in my eyes, even past the tears of happiness that was welling up.

"Me too," I whispered back.

The elation in his eyes shone so bright it was equivalent to the sun in the middle of August. Pride inflated my chest as I congratulated myself on opening up to him even as I was shaking inside. I wished Jordan would come back so I could tell them both how much I loved them or how much I wanted to be with them and not just as a sub. As a friend, a lover, and hopefully one day as a mother of their children.

I knew marriage was out of the question and still I didn't even care. I just wanted to be with them and that was enough commitment for me. I laid my head on his shoulder again and listened intently for the sounds of crunching sand indicating Jordan was on his way back.

After what seemed like forever, my patience had worn thin and I still didn't hear anything in the darkness that permeated the beach.

"Where is he?" I finally broke.

"Sometimes it takes him awhile to get the flash backs to go away," Jack stated sagely.

He wasn't looking at me or out towards the beach as I was, instead he was staring at his foot that continued to push the swing back and forth.

"Flash backs from when you guys were in the army?" I asked.

Jack's face twisted in horror. "We were in the Marines, Elizabeth."

I rolled my eyes irritably. "Whatever, Jack, honestly. One military branch is the same as the next isn't it?"

"No, no it's not, young lady. Army is full of whiny little bitches that kept having to call us to come and get them out of whatever their boneheaded commander had gotten them into," Jack growled at me.

I winced at that insinuation and had to stop myself from shaking my head at him trying to come to terms with exactly how important this really was to him.

"Alright, Marines," I said trying to sound as agreeable as I could.

"Thank you. Yes, the flash backs are from when we were on combat missions in the Marines."

I nodded and snuggled closer to him feeling the tension that was twisted into each individual muscle until he felt like a flesh covered wall sitting next to me, hard and unyielding. I understood the problem mostly because I'd experienced it myself soon after I'd finally run away from my father's house. Rationally you knew you were safe but for a split second your body and mind get thrown back to when you weren't and you react instinctively.

"So when do you think he'll be back?"

I was even more anxious to have him in my arms and hold him close just to make sure he was alright.

"I don't know, sweetie," he said honestly.

I could hear the strain of worry in his voice as well and it reflected my own. It made me realize that Jordan wasn't the only one with major issues here.

"Did you have the flash backs as well?"

Jack sighed as if I'd hit a nerve with him which answered my question without him having to even speak, but soon he did anyway.

"Yes, but not as bad as Jordan's. I got back stateside after the last mission and went to speak to my grandfather about the dreams. When you have dreams like we have, they are more than just dreams. We see them as spirits of those who have died. I still believe they are haunting me sometimes but my grandfather was right, the dream catcher did help with the nightmares."

His eyes were gazing off into the distance almost as if he could see the spirits in front of him as he spoke, like his words had risen them from the grave. Then he shook his head and the haunted look disappeared.

"Why is Jordan's so much worse?"

"Because Jordan carries burdens he shouldn't. He always had since the first day of boot camp. If someone got hurt or flunked out Jordan would take it personally."

"Why?"

I was horrified to think of someone taking so much on to himself, especially a wonderful, caring man like Jordan.

"Jordan's one stubborn bastard, Lizzie. The last mission we ever went on resulted in those scars on his chest. Our escape route was blocked and we ended up getting into a hand to hand combat situation. We got out, but just barely and he refused to let me do more than bind the wound so it wouldn't bleed all over him," Jack explained.

I grasped his hand tightly as I watch the haunted look return to his eyes, I knew I should just leave it alone and let it go. I also knew things like burdens and ghost were easier managed if they were shared.

"Why wouldn't he let you do more than that?" I asked slightly horrified and angry at Jordan for that piece of stubbornness.

"Because he refused to stop as long as our unit was in danger," Jack said.

He chuckled a sardonic chuckle before getting lost in his memories once again and the half smile on his face quickly melted away as they overwhelmed him. I kissed his shoulder and he popped out of them with a quick blink of his eyes.

"He was a slave driver, Lizzie, but it saved our asses even as it almost cost him his. I can remember sitting next to his hospital bed cussing him out left and right for being such an asshole and asking him time and time again if it had been worth it. You know what he said when he woke up?"

"What?" I asked leaning closer fascinated by the story as much as I was terrified for my men.

"He told me as long as all of his unit was safe it would have been worth dying for. I never understood that kind of devotion. But now, looking at you, I finally do," Jack said, his intense eyes staring me down.

My heart melted into a puddle of mush right there in front of him. I couldn't stand even a hairs width of space between us so I crawled up and straddled him as best I could on the bench. I laid my shins flush with his legs so that I could press my upper body against him and lay my head on his shoulder. He immediately wrapped his arms around me and held tightly as if I was his lifeline, not that I blame him because that's how I was feeling right now as well.

Jordan was gone.

He was going through something that I wasn't sure if I could help even if he'd let me help him. I was left feeling sad and alone, though with Jack's arms around me it helped relieve some of those feelings and I hoped it was doing the same for him.

I felt him lift a hand up and sweep my damp hair out of the way so his lips could find my throat where he dropped small kisses. I tipped my head to the side to give him better access all the while my blood began to boil.

A little nibble sent my breath rushing out in a loud gasp as I arched into him begging for him to do more. His nibbling kisses ran up my neck to where it connected with my ear and he let out a hot breath that sent shivers down my back.

"Take your clothes off. I need to be in you now," he growled into my ear.

I heard his voice border on desperation as he whispered into my ear and my heart squeezed with pain for him. I leaned back and looked into his eyes trying to decipher the misery in his voice, all I saw was the haunted look in his eyes and wanted to do anything to remove that haunted look.

"Are you sure, Master?" I asked wanting to make sure this is really what he wanted.

His hand reached up and gripped my damp hair which easily twirled around his fingers giving him a strong dominate hold.

"I want to forget the horrible memories and replace them with sweet ones of your wet pussy clutching me," he said.

I saw a frantic craving in his eyes and even the woman in me that almost resented the submission couldn't tell him no. I wiggled off his lap and turned to walk into the house, but a quick grasp on my arm stopped me. I turned back to him with a confused look trying to find out what was stopping him.

"Out here," he demanded.

Leann Lane

Chapter Twenty-One

My mouth hit the ground. I snapped it shut on the inarticulate sounds that came out of my throat as I tried to protest and tried to stop myself at the same time. I knew protesting was the quickest way to get a punishment.

I reached down and unbuttoned my pants, slowly pushed them down until I could step out of them and kicked them aside. I saw his eyebrows raise when he caught sight of my plain white undies. I had packed a crap load of them for this trip, they had been my way of protesting all the sexy little outfit's Jordan had put me in over the last year.

"What happened to the silk panties Jordan was always going on and on about?" he asked.

I crossed my arms and glared at him with malice, that was until his eyes darkened with a silent reminder that I needed to watch my attitude.

"I didn't see any need to bring sexy underwear since it was supposed to be just me up here," I said on a sigh trying not to let my irritation get the best of me again.

"I'm glad to see you hadn't had any intention on sharing that sexy underwear with anyone else. On the other hand, all your plain lifeless clothes will be burned as soon as we return. Even if I have to shove them into a garbage can and light the match myself."

Despite the insanity of his words, I had no doubt in my mind that he wouldn't actually do it. Even worse I knew Jordan would help him since he had the same reaction to most of my comfy clothes the first time he came to my house.

I wasn't as bad as Mia, whom I could have sworn was totally uncoordinated with her clothes. I save the wild outfits for nights out and the proper but more flattering clothes for my office. Then there were the ones I held on to purely for days where I really didn't want to take the time to worry about my clothes. Unfortunately for my Doms those 'lifeless' clothes were the ones I had brought with me this week whether they liked it or not. However, instead of arguing with him I just nodded and let him think the battle was won this time.

He motioned for me to stand in front of him as he reached deep into one of his pants pockets digging for something. Quickly, I stepped in front of him and linked my arms behind me. I kept my eyes on Jack as he found whatever he was searching for in his pocket and palmed it as he turned his gaze back at me for a long moment.

"Are you wearing a bra?"

"No, Master."

He gave me a pleased smile and nodded his head in satisfaction.

"Good. Take off your shirt."

I grabbed the bottom of my shirt and pulled it up quickly before I could lose my nerve. I threw the shirt behind me and shivered as the cool air pierced my rapidly heating body. Although in the end I didn't know if the shivers were truly from the cold air or from the intense look of desire that was burning from his eyes. My nipples rapidly tighten into hard tingling points and I fervently wished he'd reach out to play with one of them just to relieve the aching a bit.

He scooted to the edge of the bench until I was positioned right between his legs and then snapped his hard thighs closed so I was unable to move back or forwards as he finally revealed the thing in his hand. It was a large sliver flip blade pocket knife and with one smooth motion he flipped it open. He kept his eyes glued on my face watching it closely for signs of pain. I sucked in a breath, as a sense of panic began to rise as I watch him check the sharpness of the blade before leaning forward and laying it flat on my thigh.

My heart thumped hard against my chest as I tried to still the shaking in my body at the feel of the cold hard steel slowly being dragged up my leg. My mind went blank as my whole body centered on the knife and the pounding arousal combining with the fear that was beating its way through me. They produced a potent mixture that was taking my breath away and making me wet. In my rational mind I knew Jack would never hurt me and yet knowing he was so close, so able to hurt me if he wanted to was a heady feeling, the fear, the desire, the unpredictability of it.

The blade slowly slid under my underwear until it poked out of the top and with a quick twist of his wrist it cut right through the material as if it was nothing but butter.

A noise popped to the back of my throat yet I bit it off short as I watched him proceed to do the same with the other side and my panties floated to the ground. A small pathetic bundle of material that had once been the last remaining barrier between us.

"Master?" I breathed out.

"That's much better, little sub," he said satisfied.

He carefully folded the knife back up and slipped it into his pocket before standing up and pulling his own pants off. My eyes flew to his cock which was hard and laying flush against his stomach reminding me once again how large he was. I bit my lip, hoping now would be the time I'd finally get to taste it but he just chuckled and sat back down.

"Not this time, sweetheart, I meant it when I said I needed to be inside you."

I felt a twinge of disappointment, but shoved it aside knowing that whatever he deemed to give me was going to be amazing. He gripped my hips and lifted me up to slowly lower me down on his cock.

"Oh, little sub, you are so wet it's going to be no problem sliding my cock inside you," he whispered almost in awe.

Normally I would have needed more foreplay and was shocked to find he was right I was so soaking wet he slid in easily. We both let out a groan as soon as he was buried to the hilt deep inside me. He loosened the hold on my hips only to grab my hands and pin them behind me with one of his giant hands. He pressed the restrained hands into my back forcing it to arch against him and he took advantage of the position to bury his face in my breasts.

"God, Elizabeth, you smell so good," he whispered against my skin.

"Thank you, Master. You don't smell to bad yourself," I panted out.

I was holding myself in check trying hard not to move against the penetrating member that was tormenting me deep inside. He chuckled, his hot breath bathing my skin clashing with the cold air and causing goose bumps to break out all over. My nipples tightened impossibly more and the tingling became tenfold causing me to press forward a bit more to encourage him to pay them some attention.

As a Master, however, he ignored my nonverbal plea and began to kiss and lick the valley between my pinning breasts. I gave a soft moan and leaned back into his arms letting him take the brunt of my weight so I could just enjoy the attention he was showing me. The movement caused him to shift inside me and making my inner walls contract a bit. It produced a deep, lust filled, growl from him and made my inner sub did a little dance at causing such a passionate reaction from him.

"Do not move, sub."

His irritated snap cut my inner dance off at the twirl and instead threw her into a pouting stage.

"Yes, Master. I'm sorry," I whispered back.

His tongue went back to explore the little valley as I tipped my head back. I tried hard not to squirm when he came to the sensitive spot underneath my breasts. He didn't help my efforts at all, because when he realized my stiffening meant I liked it, he proceeded to give each side a little nip wringing a small cry with each bite of the teeth.

Finally, after what seemed like a viciously long pause, he pushed off sending the swing moving causing him to shift inside me. Not necessarily thrusting just shifting back and forth. The movement was unusual yet not at all unpleasant.

"Do you like that, baby?" I heard a voice come from behind me.

I turned my head to see Jordan walk up, his eyes already blazing with heat as Jack continued to push the swing. Jordan stopped a short distance behind me and began to remove his pants as well, immediately showing off his rapidly hardening erection.

"Turn her around, Jack, I want her sweet mouth on me," Jordan demanded harshly.

Jack let my arms free and lifted me up, quickly turning me around so that I was sitting reverse on him. My feet dangled with my toes just barely touching the wood on the porch. He slowly lifted me up and positioned me so I could slowly descend once again onto his cock as he pinned my arms behind my back again and pressed me forward.

Jordan stepped up to me gripping his bulging erection in his hand so he could hold it up to my mouth, eagerly I opened up and took him in as deep as I could, licking up the entire bottom part of the shaft so no part of him was left dry. I watched as Jordan tipped his head back and released a harsh moan from deep within his chest. I felt a sense of pride and joy run through me at the beautiful expression of passion that was crossing his face.

Jack started swinging the bench again and this time it was causing him to press up against the sweet spot deep inside me. A muffled cry burst from my lips at the wonderful pressure that was building. In one swift motion Jack planted his feet on the porch and released the hold he had on my arms only to take hold of my hips.

"Put your hand between your legs, Elizabeth. I want you playing with that clit," Jack growled.

I mumbled my affirmation and slide my hand down slipping it between the swollen lips, slightly amazed at how wet I was. I couldn't help but slipping my hand back a little farther to touch the spot where we were connected. I laid my hand against his cock as he continued to move in and out of me, fascinated by the feeling of how my body was opening to accept his without hesitation and how he was coated from tip to base with my own juices.

"Your clit, girl," Jack growled.

I moaned in disappointment not ready to give up my intriguing find just yet, but a light sharp smack on my ass had me quickly removing my hand and touching my hard responsive nub that was straining from its hiding spot. I ran my finger around it softly, finding it too sensitive to caress directly. Still the slight contact had me pressing back harder against Jack and sucking harder on Jordan who let out a harsh cry.

"God, baby girl," he groaned as soon as he got his breath back. "Do that again."

I wasn't sure which one he meant so I did them all just to make sure and simultaneously we all groaned. Jack's hold on my hips tighten and Jordan wrapped my hair around his hands like a set of reins, as if by some unspoken agreement we all decided it was time to move faster.

"Keep your mouth open, Lizzie, I want to be able to fuck it and I don't want to have to get the O-ring gag," Jordan growled.

Immediately I opened my mouth as wide as I could, not wanting him to get out that particular gag which would force my mouth to stay open no matter what.

Their pace soon became so fast and erratic that my poor hand was having trouble keeping up. Eventually I just pressed down on my clit and let their motions move my hand. My small cries were quickly becoming screams as I felt my climax rushing towards me. When it broke through I clamped down hard on both of them wanting to take them along with me into the spinning world of pleasure I was floating in. Jordan thrust deep into my mouth before he stiffened and let out a gut wrenching moan as he spurted his seed down my throat, at the same time Jack began to thrust harder sending little shock wave through my already clutching channel sending me off to an another climax as he found his own as well, my name being yanked from his lips.

I slumped down against Jack's legs, panting and boneless, and more satisfied than I'd ever felt in my entire life. Jordan slowly pulled out and padded inside while Jack slowly pulled out of me and picked me up again cradling me to his chest as if I were the most precious thing in the world. I snuggled up to him and laid my head on his chest listening to his heart beat as it began to slow. I was deep in thought and enjoying the comfort when Jordan came back out with a blanket and a warm wash cloth. Jack handed me over to Jordan before getting up and running into the house himself.

Jordan wrapped me in the blanket and then used the warm cloth to wash my face off, before opening the blanket and spreading my legs so he could clean between them. I hid my face in the crook of his neck embarrassed about the intimacy of having him clean me in such a way. I kept my eyes averted until I felt him bump my head with his shoulder. I looked up and saw amusement in his eyes as he assessed my expression for a moment before removing his hand.

"I never thought I'd see anything that would embarrass you, baby girl," he commented as he shook his head.

My face burned once again, "Isn't it my job to clean you two up?"

"Normally, yes. But right now we both want to take care of you."

"Okay, but can you leave such caring up to me from now on?" I asked irritably.

Jordan chuckled as he easily lifted me up and carried me into the house. He sat me on a chair in the kitchen while Jack, who looked cleaned up himself and had a clean pair of sweats on, got me a cup of coffee then began shuffling around making several sandwiches. I felt a hand on mine distracting me from my intense scrutiny of the sandwich making process. It never seemed to be so admirable until I saw Jack doing it, though it just might be because I was suddenly starving.

"Are you alright, love?" Jordan asked as I turned my attention to him.

"I should be asking you that very same question," I said with a mocking grin.

"I am now," he replied with a gentle squeeze of my hand.

I searched his eyes trying to see if he was telling me the truth, I looked for any sign that he was still haunted by whatever had chased him out of the house earlier. No matter how much I stared I couldn't see anything beyond the strong heartwarming emotion that was shining from them as he stared back.

I nodded after a moment not sure if his words reassured me or not, but I didn't question them for now, deciding to file it back for a later date seeing something else more important was at play here.

"Can I ask you a question, Sir?" I asked softly.

"You can ask me anything, Lizzie, and we're not playing anymore so you don't have to call me Sir," Jordan said one side of his gorgeous lips turned up into a smile.

I gave him a slight smile back before sucking all my courage in for the question I had to ask.

"What happened?" I asked.

Chapter Twenty-Two

The men locked eyes as Jack set the plates on the table before sitting down himself, Jack nodded as if telling him he needed to continue on with what he was about to say.

"I had a flashback from when we were serving, I don't normally have a problem with them anymore. But, occasionally it does happen and when we woke up from a very deep sleep it seemed to all come back to me in at once and I couldn't control it," he explained.

He had not looked at me the entire time he talked and his hold on my hand had become a death grip by the time he was done. My heart twisted at the thought of what they had gone through while in the service. I returned his grip just to let him know I was there for him, then reached out and took Jack's hand as well not wanting to leave him out.

Jack gave me a bright smile before turning and digging into the sandwiches he'd made, obviously Jordan agreed because he let go of my hand and began digging into his food as well.

I watched them eat for a moment before they both realized that I hadn't taken a bite and stopped to look at me.

"Eat, baby girl," Jordan demanded.

I opened my mouth to continue with my questioning and I found my words silence by a piece of food that was stuffed into it by Jack. I chewed it rebelliously as I glared at my Masters none too happy with their way of distracting me from my thoughts. I did as they asked and quickly ate my dinner because in reality, I really was starving anyway.

When we were done Jack shooed us into the living room where we sat on the couch before returning with several cups of coffee and sitting down right next to me so that I was wonderfully surrounded by my two Masters. I snuggled into Jack's side and laid my feet on Jordan's lap allowing myself to relax into the peacefulness before I ruined it.

"Can you talk about the flashback itself?" I asked slowly wanting to ask but fearful of how they would react.

Jordan paused for a moment in the process of taking a drink of his cup of coffee. I watched as his eyes seem to dilate for a second before he finally looked at me.

"Baby girl, I really don't want to talk about this with you. It's not pretty, it's not sweet. It's hard, it's bloody and it's scary. I don't want it to touch you in any way," Jordan said his voice growing harder and grittier as he talked.

I stared at him as tears started pooling in my eyes at the pain I heard in his voice. Unable to bear it, I left Jack's side to crawl over onto Jordan's lap wanting to be close to him. I needed him to know that he didn't have to carry this burden by himself anymore. His arms immediately wrapped around me, holding me with the same tight grip that he had used on my hand earlier. I snuggled closer wishing that I could disappear inside him to erase all the pain and heartache that was roiling around.

"Please just talk to me," I begged him.

"Lizzie-" he began.

I had pulled back so fast I almost fell of Jordan's lap, yet it got both of their attention.

"No, Jordan. You and Jack ganged up on me last night to force me to tell you something I'd rather have kept hidden for a long time and so now it's your turn. Spill it," I demanded poking him in the chest to emphasize the seriousness of my point.

Jordan sighed and I could feel the walls crumble as he finally gave in. Before he spoke he pulled me back into the crook of his arm and Jack scooted closer pulling my feet onto him lap where he sat about massaging them, relaxing me into them both.

"It was supposed to be the usual mission, a quick snatch and grab. A team of our boys were being held hostage by a gorilla force deep in the jungle-"

"Where?" I asked unable to help myself.

Jack chuckled as Jordan shook his head. I took that as one of those 'if I tell you I have to kill you' things so I left it alone and motioned for him to continue.

"We'd slipped in undetected past a few of the guards that were stationed and took them out silently before proceeding inside this shitty run down version of a building," Jordan continued.

His voice took on a flat note I'd never heard before. It sounded as if he was a million miles away and I wasn't sure if he was back in the jungle again, or if he was trying to distance himself from what he was talking about.

"Spider went around to the back to cover and Animal was the rookie in the group so we sent him with Sparky to locate and take out snipers and watch our asses. Jack and I went in the front and immediately were engaged with the hostiles. We heard shots as we made our way to the back where the hostages were supposedly being held. What we saw when we walked in was nothing short of a blood bath." His voice broke suddenly and he cleared his throat a few times and I saw tears fill his eyes. "All of the hostages had been killed execution style, one shot to the head of each. We were stunned by the sight. No matter what, something's you never get used to. We failed to see the man hiding behind the door and he knocked the gun out of my hand before coming after me with a machete."

I felt Jack stiffen under my feet causing me to look at him quickly and I saw his eyes close as if he had started reliving it as well.

"Spider took him out but not before he gave me this scar," Jordan said indicating to his chest.

I reached my hand out and rubbed the area as if it would help it heal the unseen wound by me just touching it.

"How did you get the one by your shoulder blade?" I asked curious now.

"Stepped in front of a bullet as we retreated into the helicopter," he said simply as if it didn't matter.

"You mean you stepped in front of me and took the bullet," Jack said softly.

"You would have done the same for me, Jackson, so don't even start feeling guilty now," Jordan warned.

Obviously this was a normal argument for them because they both went quiet and the only sound in the house was the crackling of the fire and their strong, steady, breathing. I snuggled close and soon I felt them both slowly relax underneath me. It put a small smile on my face as I began to relax as well. I heard them mummer something but I paid it no mind as I found myself drifting off to sleep again.

Chapter Twenty-Three

I awoke the next morning with a smile still on my face as I stretched and welcome the deliciously sore feeling in my body. There was not a spot on my body that did not feel as if it had one hell of a work out. Scratch that, I couldn't remember the last time a work out had caused me so much soreness. Honestly if I could bottle the men and sell them I'd make millions in the weight loss industry.

I chuckled at that last remark and started to get out of bed noticing briefly that the men were up. So I decided to take my time getting dress, looking deep into my bags to find the sexiest outfit I brought with me. It turned out to be a pair of extra tight jeans and a spaghetti strap shirt that I'd brought along mainly for sleeping in. Once dressed I looked in the mirror and sighed at my own stupidity for not bring something extra sexy along just in case. I'd honestly hadn't thought the men would follow me here and I now realized it was a stupid thing for me to think. I shrugged my shoulders knowing this was as good as it was going to get and left the bathroom in search of coffee and my men.

Once my caffeine habit was satisfied, I went looking for them and found them outside sparing in the clearing in front of the house. They had dressed in nothing else but a pair of sweats, they were even barefooted. That's sexy as hell, I thought to myself with an inaudible sigh.

They circled each other and were throwing insults left and right trying to get the other man to make the first move. At first I was a little worried that they might actually be mad, then I saw their eyes were twinkling with mirth as they were calling each other names.

They continued to circle each other like two hungry wolves around a dead carcass. Jordan had a wicked smile on his face one that I recognized from the times we'd scened and he had a particularly evil torture in mind for me. The look on Jack's face was one I had seen last night during our play, it was one of pure determination, resolve and a bit of the wicked pleasure as well.

I leaned up against the railing and took in the two as they continued sparing, landing hit after hit on each other. I was impressed that they had enough control not to seriously injure each other, yet to hit hard enough that it could be felt and counted. Jack landed a particular solid blow to Jordan's stomach causing him to groan and almost hit the ground. He was on his knees so long that I had started to get worried that he was truly hurt.

"Come on, Jor. You're getting slow in your old age," Jack taunted seemingly unfazed by Jordan's injury.

Jordan suddenly let out a breathless laugh that sounded a bit like a cough and then just as quickly kicked a foot out sweeping Jack's legs out from underneath him landing him flat on his back, the air in his lungs flew out with an audible hiss, especially when Jordan pounced on him and pinned him down.

"Old age huh? I'm what nine months older than you?" Jordan taunted back.

"Ten," Jack gasped out.

I gave a little giggle catching their attention and unfortunately distracting Jordan enough that Jack was able to toss Jordan off him and over his head where he landed with a thud on the ground next to him. They both laid still for a moment catching their breath and chuckling.

"Draw?" Jordan asked.

"Draw," Jack agreed on a chuckle.

Jack jumped up in one swift move before going around and helping Jordan up as well. They clasped hands and gave each other 'manly' whacks on the back then walked up to the porch where I stood. The light glinted off the sweat on their bodies and for the first time in my life I felt my body heat up at the sight of a man's sweaty body. Maybe I was getting turned on by the primitive sight of how they came to be that sweaty. Either way I couldn't take my eyes off them as they bounded up the stairs and proceeded to surround me, filling my nose with their spicy masculine smell and the heat radiating off them. If I had been cold, I certainly wouldn't be now nor did I think I'd ever be again.

"Good morning, my love," Jordan said swooping down to plant a heat filled kiss on my lips before passing me off to Jack who did the same.

I stepped back and leaned on the rail my legs going weak after being kissed so ardently, I gave them what I was pretty sure a very goofy happy smile.

"How did you sleep, sweetheart?" Jack asked leaning next to me.

"Amazingly well for the first time in a week," I said with a sheepish smile on my face.

"Well, with how much fun you had yesterday I'm not shocked. When we finally got to sleep last night, I slept like a log," Jordan commented.

"Yeah, and you snored like a lumberjack," Jack teased.

Jordan instantly had a wounded look on his face causing me to giggle into my cup.

"Don't laugh, baby girl, so did you," Jordan said with a little shove into my shoulder.

My mouth dropped to the ground in a suitably offended look. "I do not!"

Jack turned fast to hide the smile on his face and Jordan laughed outright as he reached out and drew me into his arms.

"No, little one, I was just messing with you. You sleep like a peaceful angel," he conceded.

But Jack didn't give up. "Yeah, a peaceful angel that likes to hog the covers."

I punched him in the shoulder and was pleased to see him wince.

"For that, you are to cook breakfast right now."

Jack's smile melted away as he stepped up to me and Jordan immediately spun me around and captured my hands behind my back. My breath caught in my throat when I realized that my joke had gone astray and now I had two angry Masters on my hand.

"Did you just give me an order, sub?" Jack said his voice deepening and his tone got very quiet.

"I-I-" I swallowed and started again, "yes, Master-I mean No, Master-I didn't mean-"

"You should know better by now then to order your Masters around. Do you need another lesson?" Jordan asked in my ear.

"No, Sir. No, I'm very sorry," I begged.

Jack reached out and pinched my nipple gently wringing a sharp cry from my lips then they watched with fascinated eyes as both nipples grew hard instantly.

"You plead well, little sub. I'm impressed. You are forgiven this time. But next time you think of giving your Masters an order, just remember that I am not afraid of reminding you of your place," Jack warned.

I felt my heart stop at the threat and the reminder of last night when he had spanked me because I was being insubordinate.

"Yes, Master," I said looking at my feet thoroughly chastised.

He nodded and stepped back allowing Jordan to let me go before heading inside the cabin.

"You need to learn to watch what you say, baby girl," Jordan warned before he walked inside as well.

I sagged against the railing as I felt my knees give out underneath me. Relief filled my whole being realizing how close I came to having another punishment. Jordan was right. I thought to myself, I really need to watch what I say. There was no way I was willing to say that out loud, though.

As Jack cooked breakfast, which I found out when I went in that it had been his intentions all along, Jordan went and showered making a sly statement about me joining him. I looked over to Jack as he opened the fridge door to pull out some eggs and I lifted an eye brow at him in question. He just smiled and nodded, waving a hand at me as he basically shooed me away.

I hurried after Jordan almost tripping as I struggled out of my clothes. A chuckled drift to me from the kitchen and a wave of embarrassment hit me as I realized Jack was watching me. I stopped and finished undressing before I went any further then took a second to fix my hair and straighten my back as I went into the bathroom. As I rounded the corner Jordan stood up from turning on the shower and gave me a pleased smile as his eyes drifted up and down my naked body.

"Jump in baby, the water's nice and hot," he said in a deep voice.

It was meant to be seductive, I knew that, yet it came out more playfully and made me giggle. This was the Jordan I knew and it warmed my heart that he'd finally relaxed again after all the stress he'd been under lately. I also felt a twinge of guilt knowing that most of the problems he'd been having could be laid at my doorstep.

I shoved those thoughts down and grasped the hand he held out as he stepped into the shower. The moment I was inside the current he shoved me under the spray and broke out into laughter as I squealed when the water hit me.

"I wasn't ready!" I complained.

"How could you not be ready, Lizzie? You joined me in the shower," he stated still chuckling.

I moved out from under the down pour and had to wipe my face before I could even see again.

"You know what I mean," I grumbled.

A gasp of surprise popped from my mouth when Jordan grasped my wrists and lifted them above my head and made me hold on to the little ledge that ran along the top of the shower wall.

"Do not move," he demanded harshly before releasing me.

I curled my fingers holding on to the tiny little ledge as tightly as I could and prayed silently that I would be able to obey my Master through whatever torture he had in his devious head. I kept my eyes glued to him while he went through the motions of cleaning up. I wanted to be angry, frustrated or even annoyed at him for just leaving me standing there, but I got to watch him as the watered ran down his body like a river making its way to the ocean. I was able to look on as his powerful, strong, hands rub each and every piece of skin making sure it was clean. It was a sight I'd never had the pleasure of before, I'd seen him naked plenty of times, but this seemed to be different more intimate.

He looked up at me from the corner of his eye and I could see the side of his mouth raise as he dropped the washcloth lower, sliding it slowly down his abs until he circled the base of his jutting erection. The muscles on the back of his hands clenched as he began to slowly pumping it up and down. I know he was just a pretending to clean it, but I didn't care at all I just loved watching him stroke himself. I couldn't figure out what I loved more the image of my hand replacing his or his head tipping back and the sexy husky groan that popped out of his throat as he did it.

My breath hitched in the back of my throat as he continued to work his cock for me. It was a beautiful and hypnotic scene that played out in front of me and I was so aroused at this point that every time he gave a hard yank I could feel it deep inside of me. I let out a moan when he groaned and my nails dug into the walls so hard that I was pretty sure that there would be gouge marks when we were through.

As my eyes stayed glued on the motions of his hands, which was why I noticed he'd finally dropped the wash cloth and the site of his stiff cock being stroked by his bare hand. I saw a drop of pearly white pop out of the tip I lost all of my control to keep quiet.

"Please, Sir. Please, I need you."

Jordan chuckled and let go before he stepped under the water again to rinse of. He grabbed the wash cloth that had been forgotten and dabbed a bit of my soap on it. The scent of my body wash, jasmine and rose, immediately permeated the air around us and Jordan drew in a deep breath.

"I've always love the way you smelled, baby girl."

He reached out with the wash cloth and began to draw it across my bared skin with slowly purposeful strokes. I laid my head back against the wall and closed my eyes loosing myself to the feel of his hands on my body. The slide of the rag across my sensitive skin had my body heating up in ways I'd never imagined.

He flitted it around my breast causing my nipples to harden immediately hoping they'd be the next thing that would be touched. They were rewarded for their patience when he passed the cloth over them. He stopped briefly, long enough to tweak them hard, harder then he'd ever had before but instead of hurting it felt deliciously wonderful. I moaned and arched my back to get more but he was gone.

He dragged it lower and lower causing my breath to come out faster and faster as my stomach tightened up in anticipation as he came closer to my soaking wet pussy. He swept the cloth across the top part of my thighs and his rough fingers gently drug across the soft pouting lips that were just begging for more. My already weak knees just dropped out from under me and the only thing left holding me up was the death grip I held on the ledge. A sharp cry parted my lips as I threw my head back, thrusting my hips out towards him a not so subtle hint for him to do more.

I cried out in relief this time as his fingers slid between the lips and found my clit that had popped out of its hiding place and practically rejoiced at the first not so gentle touch. He began to flick it hard and fast turning the buzz of heady arousal into a flaming, electrifying, sensual, whirl of pleasure. In the back of my mind I heard mewling sounds and inarticulate noises that I realized quickly were coming from me but I didn't care, I wanted more.

"Your being demanding, sub, should I take you over my knee right here? I'm sure Jack would approve, right?" he growled at me.

He'd pulled away and my eyes flew open quickly falling on Jack standing in the door way. I realized two things in that moment, the shower curtain was wide open and I couldn't even remember if we'd closed it and Jack was completely, titillating, naked. His hard thick cock was in his hand much like Jordan's had been and he was stroking it fast. The resemblance to the first night they were here was striking and even more arousing. His dark eyes were blazing with the pent up lust and locked on to the spot where Jordan's hand was touching me.

"Make her come, Jordan. I need to hear her pretty little screams," he demanded through clenched teeth.

A desperate whimper popped from my lips as my inner muscles contracted immediately and I almost felt as if I was going to come right then and there.

Jordan grabbed me and bent me over so that my hands were braced on the tub, he kicked my legs as far apart as they could go without tipping me over and with hardly any preamble he slammed into me from behind. I threw my head back and screamed, I was shocked at the ease he had slid in and I was relieved to finally not feel so empty any more.

Something tapped my cheek and I opened my eyes to find Jack standing in front of me holding his hard shaft out to me. I promptly opened up and took him as deep as I could, delighted and rejoicing that I'd finally be able to know the most intimate feel and the taste of my Master.

Jack grasped the back of my head and began thrusting in and out, taking complete possession of my mouth. I was so hot and so wild for both of them that I didn't care, the only thing I concentrated on was breathing and the building climax that my Masters were producing.

The rhythm they started built and built until it was more fervent and desperate. Suddenly it seemed as if we were all almost out of control Jordan gave a few deep hard thrust and I felt my pussy and my mouth clamp down on them and I was throw into the center of an insane whirlwind of pleasure and sensations. The world behind my eyes turned into a burst of color and I screamed around the thick cock in my mouth.

I heard the men shout and felt Jordan stiffen having found his pleasure. Then Jack's salty essence hit the back of my throat gagging me until I remembered to swallow and breath.

I sagged in Jordan's grasp and soon felt someone pick me up to put me back under the steaming water where I found myself surrounded by two muscular bodies that were gently washing me up as I slowly came back to myself.

I snuggled deep into the embrace that was keeping me upright and realized there had never been a time, before now that I felt more loved and safe.

I really did want this moment to last forever.

Chapter Twenty-Four

A short while later we were back in the kitchen where Jack promptly presented me with a fresh cup of coffee as he padded about and if I wasn't mistaken he was humming. He'd heard the first whimper from me and had shut everything down to come watch and I was glad because after all there was nothing sexier than watching a man cook.

After breakfast I decided a wonderful morning like this deserved a walk on the beach. I turned to go get dressed when I remembered yesterdays 'would be' punishment of going without clothes because I left without asking. I openly winced, knowing there was no way I wanted that to happen again. So I walked over to the men, knelt and presented my question as sweetly as I could.

"Would you mind if we came with you?" Jordan asked.

I shook my head. "Not at all, it'd be nice to have some company."

Within a matter of minutes, we were all set and ready to go. I smiled as I caught sight of their bare feet once again, if I didn't know any better I would wonder if they had shoes at all. It was an enduring show of sensitivity from the men and it made my heart melt at just the sight of it. On an impulse that I couldn't control, I stood up on tippy toes and gave them each a gentle kiss on the cheek, well gave Jordan a kiss on the cheek, with Jack it was more like strained peck on the chin because that was all I could reach of him.

Ignoring their curious looks I practically skipped ahead of them watching as the waves rolled in just barely touching my feet, I chased them in and out finally feeling a sense of freedom that was oddly contradictory to the life I was planning on living. It was quite amusing, but I relished in the moment when I felt happiness fill me completely for the first time in a long time.

I heard a deep chuckle behind me as I raced away from the water with a squeal as it rushed towards me with its cold, wet, fingers. I turned in time to see Jordan chasing me down with a wicked smile and with a single flicker of his eyes, I knew he meant to shove me into the cold water I was trying to run from. With a scream I ran off towards the woods knowing if I could reach them I'd win and be far, far, from the water I was being threatened with. I wasn't fast enough for both of them and in a single tackle we were all three rolling around in the sand.

They were chuckling as they teamed up on me to hold me down. I rapidly started begging them not to toss me in, Jack laid his hand against my lips to stop the flow of pleas.

"What was the meaning behind running into the forest?" Jordan asked as soon as I quieted.

"I know every path in the forest from here to the road. I thought maybe I could hide in there," I explained.

"You honestly think a pair of ex- marines like us wouldn't be able to find you in there?" Jordan said with a smirk.

"I know these trails better than you do. I bet I could find a good hiding spot and you'd never find me until I wanted to," I slung back at them.

Jack and Jordan laughed. "I think I feel a bit insulted. What you think, Jack?"

They let me go then stood up stepped away from me. I scrambled to my feet then slowly backing away from them in case they changed their minds and grabbed me again. Jack folded his arms over his chest with a smile on his face that was nothing short of a challenge.

"Go ahead, sweetheart. I want you to run into the forest, I'll even give you a 5-minute head start. If you think there is a place you can go that we won't find you. Go."

My heart pounded unable to believe my ears, they wanted me to hide from them? Confused and a little frightened, I just stared at them waiting for the punch line.

Jack leaned into me looking deep in my eyes, there was no joke in his. "Four minutes and 55 seconds, girl."

That jump started me and I fled down the trails as if the hounds of hell were nipping at my heels, for all I knew they were. I jumped over logs and dogged around bushes until I came to a break in the trees. It changed into a wide open circle, I looked around and around before finally spotting a dense area where I could hide. I crouched down behind the bushes and watched.

I listened intently still there was nothing, just the sounds of my heart pounding and my harsh breathing as I tried to calm it enough so I could disguise the sound. I remembered every time I'd hid from my father, if he could hear a sound, a whine, a sigh, anything he'd be able to find me. I laid my head against a rock that jutted out underneath the tree and concentrated on slowing my breathing along with my heart rate so I could hear something beyond it pounding in my ears.

Just as I was accomplishing it I looked up again and saw two pairs of legs standing on the other side of the bush.

I had been found.

My heart started pounding harder than it had when I had been running as soon as I saw the two very masculine feet come into view. I slowly looked up and up, along the hard very male bodies until I hit the two muscular bare chests that were still heaving from their own exertions. I hadn't heard them running behind me, but it hadn't taken them long to catch up to me and find me even behind the rock and bushes that I had been hiding behind. They glistened with sweat from neck to navel and each gleaming droplet fascinated me, but not enough that I didn't catch the next words out of Jordan's mouth.

"Well, I think our little scared rabbit deserves a punishment, don't you, Jack?"

My eyes flew to his face and I found myself looking back and forth between Jack grim face and Jordan's roguish grin.

"Yes. It does seem only fair since she challenged our ability to find her and then let herself be found so easily," Jack agreed.

My breath caught as I awaited their decision as to what kind of punishment it was going to be. I really didn't want a spanking this time, and had successfully managed to get out of the no clothes punishment. What now? I wondering to myself with no small amount of apprehension. So I stayed kneeling down hoping that would win bonus points on my part for being such a very good sub to them.

"I think she needs to learn the valuable lesson of being quiet," said Jordan thoughtfully.

Jack looked just as thoughtful for a moment and then nodded in agreement

"Good idea. Elizabeth, no matter what we do to you, you may not make a sound. If you do you will receive one swat each time, do you understand me?" Jack demanded.

His tone was reasonable but his words were insane. Not make a sound no matter what? I could hardly stay quiet during a movie much less whatever viciously cruel pleasure they had in mind and I could tell by the twinkle in their eyes that it was going to be outright torture whatever they were thinking up.

I nodded my understanding to them both and took a deep breath to prepare for what was coming next, but to be honest I knew in the back of my mind that I was going to be getting a few swats by the time this was over.

"Good. Come out here," Jordan ordered as he stepped back into the clearing.

I stood slowly and followed him out there with Jack bringing up the rear. The grass was soft under my bare feet, even when I dug my toes into it with anxiety it was still cushy. A fact I was very happy about since I had a feeling at some point in time someone's bare skin was going to touch it.

"Strip."

I did slowly, knowing that the anticipation would kill Jordan and excite Jack. I grasped my shirt by the hem and leisurely pulled it up and over my head, listening to the sounds the men made as my breasts immediately popped out. Jack bit back a soft curse as they bounced gently once I'd freed them of the built in bra the shirt I was wearing had and Jordan made a sound in the back of his throat that could only be categorized as animalistic.

The cool air blew lightly across my body like a gentle breath and a wave of goose bumps broke out across my bared skin making my nipples tighten and stick out immediately.

I bit back a grin of mischief at the result of the dirty trick that I was playing. Yeah, two could play this game; or three as it were. I grasped the waist band of my pants and turned around, I spread my legs knowing that as I pushed it down my ass would pop up into the air and give them one hell of a view as I bent over.

The only repercussion about this impromptu striptease was that the more excited they got the more excited I got as well. So when I bent almost completely over and presented my backside the wind swept between my legs and I could feel the moisture that was soaking through into my panties as a result of the desire pounding through me.

"Stay there," said Jack gruffly.

I grasped my ankles thankful I was so limber that this position wasn't going to kill me. He stepped up behind me and ran a finger along my spinal cord that was quickly followed by an involuntary shiver, then he slid it down the back of my underwear until he reached the wet spot that I had just noticed as well. He rubbed it softly but I could feel it as well as if there was no barrier there at all. Suddenly I heard a soft thud behind me as he hit his knees and then I could feel his breath on me gently blowing on it.

Unable to hold it in, I emitted a small almost barely there noise followed quickly by a louder cry as my bottom received a hard smack. I looked back at them from around the leg I was suddenly hugging with a little tear in my eye then watched as Jack moved back to stand beside Jordan with a shake of his head.

"We warned you, sub. No noise," Jordan said with a disapproving look.

I opened my mouth to apologize, but it was cut off abruptly by the cautioning look on Jordan's face. No noise, right. I gave them an apologetic look and bit my lip, hard, so I wouldn't make any noise again.

"Good job, now finish stripping," he ordered.

Ditching my attempt at a strip tease, I quickly climbed out of the rest of my clothes then turned back to them and was able to watch with a heated gaze as the men treated me to a striptease of their own. Though theirs was nowhere near as taunting as mine had intended to be, that didn't stop me from enjoying it.

When they were both gloriously naked, I barely had a chance to get a good look at them before they were surrounding me. Jack stood in front of me and quickly grasped my chin so his mouth could take mine in a breath stealing kiss. His thumb pried open my lips so his tongue could plunge in and begin an exciting foray with my own.

My hands flew up on his shoulders and I grasped the hard muscle there to keep from falling because at that point Jordan had dropped to his knees behind me and began kissing and biting the two firm globes that I had presented them before. He gently pulled my legs apart as far as they could go with Jack helping by wrapping an arm around my waist so I could stand on my toes and give Jordan plenty of room to play.

Jordan's fingers slowly slid up my thighs making my legs spasm a little and almost fall out from underneath me. A little noise bloomed in the back of my throat but I tightened my fingers on Jack's shoulder until my nails bit into his skin in my desperate attempt to suppress it. I heard Jack grunt against my lips and I immediately let go of my hold afraid that I'd hurt him. He pulled back the minute I had released him and looked down at me his dark eyes burning with desire.

"You didn't hurt me, sweetheart. I quite enjoy the pain of your nails digging into me, it means we're doing something right," he said huskily.

He bent his head once more but instead of kissing me, his lips made a beeline for my neck and bit it hard. He pulled away and began sprinkling small kisses around the area to soothe away the ache left behind by his teeth. My head tipped back and I almost choked on the strangled noise that was crawling up the back of my throat. It threatened to burst out when Jordan's tormenting fingers finally found the spot they had been going for.

One finger rubbed a feather-light touch across my dripping hole, rimming it, taunting me with the possibility of it pressing inside and filling my aching, empty need. I bit my lip, barely containing the whimper that was looming. This vexing finger moved slowly from the spot it had teased and slid unhurriedly up until it brushed against my distended clit that was thrusting eagerly forward from its hiding place. This time no amount of biting or scratching would hold back the cry that left my lips at that moment. A loud smack echoed through the woods along with my loud cry of pain as I was punished for disobeying my Masters. A tear trailed down my face and a whimper left my mouth when Jordan's lips brushed over the spot his hand had just smacked.

"Please stop making sounds, I don't like hurting you," Jordan practically begged from behind me.

I nodded and tried to stifle the rest of my tears that were threatening to pour down my face. Jack had pulled back and I could see the agony in his eyes as he reached up and wiped one the single tear that was still making its way down my cheek. I knew they really didn't want to hurt me and that this was just a lesson they were trying to teach me, it was just such a hard lesson and I worried that by the end of this punishment we'd all be miserable.

Leann Lane

Chapter Twenty-Five

"Thank you, baby girl. Now just relax and do not make a sound," Jordan stated again more forcefully.

I nodded my understanding, finally.

Jordan stood up at that moment then they both stepped back and I finally got a spectacular view of both of them. They were always and forever more going to be my favorite sight; either watching these two men standing together or apart it didn't matter and the fact that they were completely naked was a big bonus. The thing that fascinated me the most were the hard jutting erections that laid against their stomachs. I licked my lips remembering each individual time I'd had them in my mouth and wondering when I'd get to do that again.

I almost sighed as I stood there and just stared at them especially when Jordan turned and walked over to where I'd put my clothes. I felt my heart pitter pat as he bent over and gave me a delicious view of his strong backside. My heart rate went up even further when I watched him pick up my shirt and twist it as he walked towards me.

"We think you'd have an easier time with this if the only thing you'd have to deal with is remembering not to make a noise," he explained as he walked up to me with my shirt.

He stepped behind me and proceeded to wrap the shirt around my head immediately depriving me of my sight. My heart did not slow down one bit once he tied it securely in place, in fact it increased even more when all I could do was try to listen closely for the sounds of these men moving; the problem with that was these men were pros at moving without making a darn sound.

A breath suddenly blew over my ear making me jump and gasp. My only response from the men was a breathy chuckle that floated to me, from the other side of me, making it obvious that Jack had now joined the fun. My body was tensed with expectation as I waited and waited for the next touch to come. After a few moments of nothing I felt myself begin to relax and that's when they struck. Both of my nipples were grabbed simultaneously, gently but firmly and they were pinched between two fingers and then a rough thumb ran across the tip of it. Pleasure zig-zagged through me and each swipe of the thumb left me feeling as if someone was plucking on my clit itself; it was a sensation I'd never felt before, but truly hoped I'd feel again one day.

I bit my lip and arched my back silently begging for more, but just as suddenly as it had started, it stopped leaving me with an aching sense of loss at its disappearance. I arched my back a little more hoping they'd take a hint and it must have worked because something warm and wet swiped across one of my nipples leaving it damp. The same thing happened with the other one and when the wind blew across them, or maybe it was just a breath I wasn't sure, they tightened impossibly further and I shivered as the flame of desire burned even brighter inside me.

Hands slowly brushed down my arms and grasped my wrist to pull them up and link my fingers behind my head, then the same hands brushed its fingers down, down, down until they grasped my hips. A second set of hands gripped under my arms and the next thing I knew I was in the air right before being pressed against a hard thick body I immediately recognized as Jordan's. Instinctively I wrapped my legs around his waist, nestling his hard cock right up against my soaked pussy. I wasn't sure if I gripped him so hard with my legs to keep him close or to keep from falling; either way I held him as tight as I could even though I knew between these two strong men that there was no way I was going to fall.

I tilted my hips so that I could rub my swollen, begging clit against him and I heard him suck in a breath which turned me on even more. It must have been the same for him because the next thing I knew, I was on my back against the soft grass and my arms

186

were pinned very successfully behind my head. My legs were firmly unwrapped from Jordan's waist as the blindfold was yanked off my eyes and I blinked against the suddenly bright light until I saw his face came into focus.

"Baby girl, you are already so fucking wet I could probably just slide right in couldn't I?" Jordan said gruffly.

I nodded and silently congratulated myself on remembering not to say anything.

Jordan's triumphant smile was all the approval I needed and the returning smile on my face was just as triumphant. I relaxed and finally let go, trusting myself to do as they ordered and gave up all the control I had.

"Well as much as we both know how much you want me in there right now, I want to taste you so badly it's not even funny," he said as he crawled down my body to shove my legs open as far as they could go.

Jack sat down behind me and lifted me up so I was leaning against him. I knew he meant to make me more comfortable but the feel of his hard erection beneath my head was a giant tease. I felt the little hairs that covered his groin brush against my fingers and a very naughty little thought popped into my head and I looked up at him as I turned one hand around to grasp his cock hard and waited until he looked at me. I asked him a question with my eyes and started to pump him up and down, I was rewarded with his eyes drooping a little in pleasure and he nodded his consent almost anxiously. My actions became bolder, well as bold as I could in the awkward position I was in at that moment.

Jordan used that moment to spread my pussy lips wide and fiercely suck my throbbing clit. My hips jerked up against his mouth and I heard a sadistic chuckle come from him but he didn't stop the insanely wonderful tormenting of my clit. His performance became ruthless and merciless as he drove me to the edge with his mouth over and over again making it harder and harder for me to concentrate on pleasuring Jack or on not making noise.

I closed my eyes to give myself a blank screen to focus on and to block out the incredibly erotic picture of Jordan's blazing eyes watching every movement and taking pleasure in my hips as they jerked in rhythm to his sucking. That idea worked but didn't last long as I felt a tap on my chin jerking my focus back up to Jack.

"I wanna hear it now, sub. I want you to scream to the skies as Jordan makes you come," Jack said gruffly.

"Yes, Master," I squeaked out hoarsely.

The next sharp pull of Jordan's lips and I let out a cry as I was told to do.

"Not good enough, Jor. I don't think she really wants to come," he commented almost disappointedly.

"No, I guess not," Jordan agreed. "Maybe I should just stop."

"NO!" I cried desperately.

A sharp sting on my inner thigh had me looking down and realizing Jordan had bitten me, with a rise of his eyebrow I realized he had meant to remind me of my manners.

"I'm sorry, Sir. I mean No, please Sir. I'll scream like a good girl," I whimpered.

"Ok, I'll give you one more chance. But if I'm not happy with how loud you are, we'll stop and go back to the cabin."

I let out a relieved breath only to suck it back in when Jordan shoved two fingers deep inside me, then pressed a third against my tight puckered back hole adding an odd, amazing, pressure pleasure to the increasing buzz of sensations that were driving their way through me as his mouth attacked my engorged nub once again.

I didn't have to try to scream, the combination of the penetrating fingers and the alternating flick of the tongue and deep sucking of his mouth drove me there in an instant. I let go of Jack's cock and dug my nails into my palms as a high pitched scream was jerked from me and I immediately went flying over the edge into an ocean of ecstasy. Stars and bright colors flashed before my eyes and my breathing was haphazard at best, but Jordan didn't stop his thrusting or tormenting with his tongue until he'd wrung every last thin cry and involuntary jerk from me. I laid heavily against Jack, boneless and limp still whimpering from the hard orgasm I'd just had and the leisurely stroking of Jordan's tongue from top to bottom of my drenched pussy as if he was trying to catch every drop of my juices as they dripped from me.

He finally sat up with a Cheshire cat like grin and all but smacked his glistening lips as he looked at me.

"Still the most delicious I've ever tasted, baby girl."

I gave him a weak smile right before he lifted me up and turned me over on my weak knees. I was very thankful for his hands on my hips then because I wasn't sure if I could stay up on my own. I looked up at Jack and noticed sweet anticipation in his eyes, I didn't have to look down to know he was holding his hard cock out to me nor did I have to wait for his order though it came anyway.

"Suck me, I want your mouth on me now," he demanded in a growl that sent shivers down my spine.

"Yes, Master," I said delightedly.

I felt a nudge and knew Jordan was getting ready to finally enter me and I took a moment to just feel the completeness of having my two Masters with me.

A contented smile crossed my face then I opened wide and took Jack as deep into my mouth as I could, bracing myself for Jordan's thrust. In one smooth move he slammed deep inside me and I knew he couldn't wait a moment longer.

A muffled scream was forced from my stuffed mouth as he stretched the sensitive muscles deep inside with his hard cock as he continued to pound in me. My wet channel immediately clamped down on the thick pounding in and out of it and I clenched my muscles tighter trying to hold it deep inside while every stiff, solid, inch of him sent spasm of pleasure storming deep inside me.

It took me a bit to pull myself back from the world of sensations that Jordan was throwing me into so I could concentrate on the tasty, velvet smooth, erection in my mouth. Jack didn't seem to mind though he just started thrusting in and out of my lips that were gapping open because of every whimper, whine and cry that was involuntarily spouting from it.

When I was finally able to focus I quickly began sucking Jack deep inside and flicking my tongue around the sensitive edge at the tip, delighting in the taste of his salty skin.

I worked with Jordan's frantic thrusting to move up and down on Jack's cock and did my best to keep concentrating on what I was doing. Soon, however, I felt the rising tide of another orgasm looming and I couldn't concentrate on anything but the waves of pleasure slamming into me.

"God, she is going to come again. She's so fucking tight and wet. Fuck!" Jordan grunted through gritted teeth.

Jack pulled away and I looked up at him trying to figure out why but he was staring at me with his desire glazed eyes and I couldn't find the breath to ask him or much less care as Jordan picked up his pace and reached around to pluck at my pebbled clit. That was all it took to send me over the edge and I threw my head back and once again screamed my pleasure to the skies. I vaguely felt Jordan stiffen behind me for a moment then give a hoarse shout as he proceeded to come with several hard jerks. Panting and once again boneless from all the pleasure that was still warming my insides, I laid on the ground unable to move even if I'd wanted to.

In my daze I barely registered Jordan moving out of the way and Jack taking his place, that was until he lifted my hips and proceeded to slam into me as well. I didn't have the energy to scream or do much more then make little whining noises as he proceeded to pound into me. It blew my mind when I felt my body respond and begin to be hurtled into another star bursting climax. I wanted to protest, I wanted to cry out and to beg for mercy, but most importantly I didn't want him to stop.

This time as the surge of sensations overwhelmed me, I felt myself go limp and I let him use me however he wanted to. Still I knew even as he did he'd make sure to give me my own pleasure. When he stiffened and finally let go I felt a rush of happiness and joy wash through me that although I didn't have the strength to lift a hand I had managed to please my Masters still.

I laid heavily against the grass covered ground and closed my eyes to drift off into the aftermath of a very pleasurable bout with my Masters. I realized at that moment, that it didn't matter if I could keep up with them or not. If at the end all I was, was a pile of limp sub, I'd still manage to please them somehow.

Chapter Twenty-Six

I drifted back to myself after a moment or two and found both men had gotten dressed and somehow had managed to dress me as well. Right now they were standing over me as I still laid on the ground.

"Tsk tsk, little Lizzie. You should have known better then to pick the only place in the clearing that had any sort of coverage," Jordan said as he stood above me with his hands planted on his hips.

My head hit the ground in irritation, he was right I should have known better. I looked up with a pathetically miserable look on my face hoping Jack and Jordan would take pity on me as long as I looked terrible. Suddenly an idea on how I could get out of this with some modicum of pride attached to me. I jumped up and smack each of their arms and watched with joy as shock lite their face.

"You're it."

I turned and ran like hell and after a moment the sound of footsteps were right on my heels. They made no move to cover them up as they chased after me, but unlike them I knew exactly where this was going, straight back to the house.

I felt like a rabbit being chased by two very hungry wolves, it was a fitting similarity all things considered. My heart was pounding, my blood was boiling, and a part of me hoped they would catch up with me long before I hit the house. The sounds of tires drew me up short as I broke through the edge of the clearing, I heard a sharp whistle behind me and I turned in time to see Jordan and Jack speed up until they were positioned in front of me, protecting me from-

"Mia!" I cried as I spotted her jumping out of the car.

"Lizzie!" she cried as she raced towards me.

We wrapped each other in a giant hug and started talking and answering each other at once.

"Oh my god! What is going on? Are you okay?" she asked.

"Yes, I'm fine. We were just playing a little game," I assured her.

She giggled and wiggled her eyebrows at me. "What kinda game?"

I returned her giggles then winked at her. "Tag."

Mia went from just giggles to all out belly laughter, she even smacked her legs a few times. I bit my lip to hold mine in, I tended to snort if I laughed as hard as she was and that was something I really didn't want to do in front of Jordan and Jack. I turned to see them talking with Reed behind me, I was pleased to see that she hadn't ran off without her own Master thus not liable to get into trouble for racing out here.

"When are you coming back?" she asked drawing my attention back to her.

"I don't know," I stated honestly.

She stepped closer to me so no one could over hear our conversation.

"Are you still having problems?" she whispered.

I shook my head. "It's not that, I don't think it's up to me."

She smiled, pleased with my response and I found it funny that I'd been in this for a lot longer than her yet it felt as if she knew more than I did suddenly.

"Well, let me know because Reed has promised we could get together at the club. He wants to introduce me to the Masters and Mistress's properly. Apparently the collaring ceremony doesn't count," she said bemusedly.

I laughed at the memory of the last time we were there and Mia had almost decked a man three times her size. Reed had actually been the one to deal with it, well he did more than that, and he'd almost beat the hell out of him. Then Jack and Jordan threw him out, literally, I saw him bounce when he'd hit the pavement.

Still smiling, I linked my arm in hers and we walked over to the Masters. They were in a deep conversation that was immediately cut off as soon as we walked up. I wasn't sure if it was because they didn't want us to hear it or if it was because as soon as we got to them Mia went straight to Reed and snuggled up to his side.

I looked up at Jordan for answers but he just drew me to his and held me tightly. Jack stepped to the other side and wrapped his arm around my waist pulling me just as close. They both squeezed me between them until I felt almost as if I couldn't breathe and there was a tightness in their faces that I hadn't seen since they first got up here.

They were worried and scared, but this time it wasn't about me.

"What's going on?" I asked immediately.

"We have to go back right now, love, I'm so sorry. There's a problem Jack and I need to address immediately and it can't wait another day," Jordan said.

"What's going on?" I repeated.

Jack pulled me to him away from Jordan and made me face him. "Well discuss it when we get back, Elizabeth. For right now please go get your clothes together and get ready to leave."

I saw Mia's mouth drop when he used my given name, but I ignored her, unable to loosen the knot of worry that had twisted my stomach at the fear in his voice. Instead of arguing I nodded and headed into the house without an argument. I heard steps behind me and looked back to see Mia hurrying to catch up with me, the same worry creasing her brows as she met up with me.

"That's weird," she whispered as we walked into the door.

"I know and I don't like it one bit," I said then got to packing as fast as I could, trying hard to ignore the sense of impending doom.

We were all ready to go in less than an hour and my Masters set about deciding who would ride with me back into town. As soon as they decided that Jordan would, he demanded my keys with a look in his eyes that stated if I denied him we would apparently had enough time to use the spanking bench downstairs. I grumbled under my breath but handed them over and slouched into the front seat as he and Jack talked for a moment longer before he finally jumped into the front seat and started the car.

"Where are we going?" I asked while he was in the process of pulling out onto the highway.

"I am taking you home before I catch up with Jack at my place," he explained.

"Why don't I just go with you?" I asked feeling a dark cloud begin to form over my head.

"No," he answered firmly, "you are going to go back to your place tonight."

"Jordan, what's going on?" I asked frustrated.

Jordan just shook his head and refused to answer causing an uncomfortable silence to permeate throughout the car. It built gradually until it was almost choking me during the ride back into town. I kept my gaze out the window trying hard not to let my own anger and frustration eat me alive even as though need for answers was.

The trees whipped by faster than the blink of an eye and before I knew it the buildings of the city began to peak through, then increasingly take over and we were back in town.

We pulled up outside my apartment just shortly after Jack did and the men helped me carry my suitcase up the stairs. Then took their turns giving me toe curling kisses that promised so much more and burned my anger away in an instant.

I slump onto my couch as the door shut firmly behind them, feeling like a deflated balloon that had just whipped its way around the house. Anxiously I played with my shiny new collar finding solace in its cool metal.

After a while of doing nothing other than staring at the door wishing fervently one of them would come back in and either tell me what exactly was going on or take me to bed, at this point I wouldn't be picky, I sighed and got up to start getting things set up for the work week after all it wasn't like the night was going as I planned it anyway.

Chapter Twenty-Seven

After a long luxurious bath with a glass of my favorite wine and the gentle blaring of music, I was finally ready to go to bed. I felt proud that, in the absence of Jack and Jordan, I'd called Mia to get caught up on the gossip, the work I needed to do this week and found out that they had planned her 'introduction' for Friday. We excitedly began to plan for a shopping trip to get the perfect clothes for the occasion and to get together for lunch this week so we could continue our gossiping because I could hear Reed calling her name in the background. A smile lifted my lips as I remembered the breathless quality in her voice as she hung up. She really was very smitten with her Master and I could relate, I heard the same tone in my voice whenever Jack and Jordan were around.

My heart tugged as they crossed my mind for about the millionth time tonight, I really missed them and I couldn't help but wonder what they were doing right now. I looked down at my phone and noted with vast disappointment that I had no messages from either one of them. Glaring at the offending piece of plastic and metal I willed one of the men to call me even if it was just to say goodnight, but nothing happened. I finally gave up and gripped the phone tightly as I slowly started dialing Jordan's number, hoping that he would answer and not be to upset that I called him.

"Aren't you supposed to be in bed?" Jack's voice whipped over the phone instead of Jordan's.

I bit my lip unsure of what I should say suddenly feeling stupid for calling them, then angry for feeling stupid.

"Aren't you?" I countered.

"Is that a tone, sub?" Jack asked.

"No more than you gave me, Master. I called you because I missed my Masters and you snap at me the minute you answer the phone," I said a little offended.

There was silence on the other end followed shortly by a small curse and then Jordan's voice came over the phone.

"What's going on, Lizzie?" Jordan asked

I blew out a frustrated breath, talk about being punished for trying to be nice.

"Look, I just wanted to say hi and goodnight. I was-" I broke off feeling stupid for calling them.

"We miss you too, baby girl," Jordan said with a hint of satisfaction in his voice.

I felt myself melt under his words and a relieved smile crossed my face as I heard a knock come across the front door.

"I thought you guys weren't coming back tonight," I said curiously.

I felt myself get excited at the idea that they'd manage to come back tonight and I hurried to the front door not bothering to grab a robe to cover my nightgown figuring they'd have it off shortly anyway.

"We aren't," Jordan's voice came across cautiously. "What's going on?"

I barely heard him as I raced down the hall in a rush to welcome my Masters back into my house, I skid to a stop in front of the door and threw it open anxiously. The bright welcoming smile on my face faded the minute I caught sight of the person that stood on the other side, who was absolutely not either one of my Masters.

"Jordan, let me call you back," I said then hung up without waiting for a good bye.

I stared in horror at what stood in front of me. It was a young woman that could have been beautiful at one time, but now her hair hung in dirty greasy strands around her head and her clothes hung off her body as if they were ten times too big for her. Her eyes were on the ground and she was wringing her hands in agitation as she fidgeted almost uncontrollably. The worst part was there was something on one bandaged wrist that looked oddly like a hospital bracelet, but I wasn't able to get a good look at it.

"Can I help you?" I asked her gently not wanted to spook her.

She started mumbling under her breath and at first it just sounded like random words, all I could make out was "mine", "his" and my name.

"I'm sorry, I can't hear you. Is there anything I can help with?" I tried again.

Her wild eyes began to dash around as if looking for something or someone as she continued to mumble incoherently although this time when she said my name it was louder and sounded angrier.

"I'm Lizzie, are you looking for me?" I tried again.

Her wild eyes flew to me and blazed with insane fury making me regret saying anything at all. The look she gave me had me moving my fingers onto my phone's number pad and quickly hitting the call back button knowing I'd get a hold of Jordan's phone again. I heard an irritated voice come from my phone but I was too frightened to answer it back so I just held it tightly and hoped Jack or Jordan would understand.

"Who are you?"

"She stole our Master. He wants us, he needs us. She has bewitched him with her poisonous body," she began saying louder and louder.

"Who are you?" I repeated louder.

"She must die!" she suddenly screamed.

She let out a growl that sounded like a wild animal deep in her throat and launched herself at me. On instinct I fell backwards and landed with a thud on the floor while lifting my legs up to send her flying over my head. I felt a stinging pain in my left shoulder and looked over to see the hilt of a blade sticking out, a sense of dizziness swamp me as I watch the blood slowly begin to trickle down my arm.

I heard insane laughter coming from the living room and realized in the process of defending myself I'd let this crazy woman into my house. I rolled over to the right side trying to make sure I didn't jar the blade that was jammed into me. Stars swam in front of my face and I almost fell back to the floor but I caught myself painfully jostling my injured shoulder in the process. I moaned softly then bit my lip hoping not to call attention to myself, but I could tell by the stiffening of her back that the little noise had alerted her. She swung around facing me her gaze narrowing on me like a predator realizing her prey wasn't dead yet.

"What do you want?" I whispered from suddenly dry lips.

"He is ours, devil whore. You will not have him and once you are dead he will be free of your spell, witch," she whispered brutally.

My eyes rounded in disbelief at her words even as she continued talking quietly and frantically searching her pockets.

"Yes, we must cut out her heart, only then will our Master be free."

I realized she was looking for the knife that was still stuck in my shoulder. I leaned against the nearest wall as I felt my body grow weak with fear and, from the river of moisture running down my arm, probably blood loss. I was never very good with blood and I had a habit of fainting on the sight of it, however I made myself bolster my resolve knowing if I fainted right now I'd be dead.

I knew the moment she found where she'd left her knife because she let out a demonic screech and flew at me again. I waited until the last second and lunged out of the way allowing her to ram into the wall. A hole bloomed in the drywall as she stumbled back seemingly a little dazed and I didn't wait around to see what she was doing I ran down the hall wondering briefly why I thought it would be a good idea to only have a land line in the bedroom. I had barely hit the door to my room when I felt a hand grasp my hair yanking me harshly back.

"We won't let you get away, bitch!" she screamed.

I reached one hand up and grasped the hand in my hair, I dug my nails in feeling them break skin a little and a bit of moisture collected under my nails letting me know I'd drawn blood. Even then she kept yanking me farther and farther back into the living room, I reached back and started scratching at her arm.

"Fuck you," I growled back when she swung me around to face her.

She just smiled her evil yellow smile and grasped the handle of the knife, my vision started to go black as she pulled it out. The blood began gushing even faster and I knew in that moment I was going to die. I was determined not to go out without a fight, so I took a deep breath to clear my head and swung my foot out catching her right in the stomach just as she was arching the knife down for another stab. I caught this one right in the thigh, luckily it was only a gash and I barely felt the pain of it. She hit the ground with a whoosh and I slammed my foot down on her hand causing her to release the knife which I promptly kicked away under my couch.

I reached down to grab her greasy slimy hair and twisted it so I could hold onto it more firmly even as it tried to slide out of my hands. It was hard to keep a hold of her while she was squirming and screaming obscenities at me. She'd reached up and began clawing at my hand like I had done, yet I ignored her even while she continued to describe in great detail how 'they' were going to 'cut out my heart'.

I pulled her upwards so we were looking face to face so I could see her insane glazed eyes.

"Try it, fucking bitch. You picked the wrong girl to mess with," I snarled and watched with glee as her eyes finally held some panic.

I slammed her head into the ground just hoping to keep her dazed enough so I could run out the door, however, I must have underestimated my strength because her eyes rolled back into her head and her body went limp.

My front door burst open and two wild eyed men came flying in, scaring me half to death. The twisted look of fury on their faces made them almost unrecognizable but I knew them instantly. My body began to shake like a leaf as all the adrenaline I was living on dissipated at once and my legs gave out just as a set of strong arms scooped me up before I hit the floor. This time when I closed my eyes I welcomed the darkness grateful for the opportunity to escape the radiating pain. I didn't worry anymore I knew my Masters would take care of me.

Chapter Twenty-Eight

I awoke slowly not really sure if I wanted to welcome the sensations that were slowly returning to my body. However, the hands that I felt softly grasped both of mine caused a smile to cross my face as I recognized them even without seeing who they were. As I broke the surface I was finally able to open my eyes and looked straight into the anxious faces of my Masters.

My mind was so foggy that I didn't realize what was going on until I reached out to grasp their hands and a sharp pain radiated up my arm causing me to gasp and cry out.

Jordan's face went from anxious to angry in two seconds and I noticed Jack's face went pale just as fast. I groggily looked down for the source of pain and saw a slightly bloodstained gauze covering my shoulder, slowly the reason for my fogginess and pain came back to me.

"Is she alive?" I whispered, brokenly, my mouth really dry.

Jack nodded quickly squeezing my hand to reassure me all was well.

"Damn it," I groaned. "Next time, remind me to hit the bitch harder."

A chuckle came from the doorway drawing my attention to it and the man that stood there. He looked vaguely familiar, however, I still couldn't see him well enough, I assumed the pain medication was fogging up my eyesight as well as my brain.

"Hey thanks for showing up, Animal. We got someone here we thought you'd like to see," Jack said walking around and grasping his forearm giving him a one armed hug which he exuberantly returned.

"Hey, Chef, what's happening?" the man said then whispered something into Jack's ear which caused him to laugh.

"Chef?" I piped up.

Jordan laughed and nodded before leaving my side to go greet the new comer in the same fashion as Jack had.

"How you doing, brother?" Jordan asked as they broke apart.

"Better now. I don't think I've felt this good in years," the man replied.

I saw Jordan step out of the way so the man could come towards the bed, I made a move to sit up farther but I had to abandon it when a bolt of pain shot from my leg up to my arm and seem to radiate out through my body from there causing me to hiss in pain. Every man in the room began cursing immediately and I glared up at all of them, not even sparing this friend of theirs from the heat of my gaze.

"It's all your guy's fault, you shouldn't have brought a guest into my hospital room," I grumbled at them.

The man laughed and finally stepped up to the bed where I could see him. I gasped as soon as I recognized him even though my mind refused to believe what my eyes were telling me.

"How about family then?" he said his familiar blue eyes dancing with joy and unshed tears.

"Trev?" I whispered still not believing.

"Hey, sis."

I reached up with my good hand and touched his face to make sure he was real.

"How-? What-?" I stuttered.

"I was part of Jack and Jordan's unit in the Marines," he explained nodding his head towards them.

"The Marines? I thought you went into the Army."

Jack and Jordan laughed as Trev shook his head at me.

"Baby girl, you need to realize that there is more to the military than the freaking Army," Jordan said coming to my other side to grasp my hand.

I couldn't take my eyes off my brother for a moment because I was afraid if I did, he might disappear again and he'd be lost to me forever this time.

"Where have you been? How did you find me? Why did you stay gone for so long?" I began spouting off.

The questions kept running through my head and spewing out of me until I felt as if I would explode if I didn't get some answers. Trev went to step away and panicking I squeezed the hand I held with a death grip not wanting him to move at all.

"I'm just grabbing a chair, sis. I've been looking for you for ten years now, I'm not going anywhere," he said soothingly.

Trev pulled a chair up and out of the corner of my eye I noticed Jack and Jordan had grouped up at the door again. They were whispering between each other before seemingly coming to an agreement and turning back.

"Baby, we've got some phone calls to make so we're gonna leave you with your brother for a bit," Jordan explained before heading out the door.

"Don't exhaust her too much, Animal. She needs her rest," Jack warned him.

Trev nodded in agreement. "Once we're done here, I expect some explanation as to how my sister ended up in the hospital in the first place."

The look in Trev's eyes was a hardness that I'd never seen before, it spoke of judgment and retribution and for a moment he wasn't my brother, he had morphed into someone else and I found myself wondering if he was dealing with the same thing Jack and Jordan were.

Jack just nodded as if he had accepted the heat in Trev's eyes and was willing to take whatever punishment that was to be meted out. He quickly left without another word and I wanted to call him back but one look at Trev stopped me. I knew if he came back there would probably be a fight and I wasn't feeling up to refereeing.

"Trev, they weren't the one that hurt me," I said trying to absolve them.

"It doesn't matter, they should have protected you," Trev growled.

There were undertones of guilt in his voice that made me question whether he really meant the men or him, but before I could question it he started talking again.

"I think you have some questions you were wanting me to answer. What do you want to know first?" he asked getting comfortable in the chair.

I deciding to start with the most important one first, "Where have you been?"

"I've lived in many different places over the last few years, recently I was in Washington again trying to find some trace of where you went to," he explained.

"How did you find me?"

"Jack called the other day and asked if I'd found my sister yet. It was rather a fantastic story about how you manage to fall in with them, I would say fate if I believed in it," he said with a chuckle.

I did laugh then groaned when the movement jostled my shoulder and leg causing Trev to give me an empathetic look as if he'd been right where I was at before.

"Ow! I didn't realize you used those muscles when you laughed," I complained.

"Yeah, being stabbed has a habit of doing that," Trev commented.

"Speaking from experience?" I asked slyly.

He just laughed and stood up, he reached across quickly pressing the button to summon the nurse and I wanted to protest it but I realized my eyes were not staying open anymore. When he went to back away he set something next to me on the bed and I looked down through glazed eyes to find a bundle of envelopes sitting next to me.

"These will explain all that's happened after I left home, the rest are in the back of my car. I've never stopped trying to find you, sis, no matter how hard it became or how little the in-tel was on you I still kept trying," he promised before leaning down to kiss my forehead.

It was so much like he used to do when we were younger and he was putting me to bed that I felt tears gather in my eyes. A twinge of guilt rolled through me when I thought back about how he left and how I gave up so easily but he hadn't.

"I love you, Trev," I whispered because I was too tired to say anything louder.

"Love ya, sis," was the last words I heard as I passed out.

I awoke sometime later to find Jack was the only one in the room and it had become night once again, I hoped I hadn't slept much more than a few hours.

"What day is it?" I asked him hoarsely.

He slowly turned from the window and I saw the lines on his face which had been bad this morning only got worse.

"You haven't missed much, sweetie. It's only been a day since you were attacked, the doctor said you passed out more from shock than real blood loss," he said as he walked up to me.

I nodded satisfied that I had merely lost hours and not days over this whole ridiculous thing, but now like my brother I wanted answers.

"What happened, Jack?" I finally asked him.

He slumped into the chair next to me and scrubbed his face with his hands harshly before he finally looked at me.

"It was my fault," he said so softly I almost missed it.

"What do you mean?"

"When we were young and stupid, Jordan and I got involved with a girl named Molly. She was a bit hostile and insubordinate at first but we both enjoy a challenge so we jumped on it thinking her submission would be sweeter once we got it," Jack began slowly.

I stayed silent, I had really meant what had happened with the woman who had attacked me however this was also a story I had been waiting to hear as well.

"After a while, I discovered her hostility actually came from the fact she was insanely jealous of anybody or anything that took my attention away from her. She wanted me all to herself and she would throw a fit every time Jordan would join us. When we finally realized this Jordan and I decided maybe it was time to split up. We felt we'd never find a girl that would love us both equally," he said with such sadness in his voice it broke my heart.

Jordan came back into the room carrying coffee for both of them and gave me a firm look when I started to try to give him puppy dog eyes. I groaned in disappointment then turned back to Jack.

"So what happened after you both split up?" I asked as Jordan sat on the edge of the bed gently.

"After a while Jordan and I realized that no one was happy, so I broke it off as gently as I could and we introduced her to a new Master who had the time to spend on her and made sure she was well taken care of as was our responsibility. About a month later she showed up on our doorstep and begged us to take her back. She said she would love Jordan as long as I took her back, when we refused she went berserk and came after us with a knife. Seems to be a habit with her apparently," Jack explained shaking his head.

"What did you do?" I breathed out feeling fear for them both

"We subdued her as gently as we could. Then we called the police stating she was a disgruntled ex-girlfriend that had been stalking me and they sent her to a place that would help her," Jack finished up.

"Reed came to the cabin to let us know that someone had spotted her at the club asking questions about us. I don't know how she found where you lived but we will find out," Jordan stated, there was a hardness in his voice that I knew was meant for the person responsible for telling her.

Jack grabbed my hand gently so he wouldn't jostle my wound and squeezed letting me know without words that he was agreeing with Jordan. I gave him a sweet smile thinking about how much I was going to learn about non-verbal communication and how much fun it was going to be to aggravate him into speaking.

Chapter Twenty-Nine

The next time I awoke it was to find Jordan and Jack standing at the doorway. Jordan was whispering to him emphatically almost pleading with him, but Jack it seemed wasn't listening. His body was sagged and his arms were crossed over his chest, he was closed to whatever Jordan was saying. Jack kept shaking his head and I watched as Jordan's shoulders sagged as well like he was giving up.

"Jordan?" I said softly trying to sit up.

Instantly Jordan was at my side helping me so I wouldn't pull my arm again.

"What's going on?" I asked as soon as I was sitting up.

"Jack is being a freaking idiot," he grumbled as he sat down.

"What do you mean?"

I looked to Jack to find some answers but he wasn't there. I looked around the room for any sign of him but everything he'd left in the room was gone. His coat, his wallet, his overnight bag, all gone.

"He's blaming himself for this whole thing and thought it would be best if we split up again," Jordan said softly.

"WHAT!!?" I shouted.

I started trying to get up out of bed immediately. I swung my legs over the side of the bed and was caught by the I.V. that was still in my arm. I reached over and grasped it to pull it out when Jordan stopped me.

"You are in no shape to get out of that bed," he said harshly.

"I don't give a shit. There is no way I'm going to let one of my Masters run off like that," I barked at him trying to bat his hands off me.

"Elizabeth Moore. You are going to lay down and rest," he barked back at me and hit the nurses button.

I pressed back against him and a sharp stabbing pain shot through me and my stomach threatened to empty itself as my vision swam.

"God, freaking, dang it!" I spat out between clenched teeth and reached up to grab my shoulder.

"Stop fucking moving," Jordan growled out as he stood up to pressing the call button over and over again until the nurse walked into the door.

Jordan instantly began demanding more pain medication so I could get some rest. The nurse, unfazed by his overbearing demands, rolled her eyes and in a polite but firm tone asked him to leave immediately. I was in awe at how any woman could handle a Dom like Jordan with such ease. When she got closer I instantly recognized her from the club, her name was Alyssa and she was a Domme. She was always accompanied by her husband Kevin who also happened to be a Dom. According to the other Master's he was the only Dom strong enough to make her submit to him.

I giggled causing her to wink at me as Jordan grumbled but gave me a small kiss and left the room so she could help me get cleaned up or whatever else I needed to do.

When I was snuggled back into the bed and the pain medication well on their way to working I saw the door pop open and another hospital bed was wheeled in followed by a very satisfied looking Master. According to the nurses that wheeled them in, between Alyssa and Jordan they had managed to bully the other nurses letting him stay.

I reached out with my uninjured hand to tightly clasp Jordan's. I drifted off into sleep with, my last thought of Jack and trying to figure out how I was going to bring him back.

Tomorrow brought friends and family from The Dungeon coming to check on me and by noon that day I was exhausted but I'd never felt more like a family than I did that day. Mia stopped in and brought me a latte, which she apparently had snuck in under her coat. She waited until the nurse Alyssa and my Master left the room before she gave it to me, unfortunately Jordan walked in before I was done with it and threw it away then threatened to call Reed if she did it again. When Alyssa over heard this she leaned over and whispered into Mia's ear, whatever she said had her scrambling out the door before she barely said goodbye.

The last person to stop by was Bethany she was a little tiny slip of a girl, skinny but in a well-toned way and her hair was so dark it made her skin look pale giving her a slightly porcelain look. But don't underestimate her, I'd seen this little slip of a thing take a whip to a Dom that was abusing a sub before the moderators could get there so I knew the strength she carried. She was also the one who told me about the club in the first place, as more of prank than anything. Today she looked terrible, so guilty and forlorn that I immediately reached out to her, but she shook her head and walked right up to Jordan.

"Master Jordan, I need to talk to you," she said softly looking down at the floor.

"Yes, little sub, what is it?" Jordan said gently observing the same emotions on her face.

"I wanted to let you know that-"

She hesitated then seemed to brace herself for whatever she was going to say next. "I'm the one who told that bitch where to find her, I'm sorry and I'll take whatever punishment you wish to dole out before I finally quit my membership at the club."

My jaw hit the ground as she confessed and instead of the anger I thought I'd feel for the person who had told Molly where I lived, I felt sadness and sympathy for her. It was obvious she was killing herself with guilt over this so I couldn't bring myself to even be a little angry at her.

"What happened?" he demanded standing up to his full height.

"She came in and started spouting how she was your sister and she needed to find you because it had something to do with your mom," Bethany explained patiently.

She didn't make excuses for herself, I noticed, she knew she had been duped and she was willing to take whatever consequences they had deemed worthy for her. I looked up at Jordan silently begging him not to punish her too much even though I knew that no matter how much I begged she would be punished none-the-less.

Jordan face looked thunderous for a moment but as our eyes connected and I silently pleaded with him for understanding, it melted away to reluctant acceptance.

"Show up this weekend. Master Reed and I will discuss it and decide on your punishment, but until then you will not, I repeat, will not quit the club. If you feel it necessary after your punishment then so be it, but it will be of your choice not ours," Jordan said.

I nodded agreeing with Jordan's orders for Bethany satisfied with the idea of her waiting for almost a whole week before she found out her punishment. The long agonizing wait would be a punishment in itself. Bethany, who had always been known as the definition of a bratty sub, did nothing more than say 'yes Master Jordan' and walk out.

Love for my Master swelled in my heart until I thought it would explode. He had showed compassion towards a person who knew that she had made a grave mistake and had still come forward, at the same time being strict about the rules knowing that no good would come from disregarding her serious breach of club policy.

"Thank you, Sir," I whispered.

"You're very welcome, sub. Thank you for not interfering even though I could see that you wanted to very badly," Jordan said with a light chuckle. "Besides at this point, I think the punishment will be more of a relief for her."

I had seen the pain and the guilt clouded in her eyes and I couldn't help agreeing with him. By far the worst emotion I saw had been the abject loneliness that had tried to hide in the depths.

"She needs to find a Master," I said softly.

"Don't you dare think of setting her up, my love. The last thing I need is to hear from the other Dom's that you are starting to meddle," Jordan warned me.

210

I laughed softly and shook my head. "No way, I've got enough to handle I don't need to add match making to it."

"Good, I promise to keep you busy for a long time to come so you never get the urge to start something like that," Jordan promised.

Leann Lane

Chapter Thirty

I paced the living room one more time, which was a feat considering I was still on crutches. That and the living room was huge, I had moved into Jordan's condo so he could help me after I got out of the hospital and I had found myself wondering why I hadn't done it before. He had twice the space I had not to mention Mrs. Lichten seemed to take some joy in taking care of someone again; if that's truly what her grumping meant.

"I don't care, Jordan, this is ridiculous! Have you tried calling him again?" I asked, frustrated.

"You know I did, Lizzie. He's still not answering," he said sounding kind of lost.

I stopped in my pacing to look over at him and my heart twisted in pain. He was sitting on the couch with his elbows brace on top of his knees and his head buried in his hands. He looked depressed, defeated, and almost hopeless and I knew this was killing almost as much as it was me. I maneuvered over to sit down next to him and poked him in the arm a couple of times until he finally gave up and pulled me into his embrace. We sat on the couch like that for a long while not talking, each of us sunk into own thoughts.

"Do you know where he is?" I asked breaking the silence.

Jordan shook his head draping a free arm over his face like he was trying to hide from reality. Still he said nothing and I could feel the rage building up in me as he continued to hide his eyes.

Unable to take it anymore I let out a frustrated screech and slapped Jordan's leg.

"Ow! What the hell?" he cried pulling away from me.

"You are the Master here and I am the sub, but right now you are acting like a whinny little boy who's lost his favorite toy. Man up, would ya?" I practically yelled at him.

He looked at me with shock and awe in his face before he started laughing. I smiled back at him happy to hear his laughter again. Before I could join him he grabbed my arm, gently of course, and pulled me across his lap; one arm locked over my upper back and the other one held my legs down.

"Are you alright?" he asked immediately.

I bit my lip to keep the words I truly wanted to say to him inside and just nodded.

"Good, let me know if I hurt your arm or your leg but otherwise I don't want you to make a sound. You are being punished for talking to your Master in such a disrespectful tone."

Biting back a whimper, I buried my head in Jordan's leg.

I heard him rustle in the drawer next to the couch until he pulled something out. He flipped the skirt up that I had been forced to wear because of the bandage on my leg and I felt something metal brush under the sides of my underwear. With two quick snipes my underwear was cut off of me again.

"Come on! They were a thong!" I cried trying to sit up off his lap.

A quick hard smack on my backside causing me to cry out more in surprise then pain.

"I said not a word, sub, and do not try to get up again. I will not have you hurting yourself because you want to be stubborn," he growled. "I know it was just a thong, but it doesn't matter to me if I wanna cut it off, I'll cut it off."

I stilled and took a few deep breaths then nodded my understanding.

"Good girl. Now for your punishment, I'm gonna take a page out of Jack's book. You are not getting your underwear back for the rest of the day," he declared proudly almost as if he was patting himself on the back. "Now you may speak."

He helped me sit up and took the scraps of material away, throwing them into a nearby garbage. My mouth was still hanging down as I sat on the couch waiting for the catch.

"But-but-but, I've got a doctor's appointment today. They will want to look at my bandage,"

Jordan shrugged and looked back at me over his shoulder. "Be careful how far you lift your skirt up."

I screeched in anger but all I got back from him was a deep chuckle that floated back to me as he left. As soon as I knew he was out of ear shot a giggled a bit, honestly I really didn't care what he had done, all that mattered was I had my Master back and hopefully had given him an incentive to find Jack. All I could do now was cross my fingers and wait.

Jordan came and got me from the kitchen an hour later to take me to my doctor's appointment, before we left the house he demanded for me to lift up my skirt and show him if I had not put anymore underwear on. I grumbled but did as he asked and tried to hide my flushed cheeks when Mrs. Lichten turned back to the stove quickly and pretended to be busy. I was only soothed by the fact that Mrs. Lichten had a bright blush crossing her cheeks as well. I mumbled an apology her way and was out in the car before Jordan even had his jacket on.

The drive to the doctor's office was tense and uncomfortable and the wait in the doctor's office was nerve-racking. The worst part was the thought that any moment now a strange doctor was probably going to get a sneak peek and automatically decide I am a slut.

I groaned and hid in my hands until the door opened up.

"Hello all!" said Alyssa the nurse from the hospital as she walked in.

She showed us to a room and began taking my vitals before I finally let out the breath I was holding.

"What are you doing here?"

"My husband owns this clinic so when someone calls in sick, I'm the one he calls. Today Jordan ask specifically for me," she explained.

"Oh," was all I could say.

"I thought it'd be easier for you if you had a nurse who understood us," Jordan explained.

I gave him a small grateful smile, forgiving him a bit for the punishment. Alyssa gave me a curious look but said nothing and began her examination. When she asked me to pull up my skirt so she could examine the bandage on my leg, I hesitated.

"Umm... you see I've... Mas... Jor...？" I stuttered trying to find a way to explain for what was going on.

"Lizzie was disrespectful and is currently being punished," Jordan said to her.

She laughed and shook her head at me. "Sweetie, just pull up your skirt. I've seen it all, been in bondage a long time and had my fair share of punishments as well as given them too."

I wanted to ask her about that first part but I figured this was not the time to do so. I pulled my skirt up above my thigh and bunched it between my legs, trying really hard to keep as much of me covered as I could.

Alyssa just shook her head. "Unfortunately I need room to work, hon. You're gonna just have to bite the bullet and lift your skirt higher."

I glared at the top of her head hoping to see her wither under my heated gaze until I heard Jordan clear his throat. I glanced his way and his eyes informed me that I was coming dangerously close to another punishment. I looked away and lifted my skirt up, leaving myself completely bared to her gaze much to my mortification.

"Mmm, she does look very tempting, Jordan. Are you sure you don't want to share her?" Alyssa commented with a hopeful note in her voice.

My eyes flew back and forth between Jordan and Alyssa as I watched him seemingly contemplate what she was saying. I was never as relieved as I was when he shook his head.

"Sorry, my dear, I don't think she swings your way."

Alyssa's shoulders slumped disappointed. "Damn. It's so hard to find a good bi-sexual sub."

A bell went off in my head. "Bethany is."

Jordan looked stunned for a moment then a bright smile crossed his face. "Is she really? Weren't you just saying that she needs a good firm Master?"

I nodded emphatically.

"Alyssa, I think we need to talk after your done gawking at my sub while pretending to change her bandages," Jordan said.

They both broke into peals of laughter when they saw the shock on my face as Alyssa held up her hands having been caught.

"Now about those crutches..."

"I know where Jack is," Jordan said once we got back in the car.

I almost didn't say anything back to him. I wanted to give him the silent treatment for allowing that nurse to embarrass me so completely like that. Although, I wouldn't have been surprised if that had been part of the punishment. In the end I wanted to know what was going on more than I wanted to punish him so I caved.

"When do we leave?"

"We are not going. I am going, you are staying home and let Mrs. Lichten help take care of you," he said in a firm tone.

I felt a bolt of pleasure run through me at the fact he called his condo our home, it certainly was after the last few days over there.

"If you're going then I'm going. He's my Master as well, Jordan. I want to go get him and I'm sure if you go back and ask Alyssa she'll tell you I'm strong enough," I said stubbornly.

"Lizzie, you are not going."

"If you don't let me go with you, I'll sneak out of the house and follow you," I warned him.

"No, you won't."

Chapter Thirty-One

"I can't believe you crawled out the window," Jordan said for the hundredth time.

We had flown into Phoenix late last night and then drove out to the house where Jack had been staying at. Apparently he had gone to his grandfather's house, a place according to Jordan he hadn't been to since his grandfather had died.

"I told you not to leave me behind," I reminded him with a sweet smile on my face.

"Lizzie, that's not the point. The point is you could have gotten hurt and you didn't even care."

"No, Jordan, I do care. But you didn't care that I wanted to go with you to get my Master back. Look, I love you, but without Jack it feels incomplete."

The car swerved and I gripped the seat a bit looking over at Jordan quickly to see if what the hell he was doing. He pulled the car over on the side of the road and looked at me with a shocked expression on his face.

"You love me?" he breathed out.

I paused trying to figure out what he was thinking then finally giggled. "I thought you already knew that."

He grabbed me, careful of my shoulder that was already a bit sore from the long trip, and pulled me to him until I was just a breath away.

"Say it again," he demanded.

"I love you," I whispered.

He stole the last words out of my mouth with a deep kiss. His tongue thrust inside as if he wanted to taste the words as they left. I melted into him and poured all my love into the kiss hoping he'd feel it to the depth of his soul.

Finally, he pulled away and caressed my face, the love he held for me shinning in his eyes.

"I love you, Lizzie," he whispered back.

I smiled radiantly at him. "I know."

He laughed joyfully before setting me back on my seat with another gentle kiss then steered us back towards our destination.

Jack was waiting for us on the porch of a small rancher style home. It was obviously older and had run down a little bit but it was obvious it was well loved and well lived in.

Jordan got out and came around to help me out of the car. Jack stayed where he was his hands in his pockets until he saw I was limping up to him without the benefit of my crutches. He all but raced off the steps at that point and was at my side in an instant helping me up the steps and setting me down on a patio chair.

"What the hell are you doing out of the hospital, girl?" he growled as he moved to the other side of the deck.

"Oh! So now you care?" I snapped back.

"What the fuck does that mean?" he said turning on me.

"You left! You ran all the way out here when I needed you, Jack!" I cried.

"You didn't need me, Elizabeth! I almost got you killed!" he shouted back.

I stood up and grabbed his face to make sure he was listening to me. "No, you didn't. Some crazy woman almost got killed me, that had nothing with you."

"I'm the one that made her crazy," he said sadly trying to pull away.

Implementing a move that my brother taught me, I swept Jacks legs out from underneath and stood over him. He was looking up at me with a shocked look and I could hear off in the distance Jordan braying like a donkey.

"You are making me crazy," I told him angrily. "She was insane before you met her. She was obsessed with you and co-dependent on your affections. What could you have done? Stayed with her? That's just ridiculous."

He tried to get up and I shoved him back down, sitting on him to make sure he stayed down and ignored the burning pain in my leg. His eyes flashed with desire and I felt a certain area rise up and began straining against his pants. I gave him a cocky smile and shifted a little on top of him, a move that was rewarded with a sharp intake of breath.

"I'm glad to see I'm not the only one affected," I mimicked to him.

"You're not, Lizzie. I just don't want to cause you anymore pain." he told me softly brushing a strained of my hair out of my face.

"Then come back, Jack. I'm hurting and I need my Master. Both of them." I whispered.

I leaned down so we were face to face. "I love you, Jackson."

He sucked in a breath between clenched teeth. "What?"

"I love you, Master Jack." I repeated.

His arms locked around me and he rolled me over onto my back. His lips locked with mine as if he was sucking the very words from the depth of my soul.

"Hey buddy? If we're good can we take this party inside I think your neighbors have an issue with you molesting our sub on your porch," Jordan said amused from above us.

Without breaking the kiss Jack swept me up and carried me inside to the nearest bedroom and laid me on the bed. He stepped back then and looked longingly at me as Jordan joined him in the doorway. They glanced at each other then seemed to race to see who could undress the fastest. They crawled up the bed looking like hungry tigers about to devour their prey, I stayed still hoping it was me they were about to gobble up.

Jordan was first up as he captured my lips for a deep kiss, tasting and teasing until I wasn't sure if I would ever be able to breathe again. Jack's hands swept down pulling my shorts down baring me immediately.

"No undies?" he asked on a chuckle.

Jordan pulled away and looked down at him with an answering chuckle. "We didn't have time to go back for a new pair before we left the house. She was being punished yesterday for being rude and I guess now today for sneaking out of the house after I told her to stay home."

Jack shook his head at me. "Bad move girl."

"I'm sorry, Master!" my words ended on a cry as he spread my legs and quickly dove in.

"God, I've missed your taste," Jack rasped out.

Jordan lifted up my shirt to capture my nipple in his mouth and start nibbling and sucking on it. I grasped the back of his head with one hand and the back of Jacks never wanting them to stop. My cries became louder and more desperate when Jack's tongue found my clit and began flicking it quickly as he slowly pushed two fingers inside me with a third finding my puckered back entrance.

"Mmm... I think it's my turn to be in your tight little ass what do you think, little one?" Jack said against my clit.

All I could do was let out a little moan since Jordan had chosen that moment to bite down gently on one of my nipples. Suddenly all movement ceased and I looked down to find my Masters getting up, the next thing I knew Jordan picked me up and made me straddle his lap.

"Does this hurt your leg?" he asked concerned.

"No, Sir. Its fine," I assured him with a warm heart at his worry.

"If it starts to hurt, simple say so and we'll stop."

I nodded and gave him a gentle kiss. "I love you, Sir."

"I love you too, little sub," he whispered back.

I turned my head around to catch sight of Jack crawling up on the bed behind us.

"I love you, Master."

He paused as if he couldn't believe what he had just heard then his face broke into a radiate grin. "I love you too, Elizabeth."

I smiled back at him, the sound of my given name on his lips a musical note now. With a bit of pluck put back into me I wiggled my backside at Jack.

"So are ya gonna put it in or what?"

A hard smack landed on my ass causing me to cry out and almost regret what I had done... almost.

"If you keep up this attitude I will find new and even more effective ways to punish you and I'm pretty sure Mistress Alyssa will love to help me think up a few," Jordan warned.

I smiled inwardly not letting them see how their dominance was pleasing me. I laid my head on Jordan's shoulder and pressed a gentle kiss to his neck and was rewarded with the sound of a low moan.

A drop of warm gel dripped between my ass cheeks and my breath caught as I felt two fingers press slowly inside and start to stretch it. I moaned at the sensation I was growing to love and pressed back against the invading fingers. He pulled out and pressed three fingers widening it even further intensifying the feeling of pleasurable pressure there. Jordan slid his hand between us until he found my harden nub wringing a gentle moan from me. He flicked, played, and tugged on my clit until I was almost wild with desire, begging them to take me.

"I think she's ready, Jack," Jordan said with a low chuckle of satisfaction.

"Good because I am beyond ready," he grunted.

Jordan lifted me up and easily glided into me with one swift move. My breath once again caught in my chest and my head tilted back of its own accord, but found its spot on Jordan's shoulder again as Jack pressed me forward so he could take his turn. I took a deep breath and at the sound of foil being ripped open I readied myself for Jacks cock as it pressed against me.

"Just keep breathing, baby girl," Jordan whispered into my ear and gave me a gentle kiss on my neck.

I pulled back slightly and looked into his eyes giving him a gentle smile that was filled with all the anticipation and love it could hold. He returned my smile even through the strain on his face to keep from moving. His hands held my hips in a death grip as to keep me as still as possible and I knew it was more for his benefit than Jacks. I relaxed and laid my head back in my personal pillow as I waited of Jack to press in further. He did so slowly, thrusting back and forth until a slight pop let him passed the initial ring and allowed him most of the way in. A sharp cry erupted from my throat the minute he entered, Jordan groaned and Jack bit out a curse. They stilled for a moment and I knew they were just trying to give me a second to adjust but with the heat that had built up inside I was worried I'd combust if they didn't move soon.

"Please, Masters, Please," I whimpered helplessly.

"Are you ready?" Jack asked hesitantly.

"Yes," I keened.

They started to move together for a moment. Jordan pulling out so Jack could slip in and then Jack pulling out and Jordan pressed forward. The slow steady pace pushing me beyond my control quickly until I screamed at them. I wasn't sure exactly what I said but it must have gotten their attention because Jordan grabbed my hair and locked me in a deep soul sucking kiss. Jack grabbed my hips and began thrusting into my ass hard slamming me down on Jordan's cock forcing my throbbing clit to grind against his pelvis.

Suddenly stars bloomed behind my eyes and I was forced to tear my mouth away from Jordan's in order to suck my breath back into my body then scream it out in a mind blowing orgasm that seem to encompass my entire body. Jordan quickly followed with a hoarse shout of his own and not long after Jack's own harsh growl whipped through the air as he found his own climax.

I don't remember either of them moving but the next thing I knew I was surrounded by two warm muscular bodies and my hurt arm and leg were elevated on top of them. I sighed and snuggled deeper in the bed knowing I had finally found the place where I belonged. Knowing no matter how bitchy, or mouthy, or crazy I would get I had two strong powerful Dom's at my sides. A gentle kiss was pressed to my head and a gentle squeeze given to my hand as I fell back to sleep dreaming of what was to come. A smile crossed my face as I thought of all the ways I could drive these two men crazy.

Oh yes, my Masters were in for one wild ride.

You Are Ours

Leann Lane

Meet The Author

Leann Lane is a self-published author that spends most of her time reading, writing, or spending her days with her family. Two legged and four legged alike. She lives in the mountains of Oregon where it gets a little too cold in the winter, but it also provides her a reason to curl up with her latest favorite author or her latest writing project and stay warm. If you'd like to know more visit her online and keep in touch. There is nothing she'd love more than to hear from her wonderful readers.

http://leannlanerla.wix.com/sparkyssordidtails

You Are Ours

Excerpt

It was just after Mia had just taken a nosedive on to the concrete outside the club, the same one I'd hit. It was her birthday and I'd wanted her to wear this sexy little corset I'd never been able to fill out properly and this cute little mini that showed off her assets to the max. The end all had been a set of stilettos that had been held together with a few dinky straps, I should have known better than to make her wear them. Mia had never been coordinated or graceful and I'd made her wear the worst possible shoes.

I was in a panic as Reed, the owner of the club, came out and carried her gently through the club into a room in the back. He asked Jordan to stay with me until the ambulance arrived so I wouldn't go wandering and get myself into even more trouble.

They sent me into a kitchen through the back so I wouldn't stay out in the club with everyone else because you weren't allowed in until you signed the confidentiality agreement. I didn't care, I was glad that I wasn't out there with all those people. I wanted to drown in my own self-pity. I sat at the small table, my head lying on my arms and trying hard to stem the tears rolling out of my eyes. I hated to cry, I had been taught young that crying would never get me anything, yet the anxiety of not knowing how Mia was and the frustration of my own guilt had the tears rolling at a steady pace.

I felt a hand on my shoulder and I spun around quickly thinking it was the owner with news about Mia. The owner of the hand jumped out of the way just in time as my elbow passed within an inch of his stomach.

"Holy shit!" he shouted.

"Oh my God!" I cried as I stood up. "I'm so sorry, I'm just really jumpy tonight."

He wasn't nearly as tall as the owner was, yet he still had a few inches on me, even while I was wearing my heels. His hair closely shaved to his head, however I could still tell it was a blonde. His eyes were an interesting gray color that I could get lost in. I got caught up in looking at him unable to keep my eyes off his very muscular physique. He had to have been a full six foot of solid muscles. He was wearing a white T-shirt that stuck to every imaginable surface on his chest and I was certainly imagining it. It was his muscular biceps that caught my eyes at this moment. I could easily imagine him picking me up and putting me on the counter without much work. That salacious thought sent a delicious shiver down my spine.

My eyes continued downward taking in every titillating sight like the sweet little eye candy that the man was. Most of the men that I saw here were wearing a pair of skin tight leather pants. Not this man, this man wore faded jeans with holes in them making him look as if he'd just come from a construction site, which for all I knew he could have. I noticed he was barefoot, odd for a man, yet it gave him a more heathenish appearance.

"Are you okay?" he asked, breaking me out of my admiration of him.

I shook my head to get him out of it and maybe actually remember why I was there. My mind was already foggy due to all the alcohol I had shoved into it tonight and I didn't need a hot, sexy man clouding my judgment.

"Yes, I'm so sorry. I'm just really anxious to know how my friend is doing," I said.

I grabbed a napkin off the table and wiped my face with it praying my makeup wasn't too beyond repair. I felt an immense need for this man to find me beautiful even as I chided myself for thinking such a thing about him.

"She'll be fine, I'm sure. Master Reed is going to check on her and the ambulance is on the way as we speak," he said trying to reassure me.

"Ambulance!" I squeaked, my hand flying to my mouth. "Oh no! What have I done? I just wanted to show her how cute she could look and now she's going to the hospital and -"

"Stop," he said firmly.

My mouth snapped closed so fast I almost bit my tongue off.

"The ambulance is strictly precaution. She did hit her head when she fell and Master Reed would feel a lot better if she was checked out. As for you, yes, it was a dumb thing to make your friend wear shoes she's not very adept at walking in. But you didn't push her down or trip her, it was an accident and I'm sure everything will be fine, minus the helluva headache she's going to wake up with, so calm down."

I nodded miserably feeling only slightly better. I sat back down and pulled my cup of coffee closer, they wouldn't give me anything stronger, believe me I asked.

"What's your name?" he asked sitting down across from me.

"Lizzie," I said staring into my cup of coffee miserably.

"What's that short for?"

"It's short for Elizabeth. Elizabeth Moore, and you are?" I replied irritably.

I tried really hard not to glare at him since I hated my full name and never used it if I could help it.

"You can call me Master Jordan or Sir. Whichever you prefer," he said with a shrug.

I raised my eyebrow. "Master Jordan? Now we aren't full of ourselves are we?"

His eyes darkened to a steel gray as he straightened in his chair and stared at me. As for me, I squirmed in my own, hearing warning bells going off in my head and feeling distinctly uncomfortable. I lowered my gaze to my coffee cup and refusing to look at him, caving under the harsh glare of his gaze. Suddenly he threw his head back and laughed making me jump straight up in the air.

"Yes, I am full of myself and I have every right to be. You can ask any sub here. They'll tell you I am one of the best. Do you know what that means?" he asked leaning in closer.

There was a whole table between us and I still felt as if he was crowding me. I leaned back and folded my arms over my chest and his eyes followed the movement appreciatively. I realized that my shifting had caused my breasts to swell up and almost over the top of my corset, inadvertently giving him an unhindered view of my cleavage. I dropped my arms down quickly and felt a flush of heat as he smiled at me with a distinctively predatory grin.

"No, I'm sorry, I don't," I lied.

I was desperately trying to distract him from whatever thoughts were running through his head and hoping he would drop the subject.

"Have you ever heard of BDSM?" he asked with a knowing grin.

That bastard was on to me and if I was to be honest, I'd say I was turned on by his attention. Still, I couldn't help hearing the words 'he's way out of your league' running through my head. I shook my head, as much to answer the question as to knock out the thoughts running around in it.

"It's a form of erotic play," he explained as if that told me everything.

"Erotic play? What do you mean like... spankings and ropes? Because let me tell you, I know all about those and it's not all it's cracked up to be," I spouted out haughtily.

He smiled and shook his head. "Honey, you have no idea what I'm talking about. This goes way beyond some little light rope play, so far beyond, that you may get scared."

The fire in his eyes made me catch my breath as my blood began to heat up. He grasped my hand and began rubbing his thumb gently across my knuckles each pass sending another spike of fiery heat through me.

"But feeling fear is normal. In fact, some subs say it heightens their arousal."

My mouth went dry as he across at me from under his lashes, his gray eyes sparkling with mischief. I felt a sense of annoyance as I realized he knew exactly what he was doing to me and he was doing it on purpose, the freaking jerk. I snatched my hand back and had to curl it into a ball to keep from slapping him.

"I don't enjoy being played with and I can tell you right now, you son of a bitch, yes, I know what a sub is and there's no way in hell I'm ever going to submit to you," I growled at him.

I saw several emotions cross his face anger, disbelief, and another one that made me quake. His eyes became hard as rock and his mouth clenched in determination and I felt myself stiffen.

"Oh, really?" he said softly.

'Yeah, I'm in deep shit' I thought to myself.

Because I Want To

Leann Lane

Excerpt

Chapter One

A loud thud jerked my attention away from the bills of the extremely handsome, but completely broke, Trev Moore. I had been coming to his shabby apartment every Saturday for the last few weeks, trying to help him figure out how to pay the bills before they got worse.

For the last ten years, Trev had been obsessively trying to find his baby sister. During this search he had managed to accumulate a good amount of debt. So when his Marine buddies, Jack and Jordan, got a hold of him and told him they had her he knew he had to face the music so to speak. Especially if he planned on making the move to here permanently.

This is where I come in: Vie Tremaine! Accountant extraordinaire! Savior of people's checkbooks! More often than not I am either despised or loved unconditionally.

However, all that didn't matter; bills were not the reason Trev had stormed out of the living room. The only clue to his behavior was he had just been reading a book about BDSM of all things.

"Something wrong?" I called out.

The only response to my question was angry mumbling from the kitchen and the slamming of the refrigerator door. He stomped back into the living room still mumbling and paced in front of the couch. He paused only long enough to take long pulls from the root beer in his hand. He sucked it down like he was trying hard to get drunk off of it.

It was really hard not to allow my eyes to wandering down his well-cut body as they so desperately wanted to. Especially in his tight jeans that cupped his backside like a pair of lovers hands. His t-shirt was well worn, but that was just fine with me because it hung to his shoulders showing off the broad expanse perfectly. I felt a very girly sigh try to fall from my lips, but I forcefully swallowed it back. Still waiting, I watched his strong neck muscles work as he chugged the drink down until it was either completely gone.

"I cannot believe my baby sister is actually into that bullshit!"

Well, that answered that question.

"I can't believe I never knew Jack and Jordan were like that!" he shouted and waving his hand accusingly at the book he'd thrown across the room.

"What? Bondage?" I asked just for clarification.

"Yes! Who in their right mind would want to be tied up and fucked like that?" he continued as he stomped around.

I assumed he was looking for something else to throw. But with how little he owned, there was no way he was going to find anything. For example, when I'd first started coming here I had to bring my own cup.

"I think your overreacting, Trev," I told him in a calm tone.

"Overreacting... OVERREACTING?! It's bad enough that my sister has two... two..."

"Lovers?" I supplied helpfully.

"Yes! And now I find out that they could possibly be *whipping* her on a regular basis! And what the hell is blood play?" he cried.

In his rage he scrubbed his hand through his sandy blond hair that was almost exactly like his sisters. Sighing in resignation I almost ran my hand through my own shoulder length brown hair. Master Reed had asked me to help Trev with whatever he needed. So I'd helped him find an apartment, do a bit of job hunting and showed him a few interesting places around town. Somehow I'd never thought the in's and out's of bondage would be on my list of things to explain to him.

I rubbed my forehead trying to figure out what I could say to help him understand something as controversial as D/s. Nothing brilliant and life altering came to mind, unfortunately. I groaned silently in frustration. Being tongue tied was not unusual for me; I really was better with numbers than I was with people. I had recently found out that people had started calling me Ice Princess;

everyone apparently mistaking my shyness for coldness. Of course it didn't help that the very few times I was asked to play I hadn't been able to respond. I shook myself out of the memories of the last few depressing, horrible experiences.

On the other hand, I'd never minded coming over to Trev's. I enjoyed the short conversations we've had and the fact he never demanded more than that.

Until now.

"Look, it's honestly no big deal," I began.

"No big deal? Vie, my baby sister is a willing part of an abusive relationship!"

"It's not abuse, Trev. It's a lifestyle choice! There is nothing happening that she hasn't agreed to," I tried to explain.

Trev stopped pacing and gave me a suspicious look.

"You sure are defending this pretty hard. Are you into this crap as well?" he snarled at me with his bright blue eyes flashing.

My back straightened with anger at his insult.

"Yes, I'm into this *crap* as well," I told him in a cold tone.

He sauntered over to me and bent down until our noses practically touched. His blue eyes flashed with anger and something else… something hotter. A flare of interest was hidden by all the anger and contempt.

"So, you like to be tied up and tormented as well?" he growled.

My mouth opened and closed like a fish out of water. No words, no sounds came out even as I heard my answer screaming in my head.

"So, if I was to cuff you to my bed right now and take advantage of you, you'd let me? Even if it was for no other reason than to use you as my very own little sex toy."

Did I detect a bit of hope in his voice? I wondered to myself. Unbelievably my body started heating up in response to his words. Saying I was startled by my own reaction would be putting it mildly. Dirty talk was something that had always been a laughing point for me up until now. Now, the intensity in Trev's eyes combined with his words sent shivers down my spine and my thoughts scattered.

Swallowing a few times to get past the lump in my suddenly dry throat, I tried once again to say something. I was desperate to distract him, and myself, from the sexual tension that was escalating in the room. It would be insane to allow myself to get mixed up with a man like Trev. He was sexier than sin and more than enough for any hot blooded woman to want. But, he was also way out of my league. Not to mention he viewed my kink as something to despise. Not exactly a great basis for BDSM.

Yet, there was nothing I wanted to do more right now than to crawl on my knees into his bedroom and see if his intensity carried over in between the sheets. Dark, forbidden fantasies that had been teasing my brain since I met him began to play like a slide show. My eye lids drooped down and I felt myself begin to sway towards him.

The shrill ring of his phone rescued me from this lust induced trance. He stormed over to where his cell phone laid and snapped it up so fast I thought he was going to break it.

"What?" Trev snapped into the phone.

He frowned and stepped into the kitchen beyond hearing range. Away from his intoxicating presence my senses came back. Panic consumed me and I seized the opportunity to round up my stuff so I could make a hasty exit. Maybe once I got away from this place I could convince myself that, despite the racing of my heart and the dampness of my panties, there was no way I could get together with this man.

The door behind me creaked open before I was even half way down the hall.

"Vie? Why are you leaving?"

My heart raced as something in his voice stopped me in my tracks. It was the sound of disappointment that Masters usually had with their subs when they were in trouble. If I didn't know any better, I would think he was upset because I was leaving.

"Oh, I thought we were finished," I said happy that my voice didn't shake.

He stepped closer until he was towering over me and for the first time in a long time I felt small. That was a hard feat when you were 5' 9" and definitely not model thin. But he accomplished that easily with his broad muscular shoulders and a thick waist that just begged a woman to wrap her legs around it.

God, knock it off, idiot! I scolded myself. He's not interested in you he's probably just wondering what needed to be done now with his finances.

"You're good to continue job hunting this week," I said more confidently.

He turned around and ran a hand through his hair, obviously frustrated.

"I'm not having any luck with that, Vie. There's just no work for an ex-sniper that has been searching for his sister for the last ten years. I've always sucked at computers and don't have the patience to learn."

I put my hand on his shoulder sympathetically. "Trev, it'll take time, but you'll get there. Don't be so hard on yourself."

He looked at my hand on his shoulder then followed its arm back up to my eyes. Suddenly I knew it wasn't job hunting on his mind and I snatched my hand away as if it was burned. I felt my face flush and my gaze dropped to the floor. I hastily took a few steps back, trying to put some space between us. Trying even harder to ignore the ingrained need to submit to him. Every fiber of my being knew he was a Dom and with a little training he could definitely be a Master. I wasn't sure how they went about training for that. *Did they have online classes?* I wondered silently.

I cleared my throat to break the tension since he had not said anything nor had he taken his eyes off me. I felt like a scared rabbit that was hiding in its hole being stalked by a hungry wolf.

"Well, I should go," I finally said stepping away slowly. "I've gotta get ready to go to work."

I thought for sure he would back off and let me leave, but he surprised me by pursuing me. My back hit the wall that was covered in cheesy flowered wall paper that was peeling and barely recognizable. Normally I would have been very concerned about the stains that were being rubbed on to my white shirt. But with this sexy and very intense man giving me his full attention I couldn't bring myself to care about anything else.

His hands braced themselves on either side of me, he dipped his head down until he was just a breath away. I was immediately surrounded by his hard unyielding body and I became intoxicated once more by the scent of him. He surrounded me in his clean masculine scent and I could feel myself drowning in it.

"I thought you said you'd let me cuff you to my bed," he whispered.

I almost choked. "I- I-"

"You what?" he asked.

"I didn't think you... I didn't know you meant you specifically," I stuttered out.

He gave me a sexy chuckle that I'd never heard from him. Its deep baritone sound made my stomach clench as it seemed to embody every naughty thought that was going through my head at that moment.

"I do believe the question I posed to you was, if *I* cuffed you to *my* bed. I think that it was very clear that I meant me."

I suddenly felt as if there would never be enough air in the world to make me start breathing again. *Surely he couldn't be serious?* I thought to myself, although I wasn't sure if it was a hopeful or a fearful thought. Maybe it was both? Either way it made the nerve endings tingle in awareness.

I open my mouth but whatever I was going to say was stolen away by his lips. I hadn't even seen him move but suddenly his lips were on mine. Not just on them, he seemed to be devouring them. Stunned, I couldn't move. Never in a million years would I have imagined Trev kissing me.